CUNNINGHAM'S REVENGE

Cunningham's Revenge

Duncan MacNeil

Walker and Company
New York

Oz Edition

Copyright © 1980 by Duncan MacNeil

First published in the United States of America
in 1985 by the Walker Publishing Company, Inc.

Library of Congress Cataloging in Publication Data

MacNeil, Duncan, 1920–
  Cunningham's revenge.

    1. India—History—19th century—Fiction. I. Title.
PR6063.A167C8 1985   823'.914   85-3152
ISBN 0-8027-0847-1

Printed in the United States of America

10 9 8 7 6 5 4 3 2 1

One

For weeks past there had been a steady movement into the area east of Peshawar. From north and south natives had come singly and in groups, bearing ancient rusty rifles. They had melted into the hills, into little-used passes and into caves, avoiding Queen Victoria's patrols. Largely, they had come at night, and with them had come heavy artillery, terrible old pieces that looked as though the first discharge would shatter both guns and crews. Some of the movement had been noted by the patrols from time to time, and reported to the Commander of Her Majesty's First Division in Nowshera, but the sightings had not in fact been many and Division had tended to be unworried. Natives, after all, had a habit of moving about the country; and the guns had not been spotted at all, thanks to inbred native cunning and vigilance and a degree of camouflage. Nevertheless the orders from Division had indicated a need for extra alertness on the part of all patrols, and in their cantonment two miles westward of Peshawar, the 114th Highlanders, the Queen's Own Royal Strathspey were taking Division's warning seriously. Curiously enough, the sector to the north-west of the cantonments running through to the Frontier with Afghanistan appeared peaceful beyond its normal wont; in that area the patrols had reported no unusual activity or gatherings of Pathans, and, riding out for exercise with Fiona Elliott, Lord Brora's niece, James Ogilvie equally found nothing to disturb the even tenor of the North-West Frontier. Away to the north towards Dargai the colouring of the hills was superb as the sun that late afternoon began its decline over the peaks of the Afghan ranges rearing westward. And outlined against them the girl looked superb also: tall, rangy and with a touch of the arrogance that characterised her uncle, she sat her horse well. She had been a rider from childhood, and had the look of one who was more at home upon four legs than two. Rider and mount were one: she was much better with horseflesh than was James Ogilvie.

He was about to offer some complimentary remark when instead he turned sharply towards the south-east, frowning. A heavy rumble had come, forebodingly, and was followed by another. Ogilvie recalled the reports, vague enough ones to be sure, about the native movements . . . he pulled up his horse, and the girl caught his eye.

She asked, "Thunder?"

Ogilvie gave a short laugh. "Not thunder, Fiona. Gunfire. Heavy artillery, somewhere around Peshawar."

"The cantonment, do you suppose?"

"I've no idea, but I don't like it." Ogilvie glanced around at the lengthening shadows of late afternoon. "Time we rode back anyway."

"To do your duty, James?"

There had been a touch of something like irony in her tone, and there was a sardonic look in her eye, a tinge of amusement at the automatic response of a soldier to the sound of guns: she did not yet know the North-West Frontier of India, sternest and most demanding of any of the outposts of Empire, tinder-dry to take sudden and unannounced flame from the smallest spark. Ogilvie said, "That's the idea. The faster we ride in, the better. Keep your eyes skinned, and keep close to me."

"Race you," she said, and allowed him no time to tell her not to be a fool. Spurs touched her horse's flanks and she was away, hell-for-leather towards Peshawar. A laugh floated back as Ogilvie pounded on behind. There seemed to be no fear in her at all: something else she shared with Lord Brora, along with his mule-like obstinacy. Ogilvie caught her up, then kept as close as possible. After they had dropped down upon the track running through from Peshawar to the lofty Fort Jamrud guarding the entry to the Khyber Pass, a mounted patrol was sighted riding from the direction of Peshawar, and as they closed Ogilvie recognised Colour-Sergeant MacTrease, sweat-lathered, trewed and awkward in the lead of his Mounted Infantrymen.

MacTrease saluted. Ogilvie lifted his plain-clothes *topi* in response. MacTrease said, "I was ordered out by the Major, sir, to look for you and the lady, and bring you in." He sounded breathless.

"What's going on, Colour?"

"An attack on the city, sir, is all I know."

"And the cantonment?"

"All well, sir. Up to the time I rode out, that is. The regiment's standing-to, of course, sir."

Ogilvie nodded. "Right, thank you, Colour. Miss Elliott in the centre, if you please, and then we'll not delay."

MacTrease saluted. "Aye, sir. The Major's compliments, sir, and he wishes words with you as soon as you ride in."

"Very well."

With Fiona Elliott in the centre, the mounted patrol turned for the east and rode fast for the Royal Strathspeys' cantonment. Ogilvie reflected on Major Lord Brora and the likely content of the forthcoming 'words' with him. Ogilvie had had his Colonel's permission to ride out, and Fiona's mother's permission to take her daughter with him: but Brora, Lady Mary Elliott's brother-in-law, was as ever, Brora and tended, perhaps not unnaturally, to see himself in the room of the girl's father, his now deceased brother. Tact might possibly have dictated a need to seek Brora's permission also, but if so it had not dictated in time. Now there were overriding considerations: much blood would certainly be flowing in Peshawar, and it was likely enough the Scots would be in action shortly.

* * *

Riding in as the guarded gate was opened for the patrol, Ogilvie found that all was quiet in the cantonment, though the regiment was spread out by companies around the perimeter, their rifles loaded and ready, while the Maxim

7

detachments were standing by their guns in the centre of the barrack square, on the alert to be deployed when the orders should come. As Ogilvie dismounted and then gave Fiona a hand, Lord Brora emerged from the Mess ante-room, saw Ogilvie, and shouted at him across the parade-ground.

"Captain Ogilvie, come here."

Ogilvie marched across smartly. Brora stood with his head held back, disdainful yet magnificent in his very size and bearing, the kilt swaying gently in a cool breeze from the far distant Himalayan snows.

Ogilvie halted. Brora sniffed and said in his harsh voice, "Well, Captain Ogilvie, you've seen fit to take my niece into danger and now I wish to know why."

"Hardly danger, Major, in the direction I took. The area's well patrolled and—"

"Don't damn well argue with me, if you please, Captain Ogilvie, I am Lord Brora, and I say you took her into potential danger, with no damn chaperon moreover, and that the danger has come to pass – the reports from Division should have been enough to warn you that trouble was in the air."

"Lady Mary—"

"My sister-in-law does not know India, and is in no position to give permission. Do I make myself clear, Captain Ogilvie?"

"Yes, Major. I apologise."

"So I should think, blast you!" Brora shouted angrily. "The girl's been in cantonments but a fortnight, and you've danced attendance upon her like a subaltern of the palace guard hoping to bed one of Her Majesty's ladies in waiting. It shall stop, d'you hear me? It shall stop! You are an infantry officer, not some bloody popinjay doing a drawing-room dangle."

Ogilvie, aware that the Major's words must have been heard by every man on stand-to, had difficulty in keeping his fists to his sides, let alone in refraining from answering back. He gave no answer; but, catching sight of the Colonel's runner hovering awkwardly behind the furious second-in-command, he said, "I think you are wanted, Major," and indicated the runner's presence.

8

Brora swung round. "Well?"

The man saluted. "The Colonel's compliments, sir, and he wishes all officers to attend the battalion office at once, sir."

"Very well, and in future kindly do not *eavesdrop* upon gentlemen's conversation."

"Sir!" Colouring, the young private saluted again and doubled across the square to pass on his message. Brora swung away from Ogilvie and stalked back to the battalion office. Ogilvie followed, and found the Colonel, Lord Dornoch, seated at a trestle table with the Adjutant, Andrew Black. Black got obsequiously to his feet as Brora entered, and hovered like some sycophantic footman until the Colonel had bid Brora sit. Dornoch smiled at Ogilvie.

"Back safely, James, I'm glad to see."

"Yes, Colonel."

He was waved to a chair. One by one the rest of the Scots officers entered, together with the Regimental Sergeant-Major, Mr Cunningham. When all were present, Dornoch got to his feet, his face anxious and his eyes weary but his back as straight as ever. Word, he said, had come through to Brigade from extended patrols. A mass of well-armed natives had poured out in torrents from the hills to the north, south and east of Peshawar, standing clear of the western side initially, no doubt so as not to attract interest from the British cantonments until they were ready. They had quickly spread out to form a siege line round the city, which was believed to be totally surrounded by now. "The attackers are Hindus from the Punjab – from Lahore and Amritsar it's believed – and they've been joined in strength by forces from Kashmir. It seems we face a religious war, Hindu against Muslim. Division has already been in contact by the telegraph to Brigade – the attack is not upon the Raj—"

"Yet," came the arrogant voice of Lord Brora. "It'll not be long before the buggers take it into their damn heads to mob the cantonments, Colonel."

Dornoch shrugged. "Naturally we must be ready for that, but General Fettleworth seems inclined to doubt the proposition. I and the Colonels of the other regiments in cantonments are ordered to maintain defensive positions around the clock but not to extend beyond the cantonment area – that is, as I read the orders, not to make any attempt to penetrate Peshawar and possibly exacerbate the situation."

"In other words, Colonel, we turn our backs upon the bloodshed in the city?"

"I'm afraid we do, but I think General Fettleworth would prefer to say that we are to display a masterly inactivity until such time, at least, as the situation clarifies—"

"Or deteriorates." Brora stared around as though seeking support for a more warlike view of events. "Frankly, I don't see how the Raj can sit back and allow an outrage to take place upon one of its cities! And there's another considera-tion, Colonel, is there not – the town patrol?"

Tight-lipped, Dornoch nodded: a half company of the 114th, under Robin Stuart, was currently providing the Peshawar town patrol and would doubtless be under attack in the streets and in the city guardroom itself. The Colonel used his cane to tap the briefly-worded orders on the trestle table. "You may be sure I've not forgotten our men," he said quietly, "but Division has spoken, Major, and that's that. In my own view, we would in fact achieve little by putting troops into the city merely to suffer the cross-fire from both Muslim and Hindu and incur the hatred of each, but the situation's very fluid and further orders could come at any time. I understand Division is sending in Political Officers to put their ears to the ground and report. The moment I have more information, you will all be informed. Mr Cun-ningham?"

"Sir!" A ramrod arose from the seated group.

Dornoch gestured the RSM to sit again. "You'll keep the whole battalion standing-to until further orders, Sarn't-Major, but as soon as the situation allows I'll relieve the men by companies. For the present meals must be taken at their stations, and after nightfall one man in two may sleep at his post in four-hour watches."

"Aye, sir. And the married quarters, sir?"

"After nightfall, Mr Cunningham, you'll double the guard on them, all men to remain awake and fully alert. And you'd better arrange to have the *chaukidahs* relieved from their

10

night watch and confined in the go-down. They're probably loyal enough, but I'll not take chances in this situation." Dornoch pulled out his watch. "That's all, gentlemen, thank you. I'll just remind you that the officers will also take their meals at their posts. I'll not expect to see any combatant officer in the mess or ante-room.

*   *   *

There was a strange, uneasy atmosphere; one of much foreboding. There had been sporadic gunfire distantly, but on the whole there was a brooding quiet. When Ogilvie had ridden in with Fiona Elliott and MacTrease's patrol, he had heard rifle fire from the city but no further heavy artillery barrages. The roads in the British cantonment area had been totally devoid of natives; those in British domestic and semi-military service within the Royal Strathspeys' cantonment had been grave-faced but watchful, carrying out their duties normally but seeming on edge as well they might: their sympathies might or might not lie with their brethren fighting in and around Peshawar, but in any case the sahibs were regarding them with suspicion; and mistrust was in the air, the same sort of mistrust as Dornoch had manifested when he had ordered the withdrawal of the native nightwatchmen.

When the officers had been dismissed, Ogilvie had been called back by the Colonel, who had sat in silence for a while thereafter, puffing at his pipe. Dornoch's face was deeply lined: the long years of Indian service had left their mark, and each campaign had added more grey to his once-black hair. The Empire and the Queen's service was his life, but the lives of Scots killed in action – and there had been too many since the regiment had first left the depot at Invermore for Portsmouth Hard and the troopship for Bombay – those lives he always accounted his own responsibility and felt each one keenly as a loss to the regimental family. Now, no doubt, he saw more coming up; the Royal Strathspeys would not be long from the fight once the trouble spread, as in India it seemed inevitably to spread once the first fire was lit. But

11

Lord Dornoch didn't start on matters purely military. Tapping out his pipe, he said, "I happened to overhear the Major's words, James. Be assured I have made it quite clear you went with my permission."

"Yes, Colonel."

"A most charming young lady."

"Very, Colonel."

"If at times a trifle forthcoming . . . but blood will out, and that's natural," the Colonel added with a whimsical smile. "I want you to remember this, James: if an attack should come, as come it may and never mind General Fettleworth's views, the women on the strength in married quarters will be defended to the last. All of them. No favour will be shown. This, those of us who are married have long understood and accepted. The women are the charge of the whole regiment, not of any individual. I think you have already become . . . attached to Miss Elliott, and perhaps she to you. That's why I'm giving you a pijaw, James, such as I make a practice of giving to any officer or man who marries on foreign service. I trust you'll not take umbrage?"

"Indeed not, Colonel."

"Then we'll make no more of it," Dornoch said briskly, seeming relieved that the matter had been disposed of; and he had gone on to make brief reference to regimental affairs before dismissing Ogilvie to join his company. Leaving the battalion office, Ogilvie found himself wondering if his developing feeling for Fiona had shewn itself too strongly. There had been some badinage in the mess, or more strictly in the ante-room, but the Colonel appeared to be taking matters beyond their due weight; and Brora also, perhaps. Brora's recent outburst could have signalled the fact that he failed to see Captain James Ogilvie as a future nephew-in-law, notwithstanding the strong Ogilvie tradition in the regiment, which had been commanded in their time by both the grandfather and the father, whilst Sir Iain Ogilvie, long since promoted to the General Staff, currently lorded it in Murree as Northern Army Commander. Brora's objections were purely personal and purely spiteful: twice now, in attempting to jeopardise Ogilvie's career – once by instituting Court Martial proceedings on a largely trumped-up charge – Brora had found his impetuous temperament rebounding upon himself, and had thereafter simmered, sometimes gently, sometimes not. Crossing the parade-ground towards the sector of the perimeter held by B Company, Ogilvie put the matter out of his mind; but received a small set-back in his resolution when he saw Fiona, with Lady Mary, making towards the married quarters from Dornoch's bungalow, where the ladies were staying since Brora, as a single man, had not wished the bachelor ways of his own bungalow to be disturbed. The girl turned and waved when she saw Ogilvie, and Ogilvie return-ed the gesture with a formal lift of his *topi*. The ladies disappeared; after he had spoken to his subalterns, Ogilvie went to his quarter to change into uniform. It was while he was changing with the aid of his bearer that he heard the rising murmur of sound from the distance: a sound of shouts, cries and rifle-fire that was coming closer from the direction of Peshawar. Outside on the parade-ground a bugle blew. Grabbing the remainder of his uniform and dressing as he went, Ogilvie ran onto the verandah and jumped down. Beyond the cantonment gates a cloud of dust was rising, and there was concentrated rifle-fire now, volley after volley coming from behind the dust-cloud which was speckled with red flashes as the rifles spoke. Then there came the thunder of hooves as a squadron of native cavalry of the Indian Army charged through the rising dust, full tilt, with guidons streaming, into the mouths of the rebel rifles.

Two

Afterwards, there were many dead: the squadron of the Guides had been backed up by two squadrons of the Bengal Lancers, and all three had hacked their way into the mass of natives, spitting men on the lances and slicing with the bloodied sabres. Many of the cavalrymen had fallen, but the objective had been achieved: the natives had been driven back and then the infantry had gone in to press home the British advantage. Two companies of the Royal Strathspeys had been ordered out, and together with support companies from the York and Lancaster Regiment and the 1st Dorsets they had doubled behind the running rebels, firing point-blank over fixed bayonets. When the native rout, at least for the time being, was complete and the roadway littered with bodies, the bugles sounded the cease fire, the companies were withdrawn into cantonments and the medical sections went out to bring in the wounded in the *doolies*.

As Ogilvie came through the gate with his company he was overtaken from the rear by the Regimental Sergeant-Major, whose uniform tunic was dark with sweat. Cunningham had accompanied the pursuit and, as ever, had been a tower of strength in the brief action, seeming to be everywhere at once, encouraging the newer drafts by his personal example and never holding back, apparently scorning the bullets that had come zipping through from the native horde. Cunningham was a man to be grateful for; a good sergeant-major was the making of any regiment, and Cunningham was the best there was. Ogilvie joined him, detaching from B Company as his senior subaltern marched the men back to their defensive posts along the perimeter.

"What d'you make of it, Mr Cunningham?" he asked.

"Well, Captain Ogilvie, sir, the devils are not going to let it rest. They've been beaten off for now – but they'll be back."

"We'll be watching for them."

"Aye, we'll be that, sir. I shall see to it that the men are alert." He would, as Ogilvie knew; Cunningham never

14

seemed to sleep, was always at hand when needed, jealous for the reputation of the 114th and caring for the men. The RSM went on, "We should have an eye for detail now, sir. There is the question of the *nappis* and *chikkos*."

Ogilvie grinned. "Who might murder us in our beds?"

Cunningham gave his moustache a tweak. "Many a true word, sir. I have it in mind that bed-shaving should be suspended."

"And have the battalion paraded with bristly chins, Sar'nt-Major? Whatever next!"

Cunningham gave a laugh. "You and I, Captain Ogilvie, both dislike unshaven men. But safety must come first. It's not been unknown in the past for a native uprising to be much helped by the *nappis* cutting the offered throats."

Ogilvie nodded. The privilege of being shaved whilst still recumbent in their beds was one much prized by the rank-and-file, who were by no means accustomed to such luxury in barracks at home, and the ritual was unvarying: each morning at 5 a.m. the *nappi,* or barber, would enter the barrack-room with his attendant *chikko,* the latter bearing water heated by charcoal. Each sahib was lathered by the *chikko* ready for the *nappi's* blade, and for long enough was at the native's mercy. In point of fact, the very size of the barrack-rooms with their many occupants was a guarantee of safety, but the officers in their individual bedrooms could be picked off piecemeal. Cunningham was right. Ogilvie said, "You'd better have a word with the Adjutant, Sar'nt-Major."

"Sir!" Cunningham gave a swinging salute and his kilt swirled about thick, sun-burned thighs as he turned away. As he did so, the sound of a disturbance came from the direction of the married quarters: shouts, rifle-fire and then a high-pitched scream, a long-drawn sound of agony. Their revolvers in their hands, Ogilvie and the RSM ran for the married quarters.

*   *   *

15

Ten miles to the east, Lieutenant-General Francis Fettleworth, Commander of Her Majesty's First Division in Nowshera and Peshawar, was called from his wife's drawing-room where he had been enjoying a pre-dinner glass of dry sherry. Brigadier-General Lakenham, Chief of Staff, had received urgent despatches by the telegraph from Peshawar. Attended by his ADC, Bloody Francis, as Fettleworth was known throughout his Division, proceeded to the study where Lakenham awaited him, his face grim.

"Well, Lakenham, what is it now? Am I to be permitted no peace?" Fettleworth dabbed at his cheeks with a linen handkerchief and looked petulant. "I trust the matter's important."

"It is, sir. The situation in Peshawar has worsened appreciably—"

"Damn natives!" Heavily, the Divisional Commander dropped into a chair. "Well, go on, then, dinner will be ready shortly and I dislike keeping my wife waiting."

"Yes, sir." Lakenham, tall and spare where his master was short and fat, spoke harshly. "The attackers have spread westwards and there has been action in the cantonment area – repulsed, I'm glad to report, with heavy casualties to the natives—"

"And our men, Lakenham?"

"Ten dead, thirty-five wounded."

"Not too bad. Anything else?"

"I'm afraid so, sir. The married quarters of the 114th Highlanders have been under attack. There have been casualties. Four privates and a lance-corporal of the guard badly wounded – and two women dead."

Fettleworth put his head in his hands for a moment, then looked up with glassy eyes, staring at nothing. "My God. Anyone of importance? I note you said women, not ladies." In the army in India, only officers had ladies: NCOs had wives, the rank-and-file had women. "Well?"

Lakenham said, "I used the first word that came into my mind, sir. One was the wife of a corporal – a Mrs MacDade. The other was Mrs Cunningham."

Fettleworth looked blank. "Cunningham?"

16

"The wife of the Regimental Sergeant-Major of the 114th, sir."

Fettleworth clicked his tongue, shook his head and for a moment looked immensely sad, a condition from which he made a fast recovery. "Oh, dear, I'm most sorry, most sorry. You shall send my condolences, Lakenham, by the telegraph. At once. A senior warrant officer's wife . . . there will be a full military funeral and balls to the natives. Pass the necessary orders to Brigade in Peshawar, if you please, Lakenham, and to the Colonel of the 114th – Dornoch, isn't it?"

"Yes, sir." Lakenham paused, his eyes cold. "I think your dinner must wait a little longer yet—"

"Oh? Why, may I ask?"

"Fresh issues have been raised, sir. The British have now come under direct attack in their own quarters."

"Yes, but we can cope, Lakenham, can't we? It's still purely local, isn't it?"

"At this moment, yes. But Brigade in Peshawar awaits your orders as to what the reaction should be. With respect, sir, I advise that you yourself now seek orders from the GOC in Murree, who may find it expedient to consult the Commander-in-Chief."

"Yes, yes, you may well be right." Looking put out, Fettleworth drummed his fingers on the polished leather top of his immense desk. "Well, there's no immediate rush, Lakenham. Draft a despatch, will you, and I'll read it after dinner." He got to his feet and as he moved for the door his words floated back towards the Chief of Staff over his shoulder. "My *khansamma's* preparing a splendid salmon, don't you know . . . brought in relays of ice by the troopship to Bombay . . . all the way from Scotland . . . part of the Highlands where that feller Dornoch comes from. . . ."

*　　*　　*

In the Royal Strathspeys' cantonment the air was brittle, the mood sombre. The loss of two of the regimental wives was felt keenly. Men who in the past had believed themselves

17

picked upon by the RSM felt regret at words muttered *sotto voce* about a nagging old bastard: Cunningham, always fair, was liked and respected by both officers and men, of whom indeed few could remember the regiment without him. He was the continuing rock, the father figure, dependable and without fear or favour. His grief seemed to affect every man from the Colonel to the newest-drafted recruit from Invermore. Lord Dornoch spoke in private to both the RSM and Corporal MacDade, after which MacDade was granted access to as much rum as he wished and sent off duty for all purposes short of further attack or the full muster of the battalion to march into action. Cunningham was sat down in the Colonel's bungalow and given whisky. The two men sat in silence mostly; condolences were unnecessary: they had served and fought in each other's company for too long. Dornoch watched the RSM's face, the haunted eyes that were looking back into past days, to his marriage, as a newly-promoted sergeant serving in the depot at Invermore, to the young Mary MacAllister in service at Corriecraig Castle, home of the Ogilvies... in every sense, the 114th Highlanders, the Queen's Own Royal Strathspey, was a family, a clan regiment. On to postings with the regiment around the world, Edinburgh Castle, Hong Kong, Aden, Gibraltar, South Africa and India, Bessie – Mary's second name and the one she had come to use after marriage – always with him. Back from gruelling marches into hostile territory to find Bessie awaiting him in cantonments. The children had grown up and were in England; now, out here, the void would be the worse. India henceforward would be nothing but heat and dust, blood and battle and boredom in between... Using Cunningham's nick-name, Dornoch said, "The regiment's still in being, Bosom. It's still there, and it still needs you – always will."

"Aye, sir. I'm not forgetting that. I'll not be found lacking in my duty."

"I know you won't. I didn't mean that."

"I understand you well, sir." Cunningham set down his glass rather hard, and got to his feet, coming automatically to attention. "If you'll excuse me, sir—"

18

"Another *chota peg,* Bosom."

"Thank you, sir, I'll not. Two leads to three, and then four if a man's not watchful, and tonight I'd not trust myself."

Dornoch nodded. "It's up to you, Bosom. There'd be no blame . . . but I take your point." He reached out a hand, which the RSM took in a strong grip. "You're a good friend for any man to have, Bosom. I can't say more. Just this, perhaps: fight on!"

"I'll be doing that, sir." For a moment the blue eyes shone murder. "I'll be fighting for Bessie yet, sir, as well as the regiment, and when I get my hands on the bugger that fired the shot, I'll tear out his guts, sir."

It sounded like a simple statement of fact. Dornoch said, "One native looks much like another, Bosom—"

"No, sir. With respect, sir. Sergeant Cairns has described the man, sir. A big bastard, sir, more than six feet of him, with a great hooked nose and no hair at all on his face, dressed in a white gown and with a star branded onto his forehead."

"A star?"

"Aye, sir. When I see him, sir, I'll know him for certain."

When Cunningham had taken his leave, Dornoch was in a thoughtful mood. It was all very understandable, but personal feuds could cut across military requirements, could be at the least an embarrassment if an RSM should embark on a private manhunt as it were . . . but he shrugged his thoughts away and went to join his wife. The rest of the evening and night passed quietly; it was as though the natives were unwilling to face the combined strength of the British regiments again and had decided to bide their time. Just before midnight word came through from Robin Stuart, on the telegraph, as yet uncut, from the city guardroom: a number of British civilians had been brought in safely, the patrol had suffered casualties and all ranks had now been withdrawn to the guardroom, which was under siege. As midnight passed, Dornoch at last gave the word for a reduced readiness, and later than had at first been intended one man in two thankfully cradled his rifle in his arms and slept on the ground. Next morning there was still an uneasy

19

peace, though sounds of more firing came down upon the cantonments from the city. There was a curious sense of unreality about it all, Ogilvie thought, as the Union Flag was hoisted to the head of the flagstaff on the parade-ground, to the beat of the drummers and the wail of the pipes. When the flag-hoisting ceremony was over Ogilvie, making for his room to wash away the night's sleaziness, found Fiona coming from the Colonel's bungalow. She looked full of good health and spirit but as much as all the others had been shaken by the murder of two of the regiment's wives.

"When are we going to hit back?" she demanded, looking fierce.

"I don't know," Ogilvie answered, smiling, despite his own worries, at her manner. "Why not ask the Major?"

"Uncle David? I did. He wouldn't say. It was none of my business, I gathered. I don't believe he knew anyway," she added with a toss of her fair hair. "He said the only orders that had come through from what was it—"

"Brigade?"

"Oh yes, Brigade. The orders were just for the regiment to defend the cantonment." Fiona gave him a direct and challenging look. "Isn't your father going to do anything about it? I thought he was the bigwig in Northern India. And I thought the British always hit back." Suddenly the girl's face took on a new expression and she said, "Don't look now, but he's behind you."

"Who is?"

She laughed. "Uncle David." A moment later a shout tore across the parade-ground, and Ogilvie turned and saluted.

"If you can spare me a moment of your time, Captain Ogilvie, I'll be much obliged."

Ogilvie marched across smartly, halted and saluted again. "At your service, Major."

"Don't try to be funny, Ogilvie." Brora was scowling. "Have you nothing better to do, with the regiment likely to come under attack, than to stand and gossip?"

"I'm sorry, Major."

"Well, I have orders for you from the Colonel. Last night word came through from Division that there's to be a funeral

20

with military honours. The two women. You're to command the escort for the coffins and provide the firing-party. It will take place at 2 p.m. today, so you'll kindly stir yourself, Ogilvie – and make damn sure there's a smart turn out because more orders received half an hour ago indicate that General Fettleworth proposes attending in person, representing Sir Iain Ogilvie who's unable to get here in time from Murree."

*   *   *

Making his preparations, Ogilvie reflected that it would undoubtedly be the case that his father would wish to pay his vicarious respects to a former servant as well as support the Regimental Sergeant-Major of his old regiment; nevertheless, he felt there was more in the attendance of the Divisional Commander than a mere representation of the General Officer Commanding, Northern Army: Bloody Francis was a most transparent officer. His customary panacea, when faced with natives in a rebellious mood, was to mount a parade. Nothing, he was accustomed to proclaim, impressed the native mind, a simple mind at best, so much as a show of Imperial strength. So whenever trouble was threatened, out came the massive guns and limbers of the heavy artillery batteries, the immaculate horses of the British and Indian cavalry regiments, and the massed infantry of the line with the thunderous mouths of the brass bands and the fifes and drums in support. In the case of the Scottish regiments, the pipes and drums, to which Bloody Francis was much addicted, and today was to be essentially a Scottish occasion albeit a sad one. Bloody Francis, so conveniently bidden by the GOC to attend, would make all the capital he could in Ogilvie's view. As the morning progressed, and as the guard and escort and firing-party were drilled in cortege duties and the battalion's drums were muffled in black crepe, it seemed as though Ogilvie had been right: all the infantry regiments in garrison were to provide one company each with rifles and fixed bayonets to march behind the immediate escort found by B Company of the Royal Strathspeys; and a mounted escort of the Guides

21

Cavalry would preceed the coffins on their gun-carriages, while ahead of the whole procession would rumble a horse battery of heavy artillery. Behind the guns, and ahead of the coffins and the guides, Lieutenant-General Fettleworth, eschewing a saluting dais as being unsuitable to the occasion, would ride democratically with Lord Dornoch, Lord Brora, and Captain Black. Behind the coffins would march the RSM and Corporal MacDade; and mourning bands would be worn by everyone on parade. After the procession had marched back into cantonments, the Divisional Commander would have personal words with both the bereaved husbands, and would then return to Nowshera.

At 1.30 p.m. B Company of the Royal Strathspeys fell in under James Ogilvie to be closely inspected by the Adjutant, who moved down the ranks jerking at Wolseley helmets and kilts and criticising the set of the white pipe-clayed spats or the angle of the hilts of skean dhus. Draped with the Union Flags, the coffins were trundled out on the gun-carriages with Cunningham and MacDade in rear, and set between half companies. At 1.45 the Colonel rode out from the gates with the Major and Andrew Black and Bloody Francis himself, who had arrived in pompous state for a *chota peg* in Dornoch's bungalow at a little after noon. The Scots moved out of cantonments to the sad sound of the pipes and drums playing *Farewell to Invermore,* composed by the Pipe-Major when the regiment had left Scotland on Indian service bound. MacDade, a shade drink-taken still, was pale and wan and moved unsteadily. The Regimental Sergeant-Major's face showed strain but he moved as though nothing was disturbing him, just as if he were the RSM on parade on some entirely impersonal ceremonial occasion. Outside in the roadway the cortege and its immediate escort were joined by the rest of the infantry under Brigadier-General Shaw, the Brigade Commander, plus the cavalry and the artillery detachments. The Royal Strathspeys slow marched with rifles reversed beneath their arms, butts to the front, muzzles angled to the rear; the remainder of the infantry also slow marched, but carried their rifles at the slope. The muffled drums beat out, the highland pipes shifted to *The Soldier's*

Return. Ahead the cavalry and the guns brought up heavy dust that floated back to deposit itself over the marching men and the coffins and the trees that lined the route to the cemetery and blew across the parade-grounds of the cantonment area. The dust apart, as Bloody Francis Fettleworth remarked in an aside to Lord Dornoch, it was an impressive show.

The husbands, he announced, should be proud. Dornoch forbore to respond. Fettleworth went on, "Word'll get back to Peshawar – you'll see. It'll stop the buggers farting in church, by God it will!" He blew through the trailing ends of his white walrus moustache. "Never fails. To prove my point, there's not a damn native in sight!"

He rode on, looking pompous. Dornoch, who knew him well, was aware of the direction his thoughts would be taking: he would be thinking of Her Majesty Queen Victoria, whose military representative he was within the area garrisoned by the First Division. She would be there beside him, in her bath chair, the bun of hair sticking out behind the widow's cap, the face imperious and a hand tapping the side of her conveyance in time to the notes of her beloved pipes. If ever there was a Soldier of the Queen, it was Fettleworth; in his heart, wherever he happened to be at the time, he dwelt in Osborne House, or Windsor Castle, or Buckingham Palace, or Balmoral according to the time of year and the royal calendar, HM's right-hand General. Fettleworth would be thinking also of other things: how tiresome the damn natives were to disturb the even tenor of Division and what a lot of blasted work was going to be involved in drafting continual despatches to Murree – despatches that must be drafted with immense care since they would form the basis of onward reports not only to Calcutta and His Excellency the Viceroy, but also to Whitehall – the mighty India Office itself – and even the Court. If Bloody Francis put a word wrong, it could bounce back upon his portly person in most unpleasant ways, for General Officers, like all other soldiers both high and low, were immensely expendable persons, much more so than were the wily politicians.

*   *   *

23

When the coffins had been lowered into their graves to the murmured prayers of the 114th's padre, and the firing-party had discharged the last salute, and the Pipe-Major had played the lament *The Flowers of the Forest*, the guns and the cavalry detached at the trot and rode away and the infantry companies were quick-marched back to their cantonments. The music was lively now, to restore men's spirits and to wipe death from the slate: the Royal Strathspeys marched back to the tune of *Cock o' the North* coming stirringly from the pipes and drums until it was replaced by *Far O'er the Sea*. In the cantonment the men were dismissed to the barrack-rooms and Fettleworth went with Lord Dornoch to the latter's bungalow where the bereaved husbands were bidden to meet the General.

Fettleworth stood to greet them. He shook their hands, and Dornoch held his breath. But he need not have worried; Fettleworth spoke sincerely of their loss, of the courage of the wives who have braved Indian service and its undoubted rigours to be at their husbands' sides. England, he said, would be proud; so would Her Majesty. He cleared his throat gruffly at mention of the Queen, and his scarlet-clad stomach moved an inch upwards towards his chest. He spoke of leave, which would be granted as soon as the situation allowed. Bidden to make any special requests, MacDade asked for a posting home. He had two young children who would be better off back in Scotland now. Nodding gravely, Fettleworth said the request would be noted at Division.

"Mr Cunningham?" he asked.

Cunningham shook his head. "No, sir, thank you. There would be little point, sir. I wish to remain on Indian service with the battalion, sir."

Again Fettleworth nodded, and turned to Lord Dornoch. "You have a fine sar'nt-major, Colonel. The best. I have always admired the Scots." He blew out his moustache, then once again shook hands and the painful interview was over. Cunningham and MacDade marched out of the bungalow, put on their Wolseley helmets when outside, and marched to their lonely quarters. There was a strange look on the RSM's face – a withdrawn, unseeing look though the eyes were cold and hard as ice. In Dornoch's bungalow Bloody Francis accepted a *chota peg* from a bearer after lowering his thick body into a chair, and spoke again about the demands of Empire.

"Not all beer and skittles, Dornoch." His protuberant eyes stared at the Colonel. "How d'you assess the situation in the city?"

Dornoch shrugged. "I don't, sir."

"Hey? How d'you mean, don't?"

"Apart from brief messages from the town patrol, which is provided by my regiment, I've had no contact since the trouble started – I can make no assessment. Cannot your Political Officer help?"

"Blaise-Willoughby? Feller's doing what he can to have the city probed. He can't do more."

"Does he know the background, sir?"

Fettleworth pulled at his moustache and frowned. "I think he's been caught on the hop, frankly. Usually these things tend to cast their shadows before them . . . but this time Blaise-Willoughby seems to have been let down by his subordinates, who should have got some word through before the fuse blew."

"All the recent movement of natives east of Peshawar – that alone should have—"

"Yes. Yes, I do agree, Dornoch. Of course, I alerted Murree to the situation as I saw it, and I'm sure Murree alerted Calcutta, but we all know what Calcutta's like, sit on their damn arses in offices and let the world pass by." Fettleworth sniffed.

Dornoch asked, "Blaise-Willoughby, sir. Has he ever spoken of a man with a star branded onto his forehead?"

Fettleworth stared. "Not that I recall. Why d'you ask?"

Dornoch passed on Cunningham's report of the man who had killed his wife. "He appears to have been some kind of a leader. It might be worth while getting Blaise-Willoughby to investigate."

"Yes, perhaps. I'll refer it to him for what it's worth." Fettleworth finished his whisky, dangled his glass meaningly

25

for another. The glass refilled by the attentive bearer, he emptied it quickly and announced that he must be getting back to Division. The Royal Strathspeys' brigade would be kept fully informed as the situation developed and it might be that the regiments in garrison would be ordered in on a police action to restore the equilibrium; but for the time being he wished to await reports from Blaise-Willoughby's infiltrated officers, and the orders as yet remained unchanged: the British were simply to defend the cantonment area against any attack and were not to press any pursuit as far as the city itself. Religious insurrections, he said solemnly, were the very devil. It behoved the Raj to walk warily. He was about to take his leave when sounds of a disturbance reached the bungalow: rapid rifle fire came from the distance, from towards the city, drawing nearer. Fettleworth and Dornoch ran from the bungalow and across the parade-ground. They heard the galloping hooves closing, then witnessed the suicidal dash of a native riding a sweat-lathered black horse, straight through the gate past the barrack guard, his body pouring blood and another man laid drooping across his saddle before him. As the men of the guard opened at point-blank range, the native slid off his horse to the ground. The horse galloped on, and as it did so the other body fell, to lie face down on the parade. Men ran from the perimeter in an attempt to seize the horse's bridle. Dornoch, with Fettleworth behind him, ran towards the bodies in the dust. The rider was alive, but only just. Pain-filled eyes stared up at the Colonel as he knelt, and the lips moved.

"Sahib, I was too late . . . the Raj . . . "

Fettleworth pounded up. Dornoch got to his feet, saw Brora and the Adjutant coming up behind the General. He said, "Dead, I fancy. I think he was loyal. A pity."

"What about the other man?" Fettleworth asked.

"Dead also, sir." Dornoch waved an arm towards the huddle on the ground: the haft of a deep-driven dagger protruded from a body bare to the waist, the point of entry being just below the left shoulder-blade and angled upwards for the heart. Brora was making for him, and as the Colonel and Fettleworth approached Brora silently indicated some words burned by an iron into the flesh of the back.

The words read: *British spy of the Raj.*

Fettleworth's florid face seemed to pale and he stared down in horror. Hoarsely he said, "Show me his face."

Brora bent and lifted the body half clear of the ground, and twisted it. The dead face stared up, the eyes open and glassy. The skin had been darkened and there was much unmilitary hair, but Fettleworth apparently recognised him. He said, "He's one of Blaise-Willoughby's officers, feller named Parsons. My God!"

Dornoch's face was sombre. He looked questioningly at Fettleworth. "What now, sir?" he asked.

"Eh? What d'you mean, Dornoch – what now?"

"Blaise-Willoughby's remaining infiltrated Political Officers. If one's been found out and killed—"

"Yes, yes, I take your point. If we lose them all, we lose our intelligence. What are you suggesting, Dornoch?"

"That the time's come to take decisive action, sir. I think we should establish an effective military presence in the city before it's too late." Dornoch paused. "It's a far from pleasant prospect, to hold the ring between Muslim and Hindu—"

"And a thankless one!"

"But one I believe we must accept, sir. And I repeat – before it's too late. Nothing expands like a religious war." Dornoch lifted his head a little, sniffing the air like a warhorse scenting the smoke of battle. A cool breeze came down from the distant Himalayan peaks, wafting with it the distinctive smells of the sub-continent. "This cannot be localised, General, if we fail to take our chance to kill the bud."

Three

Returning to Nowshera and his headquarters, Fettleworth sent for the Political Officer: Major Blaise-Willoughby reported, small, sardonic and as scruffy as was normal to him. In Fettleworth's view, the Political Officer could pass for a native even when in Western clothing. The white sharkskin suit was in need of an iron and the cuffs were soiled. On Blaise-Willoughby's shoulder sat his inevitable blasted monkey, rudely named Wolseley after the Field Marshal commanding the British Army from the Horse Guards. Blaise-Willoughby was inseparable from his pet; Fettleworth had come to accept the fact of the wretched beast's existence though he detested the way the animal grinned and chattered at him, dropping peanuts fed to it by its master. There was something insubordinate in the wizened face.

"Parsons is dead, Blaise-Willoughby," Fettleworth said without preamble.

"I know."

Fettleworth stared. "You do? May I ask how? I authorised no telegraph from—"

"Quite. I wasn't referring to that, sir." Blaise-Willoughby lifted a hand and stroked Wolseley's rump. "Do I take it poor Parsons was delivered to cantonments?"

"Yes, he was. How do you know that?"

"A guess, sir. Similar deliveries have been made to the civil mortuary here in Nowshera. Morton-Walshe, Pettigrew, Hanrahan. All dead, all with knives in the back." Blaise-Willoughby's voice held no expression: he was, Fettleworth thought, the coldest of fishes. "All my agents gone – all of them. And nothing gained."

"The natives who brought them?"

Blaise-Willoughby shook his head. "They were not *brought,* exactly. There were found tied to horses that had been driven into the city . . . the town patrol brought them in, after which I identified them." He spread his hands. "We have no leads, I'm sorry to say."

Fettleworth mopped at his face and shouted at the *punkah-wallah* outside to get more air moving. "How the devil did the damn natives rumble them all – hey, Blaise-Willoughby? Did you take the normal precautions?"

"Of course," Blaise-Willoughby answered in an even tone. "I think however one must make the assumption that torture was used – indeed there is evidence of it. Finger-nails torn off – I refer to Pettigrew. Cuts and burns on the soles of the feet and elsewhere."

"You're suggesting he gave the others away?"

Blaise-Willoughby shrugged.

"That's a scandalous suggestion – Hanrahan's British! *Was* British. I mean Pettigrew – same thing. Britons don't act traitorously and I won't have it said that they do, d'you hear?"

Blaise-Willoughby said, "Every man has his breaking point, General. Even me, even you—"

"Don't be bloody impertinent, Blaise-Willoughby."

"I apologise, sir." Blaise-Willoughby inclined his head meekly, but there was a glitter in his eye. Wolseley, shifting his grip as his master bent forward, stared beadily. "We must face facts, however. It's not coincidence that all my agents have been killed, General. If none of them was made to talk, then the only other possibility is that we've a spy inside Division, and one with his ear very close to the ground indeed—"

"That's equally preposterous, damn you—"

"With respect, General, neither of my hypotheses is in the least preposterous."

"The British don't spy against their own damn side!"

Blaise-Willoughby gave a sigh of exasperation. "We have natives in Divisional HQ as well as British, General."

"H'm. Yes, I take your point. Yes, indeed. Well, if that's the case, though I doubt it since all our natives are loyal to the Raj, then it's up to you to bowl the bloody man out, isn't it? In the meantime, what do we do? What do you suggest? By the way," Fettleworth added, "something emerged while I was in the 114th's cantonment. The Sar'nt-Major's wife, the one who was killed." He explained about the star-branded forehead of Mrs Cunningham's attacker. "Does that mean anything to you?"

"A star. . . " Blaise-Willoughby pondered, frowning. "No, I'm afraid not, General. I'll bear it in mind, though."

Fettleworth said, "Well, I dare say it's unimportant really, these buggers are pretty damn primitive and like decorating themselves – like children, I always think."

"Masochistic?" Blaise-Willoughby murmured.

"Masso what?"

"It's unimportant really, General, though I doubt if even natives undergo painful decoration without purpose—"

"Oh, rubbish, you don't know the natives like I do, Blaise-Willoughby," Fettleworth said crossly. "However, to get back to my question: what do we do now, what's the next move in your opinion? The Colonel of the 114th advises positive action to hold the balance, and I'm not sure he's not right. Well?"

"Early days, General."

"Things move fast in India, you know."

"Yes, I do know. I know something else, and it's this: no one loses friends faster than he who interferes between opposing religions. We could risk the Raj by interference at this point."

"Not what Lord Dornoch said."

"Indeed?" Blaise-Willoughby raised deprecating eyebrows. "Lord Dornoch sees things, naturally enough, as a soldier, as a battalion commander. I have learned to take other views when necessary. Currently my view is this: an interposition into Peshawar at this moment could engender enough friction for both Muslim and Hindu, throughout the sub-continent—"

"To tear out each other's throats?"

Blaise-Willoughby smiled. "On the contrary – to unite against the Raj."

"Oh, rubbish – Muslim and Hindu will never unite, my dear fellow, never! That's damn balderdash."

"In an ultimate sense, I agree, they'd not. But as a means to

30

an end . . . "Blaise-Willoughby shook his head and looked pensive. "We must hold on, I truly believe, until something concrete emerges, until, for instance, we can as it were isolate the leaders and cut them out . . . and they must not be seen to be cut out by us – by the British."

"Devious," Fettleworth said doubtfully.

"Expedient," Blaise-Willoughby murmured. He leaned forward to tie up a shoelace. Wolseley teetered backwards, then recovered his balance and emitted sharp cries of anger. Blaise-Willoughby said, "Frankly my advice would be to play this *pianissimo*—"

"*Pianissimo* my backside, for God's sake talk English," Fettleworth snapped. "Damn musical terms, not manly—"

"As you say, General. Play it down, then. Wait and see."

"I don't like waiting and seeing, blast you!"

"A difficult game, I agree, and one that goes to the strongest." Blaise-Willoughby's eyes were mocking, but the sarcasm seemed lost upon the Divisional Commander. "If I might offer further advice, General, it would be that you now make a further report to Sir Iain in Murree, and await orders."

Fettleworth nodded and looked relieved. "Yes, yes, a good suggestion. Thank you, Blaise-Willoughby, that'll be all."

*   *   *

Throughout the succeeding night, sounds of war were heard coming from the city by the soldiers still standing-to in the cantonments. There was heavy gunfire, and from time to time the night sky was lit by flashes as the shells were discharged, and by the explosions as they fell upon the buildings and the inhabitants. When the wind shifted and blew from the east, the air was heavy with the stench of gunsmoke and with the appalling smell of death. Already the bodies would be rotting in the streets, and now there was real doubt as to the fate of the town patrol: the last message from the Officer of the Guard had come through a little after six p.m. That message had indicated a continuing siege of the guardroom. Now it was presumed that the telegraph line had at last been cut by the mob, and Dornoch had reported as much to Brigade, but had received no orders in return. Brigade, it seemed, was awaiting orders from Division, and Division was awaiting orders from Murree. It was likely enough that Northern Army Command had first to consult Calcutta and the Commander-in-Chief, Sir George White, and that *he* might find it expedient to consult the Viceroy.

Brora was in a fever of impatience. "British troops may be dying, Colonel, while this farce proceeds! *Our* troops!"

"I'm well enough aware of it, Major, but my hands are tied."

"With red tape! I suggest you cut it."

Dornoch gave a hard laugh. "Easier said than done. You know the chain of command as well as I, Major. Calcutta's in possession of more information than we are, in any case."

"And we mustn't rock the boat, I suppose?"

"Exactly."

Brora paced the battalion office, up and down past the Colonel and the Adjutant, his face working with angry frustration. "I call it scandalous, nothing less. The whole Brigade should be ordered in to settle the matter. Some British bayonets poked into a few black bums would have the rabble on the run in no time at all." He swung round on the Colonel. "You have your own men to consider—"

"Major—"

"You'll hear me out, Colonel. There are men of the 114th out there in the bloody town guardroom." Brora lifted a hand and pointed towards the east. "Two miles away, and we sit here safe in cantonments like a bunch of pimps in a brothel. Balls to Calcutta, I say, by the time they make up their minds it'll be too late! We're entitled to protect our own!"

"I cannot anticipate orders, Major, nor can I disobey. The orders are still not to move out of cantonments. I, and you, will obey them without question." Dornoch's face was stiff with anger, and there was hurt in his eyes. "I know you well enough to gauge what's in your mind. I warn you, if you should attempt to take any of my regiment out of cantonments on some crazy mission of your own, you will be placed in close arrest immediately. I shall say no more than that."

Brora's face suffused and he took a step towards the Colonel, his hands lifted, the fingers spread as though in a desire to throttle. Andrew Black came across quickly, and laid a hand on Brora's shoulder. Brora lashed out sideways, and Black staggered back against the wall of the room. Then Brora turned away suddenly, and strode out onto the dark parade-ground. Making for the perimeter, watching the battle fires from the city, he stopped and went back on his tracks, his face devilish in the moonlight. He went to his bungalow, shouted at his bearer to bring a *chota peg* and bring it quickly or he'd have his backside kicked. When the whisky-and-soda was brought on a silver salver inscribed with his coat-of-arms he snatched it and drank it in a gulp, banged the glass back on the salver and demanded another. This he drank more slowly, pacing the room as he did so. He stopped before a long mirror, studying his reflection: the dark, scowling face, the khaki-drill tunic – for tonight no one was changing out of ordinary service dress – with his major's crowns on the shoulder-straps, the kilt with the dark green tartan of the Royal Strathspey, the well-polished Sam Browne belt across the tunic, the regimental badges at the collar. A fine regiment, the best ...Brora shouted, louder than before, for another *chota peg*. The men depended upon their officers. They should not be let down. Besieged in the guardroom in Peshawar was a half company of the regiment ... a town patrol that was now imprisoned and under insult from native scum.

They must not be left there unsupported. They would not be.

Brora left his bungalow and marched out towards the parade ground. Fortuitously, he encountered the Regimental Sergeant-Major.

"Mr Cunningham ... "

Cunningham stopped with a slam of boots and his hand flew to the salute. "Sir!"

"A sad day for you. For us all."

"Thank you, sir."

33

"I know one thing, Sar'nt-Major: you'll not be able to wait to have a crack at the enemy."

"That's true, sir." There was deep feeling in the warrant officer's voice.

"Then your chance has come."

"Sir?"

Brora said, "I have orders from the Colonel. The town patrol is to be relieved – is to be brought out. I am to take a company, which is to leave cantonments at once and as silently as possible under cover of the dark. Do you understand, Sar'nt-Major?"

"I understand, sir."

"You may come if you wish. I shall be glad of you, but I give you no order to do so."

Cunningham said, "Of course I'll come, sir, and thank you."

"Then that's settled. Now, if you please, Sar'nt-Major, convey the Colonel's order to Captain Ogilvie. He is to withdraw B Company from the perimeter – they'll already have a full issue of ammunition – and he is to muster them quietly outside the main gate, in the roadway, where I shall be awaiting them. You will stress the need for complete silence – our native domestics are fleeter of foot than a company on the march, and must be considered untrustworthy. Carry on, if you please, Sar'nt-Major."

*　　*　　*

Ogilvie found no reason to doubt the authenticity of the orders as conveyed by the Regimental Sergeant-Major: quickly and as silently as possible he withdrew his company towards the gate, where Lord Brora was waiting with the Sergeant of the Guard in the darkness: the guard lantern, under current conditions, was not in use.

Brora said, "Captain Ogilvie, you'll move your men along the roadway to the east, independently. Fall them in two hundred yards clear, then I'll pass the orders."

"Why not—"

"Kindly do not question my orders, Captain Ogilvie, but obey them immediately."

34

Ogilvie saluted and turned away. There was a strong smell of whisky on the Major's breath, but that was his own concern. The men of B Company made their way, singly and in pairs and groups, along the road. When clear of the perimeter Colour-Sergeant MacTrease gave the order to fall in, in column of fours facing east. Brora, already waiting with the RSM, called for the officers and NCOs to gather round him. His orders were brief: B Company's task was to enter Peshawar shoulder-to-shoulder and fight their way through to the town guardroom where they were to break through the mob and enter. Further orders would thereafter be issued. The officers and NCOs were sent back to the company and Brora gave the word to double-march, running ahead of Ogilvie himself with the RSM in rear. The road lay deserted, eerie beneath the moon as the trees threw their shadows. Only B Company and a few scavenging dogs moved, but the sounds from ahead grew louder as the cantonment fell behind. Ogilvie, not doubting the Colonel's order yet, was surprised that he had apparently seen fit to give it. In Ogilvie's view, such a penetration of Peshawar needed battalion strength if not brigade; and surely – unless orders had come from above – the Colonel was flying in the face of Bloody Francis, who had been insistent earlier that action must wait upon further information via the Political Officers . . . yet what the Colonel now seemed to be doing was only what the whole battalion had wished for, and not a man of B Company would hold back when the action began, and never mind the correctness or otherwise of the order.

When the body of troops was within sight of the attackers' lines outside Peshawar, lines drawn up as though for a long siege, Lord Brora passed the order to quick march, and the advance slowed from the double. Bayonets were fixed on the march, and Brora repeated the order that the assault was to be made shoulder-to-shoulder. There would be no deployment and the men were to cut straight through for the town patrol whatever happened. It began to seem like suicide now as they approached the massed lines of the fanatics, clearly silhouetted against the fires, and Ogilvie was smitten with many doubts. There was a much stronger force than he had expected, stronger for sure than Lord Dornoch would have anticipated in the absence of any positive information. A moment later he heard a horse galloping up from behind the advance, and word was passed forward from the rear that Captain Black was riding down upon them, and yelling like a madman.

Black came past the main body of the company, and pulled his horse up alongside Lord Brora, his uniform stained with sweat despite the cool night air. "A word in your ear, Major," he said. "I am sent by the Colonel, with orders."

"Too late, Black, too late."

"Major, you are to—"

"Get out of my way, Captain Black, and that is an order." Brora strode on. As Black, helplessly fuming, kept pace with him, Brora drew his highland broadsword and flourished it at the Adjutant. "You bloody fool, do you not see that it is too late even if I were to listen?" He waved the sword ahead. "We have been seen now, and must fight our way through." The words were scarcely out of his mouth before the firing started, and a man in the leading file reeled, clutching at his shoulder and dropping his rifle, which was picked up by the man behind. Brora's voice shouted the order to resume double marching, and B Company ran ahead towards the flares and the din of battle and within a minute had reached the attackers' lines. The Scots rifles fired point-blank into the mass of natives and Brora's and Ogilvie's broadswords flailed ceaselessly, the blades becoming bloody and hung with a lace of flesh as they cut into necks and upraised arms. Behind, Cunningham was covering the rear with a terrible ferocity, making good use of his own broadsword with one hand and with the other emptying his revolver time and again into the close-packed bodies as the company forged through. The Scots found themselves assailed with all manner of weapons: the unwieldy and slow-loading rifles of the native horde, the long, snaky, rust-covered bayonets, and with sticks, stones and filth. There was noise everywhere – the artillery was still in action, and every native throat was yelling and screaming insults against the Raj. Black was dismounted now, his horse cut down beneath him. The

36

company pressed on, carrying its wounded when they could not march, coming soon between burning buildings and crashing masonry and beginning to leave the mob behind. Suddenly a ringing shout came from Lord Brora:

"Ahead there – the town patrol's ahead, marching out towards us!"

A ragged cheer went up. Ogilvie saw, in the light from the fires, the advance of the kilted soldiers with Robin Stuart in the lead with his senior subaltern, the latter with his head roughly bandaged. In the centre were several British civilians. Several men were being borne along in *doolies,* but, at first glance at any rate, the half company did not appear badly depleted. When the two groups came together, Brora lost no time in talk: he turned B Company about and ordered the town patrol to fall in behind. The march out began, through the close heat of the fires towards the encircling lines around the city, with the occasional shell exploding uncomfortably nearby. The fighting continued as the combined force approached the city's perimeter, but as the advance back went on the firing fell away and the natives in the immediate sector began streaming to either flank, yelling imprecations and turning their ancient rifles outwards and away from the Scots. Shortly after this Ogilvie realised why: over the sounds of gunfire and screaming natives, he heard the throb and beat of the pipes and drums and a minute later saw the shining bayonets of the battalion advancing to meet them. Again a cheer went up. B Company and the town patrol went forward at the double, coming clear of the enemy under a final hail of somewhat wild rifle fire, and joined up with the main body of the battalion.

Lord Brora, ragged now and bloodstained but laughing like a madman, strode forward towards the Colonel. He gave a mocking salute. "Well met, Colonel. I think you also have disobeyed orders now. In the meantime, I present you with the town patrol and some assorted British officials. Mission successful, I think!"

*   *   *

Marching back behind the pipes and drums to cantonments, Robin Stuart made a preliminary report to Lord Dornoch: the city was badly damaged and there was a good deal of looting going on by both sides. The situation was utterly confused. Notwithstanding the fact that a number of the attackers had penetrated the city, the bombardment from the heavy artillery was being maintained spasmodically, the shells naturally coming down on friend and foe alike. The patrol had lost nine men dead and twenty-two were wounded in varying degrees of severity; all the dead and wounded had been evacuated, thanks to Lord Brora. Stuart said, "We had word the Major was coming through, Colonel – a loyal native gave us the information."

"And then you marched out to meet him?"

"Yes, Colonel. The Major's saved a lot of lives. We were almost out of ammunition . . . we'd been under continuous attack once I'd withdrawn the patrols and the civilians into the guardroom."

"Yes. Have you gleaned any information as to who's behind all this, and why?"

Stuart shook his head. "No, Colonel, I'm afraid not, other than that it's Muslim – or anyway Pathan – against Hindu."

"And your assessment, your views on what ought to be done now?"

Stuart blew out his cheeks and frowned. "That's hard to say, Colonel. As I see it, there are two alternatives. Either we leave the situation to resolve itself, in the course of which there'll be a lot of slaughter of the innocents along with the rest, and Peshawar will burn to the ground – or we advance in strength and put an end to it." He added, "Of course, those two alternatives are the extremes and each can rebound on us, but I see no middle way."

Dornoch laughed without humour, a sad sound. He said, "My dear chap, you see it as a soldier, as I do. I find no middle way either! But as usual the politicians have the last word, and we must obey."

*   *   *

38

As the battalion came back through the gate, there was cheering from the company left behind on barrack guard, spread thinly round the perimeter. Helmets were waved in the air; the word spread quickly that the Major had brought out the town patrol, and from the guard company and from the others left behind in the stables and the quartermaster's stores there was a special cheer for Lord Brora, who was a bastard but had guts and had no fear of the rabble. This the Colonel noted and gave way gracefully. He kept the battalion on parade briefly after the wounded had been delivered up to the medical orderlies and the dead removed, and in front of all ranks he shook Brora's hand and thanked him. When the battalion had been fallen out, to resume post at the perimeter, he took Brora aside.

"No more will be said, Major. But I give no promise for the future should you disobey my orders again."

There was a sardonic look on Brora's face and he was about to utter when Andrew Black came up at the double, his expression urgent. Dornoch asked, "What is it, Andrew?"

"Mr Cunningham, Colonel. He's not returned with the battalion."

Dornoch stared. "Not returned? You're sure?"

"I am sure, Colonel, yes."

"When was he last seen?"

Black shrugged. "I don't know, Colonel—"

"Major?"

"I don't know either," Brora said flatly: it was plain he cared little. "I have no idea—"

"Then you shall find out!" Dornoch said harshly, his face bleak. "The battalion will parade again immediately and each man will be questioned until I have the facts."

Four

Fettleworth was in a fractious mood: his breakfast kedgeree had been off, smelling to heaven, and he had personally kicked the backside of his *khansamma* for some relief for his temper, after which he had harangued his wife for her lack of control over the household servants until she had quietly burst into tears and said she hated India and would much rather live in Cheltenham. That was the last straw: no senior officer cared to be reminded of Cheltenham and its doddery majors and colonels. Cheltenham was a high-class dosshouse in Fettleworth's view, its quiet hotels agape for generals who had been prematurely retired after failing their Sovereign in the far-flung outposts of her Empire.

"Bugger Cheltenham," he announced and flung away in a huff. Then Lakenham had arrived while he was still sitting on the thunderbox; and upon emergence from privacy he had been handed disturbing despatches sent via Brigade from the Colonel of the 114th Highlanders outside Peshawar, and Cheltenham came to mind again.

Having read, Bloody Francis poked disagreeably at the telegraph form. "This man Cunningham. Last observed by a lance-corporal . . . entering an alley and firing his revolver." He looked peevish. "Probably dead."

"Lord Dornoch—"

"Yes, yes, Lord Dornoch. The Scots are all very well, but some are quite impossible. Dornoch believes he may be upon some personal vendetta to do with his wife!" Fettleworth thumped his desk. "I ask you! All damn natives look alike and Cunningham didn't even see his wife's attacker so far as I recall. He merely took a sergeant's report of the man."

"That is correct, sir."

"Well, then! I don't know what Dornoch expects me to do about it, I have plenty of other worries, among them the fact that Murree appears to be both deaf and dumb." Fettleworth jabbed again at the despatch. "This Captain Stuart – town

40

patrol. Why am I to be tormented by his thoughts and views, Lakenham?"

"He's been on the spot, sir—"

"So he may have been, but he's a mere captain, and captains don't *think* any more than damn subalterns do. And what's his summary when all's said and done? Either we go to war, or we don't. Brilliant! Feller must be still in the kindergarten." Bloody Francis got to his feet, tugging at the neckband of his tunic, which cut deeply into the folds of his throat. "Write a despatch to Brigadier-General Shaw. There are no fresh orders as yet and patience is to be exercised. My congratulations to Dornoch on extracting the town patrol and the civilians, but remind him that his initiative, or Brora's initiative as the case may be, may prove unwelcome to Murree and he may have some explaining to do. Add that I cannot condone disregard of orders. It's really too bad—" He broke off as his ADC entered. "*Now* what is it?"

"A despatch from Northern Army Command, sir."

"At last!" With a thump, Fettleworth sat down again. He reached out a plump hand. "Let's have it."

The ADC put the despatch down in front of the Divisional Commander, who read, then blew wearily through his moustache. "We sit tight, Lakenham. We do damn all!"

"And let Peshawar burn?"

"Yes! Get Blaise-Willoughby here at once. Perhaps he can interpret all this blasted nonsense for me. And hold on to that despatch for Brigade, there'll be more to add to it when I've had words with Blaise-Willoughby."

* * *

At noon Fettleworth's despatch, in full, was received at Brigade and the Colonels of all regiments in cantonments were summoned to attend upon Brigadier-General Shaw. The conference did not last long; when Lord Dornoch rode back, he called his officers together and gave them the facts.

"Peshawar's to be left alone," he said. "Calcutta is in possession of certain information that it's no more than a diversionary tactic, engineered by the Pathans along the Frontier, who have stirred up the attack by the Hindus in the expectation of engaging the whole of Northern Army – while they, the Pathans, gather in the hills to sweep down on Nowshera, Rawalpindi, Murree itself, and all other British garrisons in the Northern Command area."

"So there's no change in the orders?" Brora asked.

"No, except that all regiments in cantonments will resume the provision of normal patrols towards Afghanistan to watch developments."

"Is an attack on the cantonments considered likely?"

Dornoch said, "It may come and we must be ready for it, but I think the danger will not be yet – not until the Pathans see we haven't fallen for the trap. When they do, then the Hindus may be stirred up to attack us. For the time being Brigade has ordered us to stand down from full alert. That's all for now, gentlemen. Captain Ogilvie, a word before you go."

When the others had withdrawn, Dornoch indicated a chair and Ogilvie sat. Dornoch said, "I have particular orders for you, James, from Division. It seems Major Blaise-Willoughby has put your name forward for a special mission. I don't like it, but there it is. I dare say you can guess what's involved, considering the initiative comes from the Political people?"

"Infiltration, Colonel?"

Dornoch nodded. "You're to enter Peshawar on attachment to General Fettleworth's Political Staff – I have no other details, but you'll be briefed fully by Blaise-Willoughby. You're to report at Division at 3 p.m. this afternoon." He paused, rubbing thoughtfully at his chin. "I have a request of my own to make, James, though it must not cut across your orders from Division. Again, I think you'll understand."

"The Sar'nt-Major, Colonel?"

"Yes. Keep your ears open. I'm much worried . . . I fear he's dead. He's an old Indian campaigner, of course, but inside Peshawar, alone, in uniform unless he managed to dispose of it . . . he'd have small hope of survival. Nevertheless, the regiment has a need to know."

*   *   *

Riding out that afternoon for Nowshera, Ogilvie reflected that the Colonel seemed quite convinced that Cunningham had gone off on a private manhunt. The theory, in fact, held a certain amount of water: Cunningham, that experienced soldier, would have been most unlikely to detach for any military reason into an alley under the particular circumstances of Brora's entry into Peshawar. The orders had been to keep together, shoulder-to-shoulder throughout. He would undoubtedly have obeyed and in any case would have realised the sense of the order. Incredible as it might seem in the case of anyone of Cunningham's rank and service, he was technically guilty of desertion if he had indeed followed his heart. It was not a happy thought. If the Colonel should, within the rigidity of thought of the army's high command, be unable to pull that particular chestnut out of the fire for him, Cunningham would be better off with a native dagger in his stomach.

Ogilvie rode on, leaving Peshawar to the south of his track. The territory, under the general surveillance of distant British patrols and outposts, could be considered reasonably safe so far, but Ogilvie was keeping fully alert for the trouble that in fact could always strike along the North-West Frontier not many miles to the west, and was apparently due to come soon. He thought of Fiona Elliott: she had been crossing the parade when he had ridden out, and he had chided her for being out and about in the early afternoon sun, but she had laughed at him, and remarked that madness was in the family anyway. "Look at Uncle David," she'd said, and grimaced. "It'll come out again in my children, I expect." She'd given him a direct and challenging look, and winked. She was undoubtedly forward; at that moment Brora had appeared and Fiona had said, "Oh, God," and waved Ogilvie away. He had watched her going back across the parade: she was long-legged, and moved gracefully, the long skirt of her dress giving her a look of gliding rather than walking. Brora was having a difficult job in his role of guardian: all the unattached officers of the 114th and adjacent battalions had flocked round Miss Fiona like bees round a honey-pot until recent events had precluded socialising. Yet it was James

Ogilvie she seemed most to favour, to Brora's chagrin. Ogilvie guessed that the Major would be glad enough when Lady Mary and her daughter left cantonments for the Simla hills, which they were programmed to do within the next three weeks by which time the summer season would be at its height. Now, of course, future movement must depend on the developing military situation, and it was possible that all the women would be evacuated to Simla at short notice. Rumour had had it that Bloody Francis had so far been reluctant to order their removal since he did not wish to appear to over-react; to do so might be to alert the natives to the fact that their schemes were known, and in any case an earlier generation of women and children had suffered in the Mutiny and the Raj had survived. . .

Upon arrival at Division, Ogilvie was taken straight to the Political Officer. Blaise-Willoughby he knew well; it was presumably because he had worked for the Political Officer on earlier occasions, and because he had an excellent command of the Pushtu tongue, that he had been chosen for this mission in Peshawar. Blaise-Willoughby confirmed this. "You've done it before," he said, "so you'll have no great problem."

"You've no one more experienced?"

"I had, but they're dead," Blaise-Willoughby answered briefly. There were other reasons too why there was no availability of officers on permanent attachment to the Political Service: one was down with dysentery, another had recently married and it was not policy for newly married politicals to be sent out on missions. And since it was essential that the appointed officer should know the operational area intimately from recent experience, no useful purpose would be served by drafting in officers from elsewhere. Somehow, Ogilvie was left with the impression that Blaise-Willoughby regarded him as second best and had to make do, but then there had always been a certain superiority in the Political Officer's manner; no combatant officer, he seem ! to suggest, had brains. He passed Ogilvie's personal orders concisely: Ogilvie was to approach Peshawar that night, in native dress and using the identity of one Abdul Satar Dawar, an Afghan from beyond the Frontier, a Pathan tribesman eager to fight against the British Raj.

"How do I pass through the siege lines?" Ogilvie asked.

"You don't. They're Hindus, as you know, and although there's known to be collusion, you could face difficulty," Blaise-Willoughby said with studied under-statement. "I dare say you've heard of the O'Kelly Drain?" He lifted an eyebrow. "No?"

"No."

"Then I'll explain. Around fifty years ago one Patrick O'Kelly, an Irishman in an infantry regiment of the East India Company, committed murder. A fellow soldier – a heinous crime, of course. He was sentenced to be hanged in public, outside the city jail, but he escaped from custody. With native assistance, he found a long disused tunnel that led from the city, below the defences and out into the country. The pursuit being not far behind him as it happened, his native helpers were apprehended on their way back from the tunnel entry and they gave him away under pressure. These natives also revealed the point where the tunnel emerged." Blaise-Willoughby shrugged. "He never appeared, nor did the men who were sent down to flush him out."

"So—"

"So he's still there, as you'll find out."

Sourly Ogilvie asked, "Is there any reason why *I* should ever come out, any more than O'Kelly and the others, Major?"

"Every reason. We now know why those men never emerged."

"Why?"

A smile flickered briefly over Blaise-Willoughby's face "*Naja tripudians,* my dear chap. Hooded cobras. They live in the tunnel."

"And you expect me to go down there?"

"Yes. Why not? I've been – I heard the story a few years ago, and I have an enlarged bump of curiosity. Of course, I didn't go unprepared, since I rather suspected the truth about O'Kelly's end. I took the remedy with me: mongeese."

"And you have mongeese handy now, Major?"

"Certainly. I'm rather fond of animals, as you know, and in India the sensible man always knows where to lay his hands upon a mongoose, does he not? You need have no worries about your entry into Peshawar, Ogilvie, none at all. Your problems start after you emerge from the tunnel—"

"Whereabouts does it end?" Ogilvie asked.

"In the garden of a rich merchant's house on the western outskirts." Blaise-Willoughby added, "It's possible the house has been destroyed by the gunfire. You may have to clear a way out of the exit, perhaps, but I don't see many difficulties there – it's a chance you must take. Once you're into the city, the rest is up to you. You circulate, and you keep your eyes and ears open."

"What for, in particular?"

Blaise-Willoughby said airily, "Oh, anything you like, my dear chap, pertaining to what's going on. You know the sort of thing that's grist to my particular mill – the extent to which Muslim and Hindu are prepared to suffer one another in the overall interest of fighting the Raj – you'll realise that's vital of course – and what their ahead plans are . . . disposition of tribes, attack routes and assembly areas, their numerical strength and size and location of their arsenals. And of course I'll expect a detailed report on the situation inside Peshawar itself." He paused. "And one thing in particular, possibly the most important of all."

"And that is?"

Blaise-Willoughby lowered his voice as though instinctively guarding secret information, however unnecessarily inside Divisional HQ. "Something's emerged. I feel I can congratulate myself, frankly. Something that links . . . your Mr Cunningham started the line of enquiry, as a matter of fact. He mentioned, as I was informed, a star branded onto the forehead of the native who killed his wife – you remember?"

Ogilvie nodded.

"A big man – over six feet – hooked nose, no hair, dressed

46

in white. And that star. I want you to watch out for him, glean what you can, and report back, using the tunnel again to make good your escape. If you can manage to take him and bring him out with you, so much the better, but I recognise that there might be practical difficulties in the way of that."

Sarcastically Ogilvie said, "Yes, there might. Who is this man, Major?"

"He's known as the Star of Islam – self-styled in the first place, I gather. Muslim, obviously. He's a fanatic – detests the Raj and has sworn to bring down British rule. Brave as a lion and always in the forefront of the fight. Foolish in a leader to expose himself, but that's his way. If, as I believe is the case, he's in Peshawar and co-ordinating this wretched business, then the Raj is really in for trouble." Blaise-Willoughby pulled out a watch and looked at it. "You'll leave here after dark mounted and with an escort for some of the way, and rendezvous with me so I can show you the tunnel, then you're on your own. Before leaving, you'll be briefed very fully on the antecedents and so on of Abdul Satar Dawar. Is there anything else you want to know, Ogilvie?"

"Yes," Ogilvie answered sardonically. "How do I ensure that the mongeese are still around when I go back through the O'Kelly Drain?"

* * *

The mongeese went with him in a stout canvas bag with air holes: a dozen protesting, kicking grey animals of varying sizes up to about eighteen inches long. They were, or would be when he was on foot, heavy. Blaise-Willoughby suggested that he might leave them bagged and concealed inside the Peshawar end of the tunnel; they should not have too long to wait for his return, Blaise-Willoughby said hopefully, since he was to acquire the maximum possible information in the shortest possible time. Speed could prove vital. Ogilvie, riding with his escort of a *duffardar* and four *sowars* of the Guides Cavalry, went over and over in his mind the briefing

47

received from Blaise-Willoughby: it had been extremely detailed and he had to be word perfect under questioning. He concentrated now on the family background and antecedents, the whole role and character of the Pathan, Abdul Satar Dawar, brigand from the Afghan hills. His ragged clothing stank realistically, his *jezail* and its snaky bayonet were decently rust-covered, his entire body had been properly stained with a dye that would last for long enough even if he didn't leave Peshawar quite as soon as the Political Officer had seemed to expect. He went on to reflect upon the military situation as outlined to him by Bloody Francis in person before he had left Division. Fettleworth had been as pompous as ever, and as patriotically bombastic, as he spoke of the vile rebels, but had to admit certain deficiencies in the state of readiness of his Division: not his fault, of course.

"Nor yer father's really. I blame Whitehall and the rise of all these blasted socialists." He sniffed. "Namby-pamby lot, so are the Liberals. There's a lot of lobbying to prevent money being spent on the army, don't know about the navy but I suspect something similar. What?"

"Yes, sir."

Bloody Francis nodded. "Thought you'd agree. I loathe all politicians, of course. Dishonest the lot of 'em! Lining their own pockets while we out here lack regiments – that's the trouble, you see. I'm fully extended as it is, providing patrols alone is an enormous drain, and now I have a whole brigade pinned down in the Peshawar cantonment, it's too bad. However, if the worst happens, we shall win through, of course, goes without saying. Murree has guaranteed reinforcements and Sir Iain's already asked for replacements from Southern Command, though God knows how long they'll take to get here, I don't."

"Yes, sir."

"Naturally, I've made certain arrangements and dispositions, but I'm sorry to say Major Blaise-Willoughby prefers that I don't tell you about them, Ogilvie. Feller's a fool . . . but there we are, the damn natives do employ nasty methods and we have to take account of their ways."

Fettleworth seemed embarrassed: he was still incensed at Blaise-Willoughby's statement that every man, even a Briton, had his breaking point under torture. After a pause he went on, "It's up to you, Ogilvie. You come from a military family and you're bound to succeed, it's in the blood. Do your best, my boy, and the Raj will be grateful. We are all depending upon you – all of us from the Queen down." It was a tall order, for a captain of infantry to save the Raj; and Fettleworth appeared to take the fact in and to realise the need for a stimulus, for suddenly he lifted a scarlet-clad arm and pointed at the immense portrait of the Queen-Empress on the wall behind his desk. Ogilvie wondered if he should salute. "Look, Ogilvie," Bloody Francis said. There was much emotion in his voice as he stared at the Mother of Her Peoples. "Let Her Majesty be your lode star, my boy! Never cease to have her in your mind! See her in the darkest hour! She'll stiffen you when needs be."

Jogging across hard country in a very dark hour, Ogilvie reflected that Her Majesty's imperious frown had seemed to be directed specifically at himself...

*   *   *

"Here we leave you, sahib." The *duffardar* pointed in a south-westerly direction. "The Major sahib waits behind the tree that you can see. If you will please dismount, sahib?"

"Right." Ogilvie dismounted and handed his horse over to one of the *sowars* who would lead it back to Nowshera. The night was black mostly, though now and again the moon peeped through the heavy obscuring cloud, and there was light in the south from Peshawar. At the *duffardar's* command two *sowars* dismounted and once again the *duffardar* addressed Ogilvie.

"A hundred thousand apologies, sahib. I act under orders from the Major sahib to behave as one would normally behave with a Pathan, in case the night should hold eyes." He gave an order in Pushtu to the *sowars* and Ogilvie was picked up bodily, and swung backwards and forwards for a while

49

before being hurled like a sack of manure from the mens'
grasp. Still clutching his bag of mongeese, his slung *jezail*
banging against his backbone, he landed heavily, bruising
himself and tearing the skin. As he picked himself up, a
stream of obscenity was poured upon him. He was, in
Pushtu, a mangy dog and the son of a cow who would have
been better served by the rope. Then the escort galloped
away, back to Division. Ogilvie made his way with his
struggling, squeaking sackload towards the tree. As he
approached it, Blaise-Willoughby was seen lying on the
ground behind the trunk. He called in a low voice for Ogilvie
to join him and said disparagingly, "Can't you keep those
mongeese quiet, for God's sake?"

"No!" Ogilvie snapped.

Blaise-Willoughby shrugged. "Oh, well, it's your funeral, I
suppose . . . though I must say I hope not."

"So do I." Ogilvie sounded as savage as the mongeese,
whose effectiveness he was beginning to doubt the more
strongly as he came closer to the area of the cobras' lair.

"Ça ne fait rien," Blaise-Willoughby said with infuriating
levity. He got to his feet, taking up a crouching stance. "Now,
follow me. It's not far . . . I didn't want those *sowars* to be
able to locate the entry, you know." They walked south for
some four hundred yards, stumbling along a deep *nullah,* a
dried-out one, in what was currently moonless dark. There
was still the glow of light from Peshawar and from time to
time the fearful rumble of the guns. The flares were fully
visible along the siege lines and the wind, from the south
now, brought the smell of gunsmoke and of burning timber.
Blaise-Willoughby followed the *nullah's* course south-
westerly towards another large tree and a hundred yards or
so beyond this he climbed out from the *nullah,* moved
forward cautiously a foot at a time, and at last stopped on the
brink of downward-sloping ground that led, so far as Ogilvie
could make out through the encircling gloom, to a thick
growth of bush.

"There," Blaise-Willoughby said.

"Where and what?"

"The O'Kelly Drain, of course," Blaise-Willoughby said

50

irritably. "The entry's under those bushes. You'll find them prickly, but never mind. The earth may have fallen in a little by now, perhaps," he added. "It's some while since I went down."

"Did you go all the way, Major?"

"Yes, of course I did."

"What if the entry's fallen in so much it's blocked?"

"Use your initiative, Ogilvie – unblock it. You have hands. It won't be entirely blocked. The cobras have to get out, haven't they?"

"They're thinner than me," Ogilvie snapped. "What's the mongoose drill?"

"Ah yes, just as well you asked. Do what I did. Release one at a time, the first as soon as you enter, or just before if you feel safer. The remainder as the occasion arises, only try not to lose them afterwards. They'll go ahead of you, they won't retreat past you usually, but if they do, chivvy them on, and round 'em up before you leave the exit. It's really quite simple."

"Good."

"Try not to let them bite you. Here." Blaise-Willoughby reached into a rucksack dangling from his shoulder. "These should help." He brought out a pair of heavy leather gauntlets and handed them over. Ogilvie pulled them on, then the Political Officer produced, with a triumphant air, what seemed to be a cylinder bound in black leather with a rounded piece of glass at one end and a metal screw-on bottom at the other. Ogilvie took it curiously: this was a recent invention – an electric torch that took its power from dry batteries contained in its body, batteries that when a slide was pulled down gave light to a small glass sphere called a bulb. It should prove useful and Ogilvie was indeed immensely grateful. There was one more thing: a British Army revolver with a hundred rounds of ammunition, all to be kept well concealed beneath Ogilvie's filthy garments and for use only in extreme emergency.

"Down you go," Blaise-Willoughby said. He reached out a hand. "Goodbye and the very best of luck, Ogilvie, and please don't take too long. You know what Fettleworth is."

"What about you? How do you get back to Division?"
"Don't worry about me," Blaise-Willoughby said. Ogilvie
didn't, much: Blaise-Willoughby was noted for his love of
walking, usually alone except for Wolseley who was not
present tonight. Possibly the monkey could smell mongeese
and didn't like them. Blaise-Willoughby waited for a moment as Ogilvie descended the slope, then vanished to begin
his homeward trek. At the bottom of the declivity, the bushes
grew immensely thick, utterly obscuring any entry, and
Ogilvie, gloved, tore away at them and grew hot and
blasphemous. Persistence did the trick; after which more
work was necessary to free the entry of clutter. His flesh
crawling as he thought of the resident cobras, he shone the
electric torch through the opening and found that the tunnel
was still intact, at any rate to the extent of the beam of light,
and was fairly roomy, though he would need to bend. It
sloped downwards, quite steeply to begin with, but Blaise-
Willoughby had said it levelled off after a matter of fifty
yards or so. It was no less than four miles in length, and
O'Kelly had got half way before meeting his death; his
unfortunate pursuers had not got so far, as witnessed by the
position of their skeletons. The tunnel, whose original
purpose Blaise-Willoughby had not been able to ascertain,
was old but well built and lined with bricks from England –
Suffolk Whites, no less. These had crumbled in places, not
many places, and the cobras, one of whose habits was to take
up their abode in ant-hills, had probably gained access in the
first place by way of such dwellings situated above the
crumbled portions.

Ogilvie untied the neck of the sack, cautiously, and
reached in. He brought out one of the wriggling, kicking
mongeese, knelt on the sack's neck to keep the rest inside,
and projected the nose of the mongoose towards the tunnel
entry. The creature swerved away and vanished into the
night. Ogilvie cursed. He shone the torch along the tunnel
again and, taking a risk, eased himself and his *jezail* through
the entry and slid downwards carrying the sack. When he
was a few hair-raising yards from the mouth of the tunnel, he
tried again with the mongeese. This time the released animal

52

moved obediently ahead, seeking cobras, and Ogilvie moved on, his heart in his mouth, eyes watchful for the serpents and body ready to block any back-tracking on the part of the mongoose. It was a terrible journey, though the going itself, with the aid of Blaise-Willoughby's electric torch, was not as bad as Ogilvie had expected even though the need to bend a tall body brought discomfort and slow progress. As each foot of the way loomed up into the torch's beam, he searched for the rising body and the spreading hood, could almost feel the sudden, speed-of-light dart that would bring the fangs and the venom. In the sack, the mongeese struggled to be free; the second released one had gone ahead and and had vanished, which might indicate no cobras in the immediate distance, though this could presumably not be relied upon. Ogilvie sweated from the close atmosphere in the long tunnel – there were air shafts, but many had become blocked – and from sheer fear of the unknown, of the sudden slither that might herald attack before he could despatch another mongoose to his protection. But nothing manifested and after almost an hour's slow but steady progress towards Peshawar he breathed more easily, feeling that providence must be on the side of the British after all, and that the cobra population had stolen discreetly away.

Then, with terrible suddenness, he saw it: the torch-beam shone onto scales, onto a lithe, silent body slowly rising as the light disturbed it, a body arched a little backwards and swaying as the hood extended round the head, a body that rose horribly from inside a rib-cage surrounded by yellowed bones, the presumed remains of Private O'Kelly of fifty years before.

Five

Shortly after James Ogilvie had left Nowshera, orders, half
expected and half not, had reached Lord Dornoch and the
other commanding officers from Brigade: Lieutenant-
General Fettleworth, on advice from Calcutta relayed via
Northern Army Command, had after all decided to evacuate
the women and children from the Peshawar cantonment.
They would be taken to Simla via the railway from
Nowshera, and military transport would reach the cantonments from Division at 7 a.m. next morning. They would
ride under strong escort: a cavalry brigade would provide
distant cover, while two squadrons of horse, with a mounted
artillery battery, would accompany the convoy itself to
Nowshera. The railway train, which would take them as far
as Kalka, would be heavily guarded by the 2nd Middlesex
who would thereafter act as escort to the bullock-carts for
the lumbering journey up into the hills from the railhead.

Under Andrew Black, the Regimental Quartermaster
Sergeant and Colour-Sergeant MacTrease, acting in the
room of the still missing RSM, made the arrangements for
the families. All were to go, including the Colonel's lady and
Fiona Elliott with her mother. Fiona made objections: she
was not going, she stated flatly. She had been in Simla briefly
before coming to Peshawar, and hadn't liked it.

"Simla's a bore," she said.

"Rubbish!" Brora snorted. "It's a healthy place, and it's
safe. All of us would give our eye-teeth to be in the hills
during the summer months, as well you know."

"Well, Uncle David, I *wouldn't*!" Fiona's eyes flashed.
"Anyway, I think it's cowardly. I feel quite secure enough in
a British garrison, thank you, and I should have thought we
could be of some help."

Brora showed white teeth in a savage grin. "In what way,
might one enquire?"

"Well . . . nursing casualties."

Brora laughed. "I rather think not! Have you ever seen the

54

results of, say, an exploding shell or the swipe of a sword, or the thrust of a bayonet in the guts?"

"You know I haven't, Uncle David—"

"Then let us pray to God you never do, for you would swoon on the spot and be a confounded nuisance to the doctor and his orderlies." Brora swung round on his sister-in-law. "Am I not right, Mary?"

Lady Mary looked down at her lap. "You usually are, are you not?" she said.

Brora glared. "It's my habit, yes."

"Alastair used to say—"

"My brother's comments fail to interest me." For a moment, as Lady Mary looked up, flushing, their eyes met. There was a curious look on Brora's face, a mixture of gloating with a touch of malice and something else that was almost lust. It was the woman who looked away and then spoke rapidly as though anxious not to discuss her dead husband further. She said, "I agree with Fiona that Simla's a horrid place, David. There's really nothing to do except—"

"Gossip," Fiona broke in. "Tearing reputations to shreds."

"Mrs Major This and Mrs Colonel That—"

"Almost standing at attention when Mrs Brigadier-General's announced—"

"Tea-parties—"

"Dances with a lot of old men who can't keep their hands to themselves, and then more gossip."

"And too much whisky," Lady Mary said. "It's too cheap and available—"

"And it leads to sex," Fiona said, and went scarlet: she had uttered something terrible, and once again Brora's face was a mixture of emotions. He ordered her brusquely to shut up and leave the room and make ready for the morning's departure and no more argument; General Fettleworth had given the order and there was no more to be said. Brora, however, had something else to say to Lady Mary and he said it after Fiona had gone to her room: the girl, he announced angrily, had been given unwholesome and frivolous ideas by Captain Ogilvie, and the association was to stop. All young officers were stallions, Brora said in a loud voice and an aggressive one, but Ogilvie was the limit. A young woman of Fiona's age and upbringing would never have so much as heard the word sex had it not been expressly brought to her attention, and – here Brora's expression changed – as for her views on whisky's effects, they were, to say the least, unexpected in her mouth . . . Brora burst out into a peal of coarse laughter, laughter with more than a trace of sadism in it. He slapped his kilted thigh, guffawing away, and said, "Dornoch had better see to it that the good doctor puts more than a dose of quinine into the Mess sherry, so that rampant natures are subdued!" Once again his sister-in-law avoided his staring eyes and Andrew Black, announced a moment later with a report for the Major, was uneasily aware of much strain in the atmosphere.

*　　*　　*

Ogilvie stopped dead, as though he had put down roots on the spot. There was no sign of the released mongoose, who stood in dereliction of duty. Keeping the beam of his torch shining on the swaying snake, his fingers shaking, Ogilvie opened the neck of the sack and brought out another animal. The cobra seemed to be immediately aware of threat: the swaying increased its tempo, and there was a loud and angry hissing sound. The forked tongue flicked in and out. The body seemed to stretch even farther from the heap of old bones, until the reptile appeared almost to be standing on tip-tail. The range of the electric torch was not great; Ogilvie, keeping motionless, believed that if the cobra should lean its hooded head closer, the fangs would touch him. But the mongoose was no hanger back: the grey fur seemed to move like a streak of lightning through the foetid air, and within seconds the animal was gripping the cobra's throat in a death bite. The snake swayed and flailed and continued hissing and the mongoose was flung this way and that but still clung grimly on, claws scrabbling, teeth inextricably pierced into flesh. It seemed an age of bloody combat before the movement of the serpent grew less and less; at last the hood subsided and the neck fell forward and the eyes glazed over. The job was done.

Ogilvie's filthy garments were soaked through with sweat and he felt too weak to move on. But move on he had to, with feet like lead as they began again to carry him into the unknown where more enfanged venom could be waiting. He edged past the dead cobra, where the mongoose was enjoying the fruits of its victory, gnawing and tugging and swallowing. That mongoose would not be moved from its meal and must be written off the strength. Nine more left now, nine that had to be enough. The one released inside the tunnel earlier had not turned up; no doubt it had deserted to the open air by way of one of the crumbled sections below which Ogilvie had passed earlier – not without difficulty though the passage was not wholly blocked.

Ogilvie moved on, more cautiously than ever. A little farther along he came upon more bones and skulls, and the remnants of uniforms – the soldiers of the East India Company's army who had been sent to flush O'Kelly out to face his hanging. There were badges in the dust and rubble, and brass buttons: Ogilvie recognised the insignia; a regiment that had been disbanded with the withdrawal of the East India Company's charter, and had re-formed as a part of the British Army – the 88th and 94th Foot, The Connaught Rangers, oddly enough Private O'Kelly's own countrymen. So served and died the men who had laid the foundations of the Raj, in darkness and by fang of serpent, or in open battle in the air above – it perhaps made little difference when the actual moment came, but Ogilvie spared a thought for forgotten families who had lost their men in this dreadful, God-forsaken tunnel; and then pressed on again. He found no more cobras and the rest of the journey was easily enough accomplished. At last, away ahead still, he saw eerie red light: the flicker of fires, he believed. As he closed the end of the tunnel he began to smell smoke, and then heard the sounds of war filtering down. Some dozen yards inside the exit, he placed the sack of mongeese on the ground with its neck securely tied, and covered it as best he could with rubble, hiding the electric torch beneath the pile.

Then, with care and in silence, carrying the *jezail,* he approached the exit, which was bush covered as the other end had been. Now there was no doubt about the source of the light: just beyond the exit, a building was on fire, no doubt the house of the rich merchant. Careful reconnaissance told Ogilvie that the exit itself was unguarded, and he pulled himself up and through the bushes, tearing skin and catching his dirty garments on the thorns.

As first his head and then his body appeared in the red light, he heard a high scream of fear close by, and he turned sharply. He saw four women huddled in a group beneath a large tree, Muslim women in veils. Three seemed to be old, one young. He called out in Pushtu that he came as a friend, a Pathan from beyond the Frontier, from the Afghan hills. He approached the women, who fell back from him but had stopped their screaming.

He gestured towards the burning house. The garden was large and the fire was at a safe distance, but the heat could be felt. "Your house?" he asked in Pushtu.

One of the old women answered. "Yes. What is your name, and why do you come?"

"My name is Abdul Satar Dawar, and I come to assist my people."

"The Pathan people?"

"Yes," Ogilvie said. "Do you support your people, the people of Islam, or have you deserted to the infidel, the British?"

All four women gave a kind of keening sound; at the end of the garden a part of the house collapsed, sagging inwards into the raging fire, and a myriad sparks flew upwards to the low-hanging stars. Fierce heat swept across, and Ogilvie repeated his question. The younger woman answered.

"From the British we earn rupees. The Raj brings us trade...but we have no love for the Raj. We have not deserted, Abdul Satar Dawar."

"And the British in the city . . . what has happened to them? And how do the people of Islam regard the attack upon them by those of the Hindu religion?"

All four women answered at once, a babble of sound from

which Ogilvie gathered that such British officials as had been in the city when the attack had come, and who had not been gathered in by the town patrol and removed to safety in the guardroom, had been set upon by the mob and killed. There had been stoning, and knives and *jezails* had been used freely. Always India was seething beneath the surface and when an eruption came the fullest advantage was taken. But there was no love for the Hindus any more than for the Raj, though word had come to the people of Peshawar that they must accept their lot in the wider interest, the interest of seizing India back from the British Raj. Peshawar, with its 100,000 close-packed inhabitants, was to be the city of valour, the lighter of the torch of freedom, and in the fullness of time Islam would emerge supreme and would break the Hindus as by then they would have broken the Raj.

Ogilvie asked, "From whom does this word come?"

"From the man known as the Star of Islam, who is descended from the Prophet himself."

"Indeed he is a man of holy descent," Ogilvie said with proper reverence. "It is he whom I have come to see, and whoever will take me to him will be beloved of the Prophet. Do you know where he is to be found?"

"This we do not know, Abdul Satar Dawar."

*   *   *

The city was a shambles; everywhere Ogilvie found heaps of rubble. Bodies lay in profusion, old and young, men, women and children, scavenged by the pariah dogs who gnawed and ripped. The stench of death was overpowering, adding its horror to the stink of the open drains. There were craters where the artillery shells had exploded, and there was still the occasional shell coming across from the siege lines outside. One landed at the end of an alley along which Ogilvie was moving, and he flung himself flat in a pile of unnameable filth, and was covered with debris as the explosion lit the night. Getting up, he moved on, not knowing where he might be going. It seemed an impossible task to find one man in this seething, bleeding city; and if the Star of

Islam had any sense, he wouldn't be inside Peshawar in any case. The guns of the attackers could kill him as easily as anyone else: he would scarcely be immune from death, however holy he might be! Stumbling on, Ogilvie felt he was living a nightmare, and living it pointlessly. Blaise-Willoughby had been a shade too clever, or a shade too expectant. Nothing could come of this crazy mission except death for himself. Currently the one thing that struck him was that Bloody Francis had been right not to have committed British troops to the salvation of Peshawar. The whole city was rotten to the core, crawling with hatred for the Raj, and was not worth one man's life. Better to let the unnatural, uneasy alliance between Muslim and Hindu take its predictable course. The signs of hate were everywhere to be seen: flags ripped down and trampled in the slimy filth of the drains, or half burned; slogans daubed on walls; the bodies of a group of British civilian officials, horribly mutilated, lying in the roadway outside the Salt Department's offices, which had been sacked; official forms and reports blew about on the breeze. The mob surged along, carrying Ogilvie before it, yelling against the Raj and against their Hindu attackers, loosing off *jezails* indiscriminately and flourishing knives and daggers. It was an unparalleled situation, and Ogilvie knew the women in the merchant's garden would be proved right: given time and success against the Raj, the Pathans along the Frontier, and the Afghans from beyond the Hindu Kush, would come down like the flood tide upon their catspaws the Hindus. Then the whole of India could become a bloodbath in which the British could sink without trace. It was true the Raj was mighty, but its might depended largely upon consent of the population. The actual armies in the field were comparatively small, and could soon be placed at the mercy of India's teeming millions, while the supply and reinforcement route from the United Kingdom was a long one and ships were slow.

Forced along before the mob, willy-nilly, his ears ringing with their shouts, Ogilvie looked up as he passed the end of the Salt Department building: he caught a glimpse, no more, of a face. In the red light from the various conflagrations he

60

believed the face to be a white one, no doubt some member of staff who had managed to hide himself away and escape the holocaust, at any rate for the time being. He moved on; he would return when he could extricate himself from the mob. An ally in Peshawar would be welcome enough if he could make contact, but in the meantime he had to carry out alone his orders from Blaise-Willoughby and find the answers wanted by Division. Currently there seemed little prospect of success. And a few moments later he saw something that sickened him: pinned to a filthy hovel's door, pinned by two bloodstained knives, was the tartan of the Royal Strathspey – a spread-out kilt. The town patrol, and Brora's expeditionary force, had brought out all their dead and wounded intact. The kilt could only be Cunningham's.

Six

The journey north from London by the railway train was a long one, but was not uncomfortable: Her Majesty had graciously made available the royal drawing-room and bedroom coach of her own train to bring her Prime Minster to Balmoral – the Marquess of Salisbury was a Conservative and very different from the dreadful Mr Gladstone, to whom such honour would most certainly not have been accorded. So Lord Salisbury with his despatch boxes, his portfolios and – regrettably – his Gladstone bag reposed in plush and fussy luxury as the royal train puffed north through England's summer fields and smoky midland cities, through Berwick-upon-Tweed with a glimpse a little later of bright blue sea beyond the Scottish border, and on into

Aberdeenshire, sternest part perhaps of Caledonia stern and wild . . . Aberdonians, like Her Majesty herself, were dour folk and the eastern half of Scotland was dour also, more dour by far, Lord Salisbury thought, than the west with its beautiful lochs and islands and sense of withdrawal from the world. In the west a man could find peace; in the east he found money being made, and Aberdonians to place it carefully and dourly in the Royal Bank of Scotland. It had been, Lord Salisbury thought as the train drew closer to the railway station at Ballater, likely enough that Her Majesty and the late Prince Albert had chosen Balmoral as their Scottish home not only on account of the purity inherent in its very name but also on account of the honest and frugal virtues of the Aberdonians themselves, for Her Majesty was by nature thrifty.

At Ballater the Prime Minster was met with ceremony: a guard of the Gordon Highlanders was paraded outside the station, while the royal carriage sent for his transport was escorted by a captain's escort of the Scots Greys. To represent the Queen was His Grace the Duke of Argyll, hereditary Master of Her Majesty's Household in Scotland and at the same time her son-in-law. During the drive to the castle, the two peers spoke of anything but of Her Majesty and of the business that brought the Prime Minster, most inconveniently as it happened, all the way from Whitehall to Balmoral. The Queen's message had been peremptory: she wished to learn from the lips of her Prime Minister what was happening in her Empire beyond the seas, and why her subjects were being placed at risk of their lives. . .

"Not placed, ma'am," Lord Salisbury said when, after moving obsequiously and with bowed head over the tartan carpets into the drawing-room, he had been greeted sharply with the direct question. "Not placed precisely—"

"Then what, Lord Salisbury?"

Salisbury gave a discreet cough. "Force of circumstances, ma'am. They were there in Peshawar when the natives struck."

"And have been *left* there."

"Some have been brought out, ma'am, according to

62

despatches by the telegraph from Lord Elgin in Calcutta. Others have—"

"Have been *left there,* as I have just stated."

Salisbury spread his hands mutely.

"Yes or no, Lord Salisbury." A heavy walking-stick was tapped on the carpet. *"Yes or no?"*

"Yes, ma'am. I'm afraid that is so."

"I call it disgraceful, and it is to be remedied."

"Yes, ma'am. But may I —"

"Our subjects left to be murdered! I am much distressed, Lord Salisbury. Why, pray tell me, have the Hindus attacked Peshawar? They are a peaceable people, are they not, until provoked?"

"Hinduism covers a multitude of peoples, ma'am, a number of races throughout India, not all of whom can truly be said to be peaceable even when unprovoked. Currently the situation is much confused and many questions are left unanswered – even Your Majesty's Viceroy is not in possession of all the facts."

"Then he is to take steps *at once* to find them out."

"Of course, ma'am, of course."

"You shall tell him so. You shall telegraph our wishes. In the meantime you shall tell me all that is known about our poor subjects in the East, and what is being done for the protection of them and of our Indian Empire."

The Prime Minister, stared at solemnly throughout by two remarkably ugly small dogs from the royal kennels, did his best to give a clear picture without provoking the Queen into irrational demands for troop movements that might prove embarrassing to her generals on the spot. India, he said, was full of intrigue and bribery and suspect dealing, and there was a swelling undercurrent of unrest that was always present and sometimes erupted in boils. It behoved the Raj to walk warily: at times to strike hard, at other times to turn the other cheek at least for a while. In the latter event it was true that lives could be lost while the cheek was averted, but the dead died as nobly as those who died when the decision was for immediate retaliatory action. They died for the continuance of the Raj; and Empire, of its very nature, embraced the spilling of blood . . . Lord Salisbury talked soothingly, and he was a Conservative, but he was unable to contain the Queen. The stick was tapped many times, and the voice rose high. There was an unseemly tantrum, stilled only when the pipes and drums of the Gordon Highlanders were heard from beyond the great windows, and the martial sounds of Scotland swept the distant hillsides with haunting savagery. The Queen much loved the highland pipes, and paused to listen, a strange expression on her face and her eyes moist. When the sound faded the tantrum had gone but the issued commands were precise, and ended in the Prime Minister being bidden straight back to London and the enactment of them. With a haste inappropriate to his great office, Lord Salisbury was returned in the royal carriage to Ballater and was pushed backwards as far as Perth, where the train was reversed for the chug south. On the day after he reached the capital Lord Salisbury, most dubious as to the royal commands, sought advice from the ancient Mr Gladstone in his country retreat, shouting his worries down the proffered ear-trumpet outthrust from a foliage of white hair.

"She's a woman," Mr Gladstone said. "She's compassionate but has a woman's judgment, which is to say she has none."

Salisbury nodded.

"She's always been tiresome, of course. Look at the way she treats the Prince of Wales. Time she retired, like me. Frankly, as Prime Minister I found her appalling, quite impossible in spite of a number of good points." Gladstone paused. "You could plead deafness, Salisbury. Ignore the woman."

"She *shouted* it," Salisbury said in an aggrieved tone. "One of her equerries heard it quite plainly, and I could scarcely have done less."

"You're the Prime Minister, my dear Lord Salisbury, not she."

* * *

Lord Salisbury compromised: he called a meeting of the cabinet and put the Queen's commands to them. In the meantime the London newspapers had carried the story of horror in Peshawar. One headline read: DREADFUL SAVAGERY SHOWN BY NATIVE MOB IN PESHAWAR AND IMPERISHABLE GLORY EARN- ED BY STALWART BRITISH CIVILIANS WHO REFUSED TO LOWER THE FLAG OF EMPIRE IN THE HOUR OF FEARFUL DEATH. London had taken this to heart, and was already wearing its heart upon its sleeve. Through the windows of the cabinet room, the noise could be heard from Whitehall: thousands of Londoners had gathered, and were singing *Soldiers of the Queen,* and *We Don't Want to Fight but by Jingo if We Do...* A soap box had been set up in the middle of Whitehall and all the horse omnibuses and hansoms had stopped. From the soap box an elderly man, white-haired, morning-coated, silk-hatted and supported by a walking-stick, clinked medals won in the Crimea and made a rousing speech. England was ready to fight back; Her Majesty's Guards could embark aboard the troopship at a moment's notice and take their bayonets to distant Peshawar and give the damn natives What For. The Vice-Admiral Commanding the Mediterranean Squadron could sail his battleships and cruisers through the Suez Canal and bombard Bombay as an earnest of what Great Britain could do when the natives thumbed their noses at the Queen. Peshawar was an important garrison, guardian of the caravan route between Afghanistan and India, and it was on the lips of everyone, as were the names of the generals of the day. If Sir George White and Sir Iain Ogilvie couldn't beat the natives, then Lord Kitchener should be sent, or Fighting Bobs, or Redvers Buller.

As the storms of cheering broke deafeningly, and as the Commissioner of Police used the telephone from Scotland Yard to report similar scenes all over the metropolis, the cabinet's decision became inevitable; and during the follow- ing afternoon, Lord Salisbury rose in the House to give the delighted Lords, and subsequently the equally delighted Commons, the news that urgent despatches had gone to His

65

Excellency the Viceroy of India with orders that Peshawar was to be relieved immediately.

* * *

Moving free of the mob after passing what was so obviously the RSM's kilt, Ogilvie, diving down a side alley that appeared deserted, circled back towards the Salt Department building where he had seen the face at the window. His thoughts were tumultuous now: Cunningham must surely be dead; if so, the regiment would never be the same again. It was impossible to imagine the 114th without Bosom Cunningham's ramrod presence. No man was ultimately indispensable, but the loss would be felt for a very long time and in the interval morale would suffer. The RSM had always seemed to be the one man who had to go on for ever – often enough, certainly, to the dismay of recruit drafts from home – the one man sure to be there still when the regiment itself faded into the mists of history, marching four-square to the sound of the pipes and drums. Yet now that his wife had gone, death may well have come easily to the RSM. In a sense what he had done was in itself an act of suicide. . .

Ogilvie moved on. He passed open doorways and gaping holes in the walls of the hovels. Dereliction was everywhere: all the inhabitants seemed to have gone from the dwellings, leaving their scanty possessions behind them. Several of the dark doorways held bodies, some, by the stench, too long exposed to the Indian heat; there was no sign here at all of anything living. Ogilvie made the assumption that all the people were in the wider streets, making up the ravening mob that roved and looted. There would be pickings in plenty: Peshawar had contained any number of wealthy traders who had grown fat under the Raj, and the lowly natives would now be making hay, not entirely ungrateful to the massed Hindu force that had given the opportunity. But in the long run, they must surely be doomed – unless the curious alliance with the Hindus had provided for a way out for the Muslim inhabitants through the siege lines, a way for them to join the Pathan hordes now presumably perched ready in the Frontier hills for their massive swoop upon the British garrisons.

Moving warily into the next alley, Ogilvie heard crying coming from one of the odorous doorways: the cry, he fancied, of a child.

He stopped. In India children were often enough a casualty of war, but an unwelcome one. Looking first to right and left, he approached the doorway. He stepped inside, cautiously, and his foot touched something soft. He bent, and felt around in pitch darkness: what he touched was a body, that of a woman, cold and still and flaccid. From the passage beyond an appalling smell rolled out, the smell of a charnel house after plague. The crying, from some inside room, continued harrowingly, a sort of keening for the dead. Ogilvie moved deeper into the passage, stepping over the body. He came to another, this time a man. Then he began to see light – once again the red light of fires moving closer, and he saw that the whole of the back of the hovel had gone and that beyond was a shell-hole, deep and black and sinister. As the light from the fires increased, he saw that the walls of the passage in which he stood were scored by splinters and that the man's body at his feet had been decapitated. The head, with staring glassy eyes, was beside the shattered knee, and beyond were more bodies reduced to remains – shredded flesh, shorn-off limbs, entrails gouged from stomachs by blast or flying metal, a hideous scene of carnage. The keening went on, and Ogilvie tracked down its source in the wreckage of a room opening off the passage to the right of him.

He turned aside and went in. There was a broken table and the remains of a chair, and on the ground was a filthy straw bed, and on the bed the sobbing figure of a young girl crazed with grief and terror. It was clear enough that she was the sole survivor of a family caught in the dreadful trap of a war in the name of rival gods.

He stared down in pity. The fires were moving closer: they could not remain in this place. He took a step forward, and bent. He spoke urgently in Pushtu, and the sobbing stopped, and the girl stared at him with big, luminous black eyes filled with pain.

"I shall help you," he said. "Come, and we shall go together."

"I shall not leave," she said. "My home is here. . . "

"Your home has gone," Ogilvie said gently but with firmness, "and now you must come away or you will be burned."

"My mother and my father and all my brothers and sisters are here and I shall not leave. My place is with them."

"They have gone to the Prophet and to Allah," Ogilvie said, feeling the increasing heat fanning his face like the fires of hell. "They wish you to live until the Prophet calls, and he has not called yet. Come!"

He bent, and lifted the girl in his arms: she was a feather-weight, thin to the point of starvation. Nevertheless she fought him with astonishing ferocity, spitting like a wild cat, tearing and kicking and gouging at his eyes. Fighting her, he felt the filthy creep of lice on his flesh. He held her at arms'-length and set her on her feet, then knelt and bent the almost weightless body across his knee. With the palm of his hand he belaboured her skinny rump, and she howled briefly with pain and indignity, but the fighting stopped.

Ogilvie grinned at her. "Now you shall behave like a true daughter of Allah," he said, "and do as you are told by your elders, and by a man who has come from Afghanistan to help your people in the name of the Prophet, and to bring tidings of help to the Star of Islam."

"The Star of Islam, the all-powerful one?" The big eyes stared. "Do you know him?"

Ogilvie said, "I do not know him in his person, but in his reputation. I am but a messenger who has come to find him. Do you know where he is, child?"

"I do not know." The girl paused; Ogilvie took her by the hand and drew her into the passage, then picked her up again and hid her face in his shoulder as he stepped over the bodies into the alley. There he set her down once more, and she said, "There is one who may know where to find the Star of Islam."

"Who?"

"One of my kinsmen, an old man, the grandfather of my mother's cousin's wife . . . a man of much faith and very, very many years."

68

"And he is in Peshawar?"

The girl nodded.

"You will take me to him?"

She nodded again. This time it was she who took Ogilvie's hand. She said, "Come. It is a long way." They set off together, making towards a wider thoroughfare at the alley's end, back into the milling crowds, passing by more bodies. The girl appeared remarkably composed now and there were no backward looks towards what had been her home. As they went, she told Ogilvie about her aged kinsman, a man not far short of a hundred years it seemed, an Afghan originally from Kandahar who as a younger man had heard the pipes of Havelock sahib marching to relieve Lucknow on the Gumti River in the great mutiny, and had fired upon the column from the surrounding hills. He was, the girl said, a man of much knowledge and many stories of the old days, a man whose hatred for the Raj was deep and intense.

*   *   *

Her Majesty's command, now formalised into governmental policy, had reached Calcutta; and His Excellency the Viceroy had sent at once for Sir George White, Commander-in-Chief in India. White had protested strongly: the orders to relieve Peshawar went against the very reason the decision had been made not to march in the first place. His Excellency agreed, and telegraphed advice back to Whitehall. The order was repeated in strong terms; Her Majesty's Government was of the view that the relief of Peshawar was of more importance than listening to the grapevine, the grapevine that said the Pathan hordes would descend upon Northern Command and shatter the Raj as soon as the troops had been committed in Peshawar. The Viceroy was forced now to concede; and the appropriate order was given to White and was then sent immediately by the telegraph to Murree, where it was delivered to Sir Iain Ogilvie by his Chief of Staff.

"It's not unexpected," Sir Iain said, "and I'd like nothing better than to see British troops scattering the bloody siege lines, but I'm not convinced it's wise at this moment." He looked up at his Chief of Staff. "It's an order, of course . . . but what's your view, eh?"

"A waste of men and material, sir."

"Yes. Only in a sense, of course. It's not been a *good* thing for the Raj to be seen merely standing by. Some action on our part should have its effect on the native mind."

"We've been into that, sir. I see no good coming from an intervention – the casualties will be enormous, in my view unacceptable. Peshawar will become a running sore." The Chief of Staff, hawk-faced and dark, stared across the room towards distant hills visible through the great windows of Northern Command. "With all due respect to her, the Queen's no strategist."

Sir Iain grinned. "But Sir George is, and he's passed the order. I have no option now."

"We shall play straight into the hands of the tribes, sir. With men tied down in Peshawar, we'll be wide open to attack."

"As I shall once again make plain to Calcutta – it rather seems as though our Whitehall masters simply don't believe what's been reported to them. However, their orders must be obeyed in the meantime. Inform the First Division in Nowshera, if you please, Williams, and tell General Fettleworth he's to make a quick and decisive job of it, no half measures. If necessary he must commit the whole Division. I'll be sending reinforcements from Murree at once, and we'll have to urge the Commander-in-Chief to entrain replacements from Ootacamund as soon as possible."

When the Chief of Staff had left his presence to draft the various despatches, Sir Iain sat back at arms' length from his desk, frowning. The order *was* a mistake, of that he was convinced; but public opinion at home in England had of course to be considered by Her Majesty's ministers and public opinion would be demanding action to relieve Peshawar and never mind considerations of strategy. And there was no doubt that it would look immensely bad throughout the world if Peshawar and its inhabitants, whether or not they were loyal to the Raj, were allowed to burn. Yet it was the job of Her Majesty's ministers at times to make unpopular decisions and not be swayed by public demonstrations – or by Her Majesty. Her Majesty could be a confounded nuisance when she was allowed her way. Her heart was in the right place, but she was impulsive to say the least...

* * *

"I don't advise it," Blaise-Willoughby said flatly. "I've said it before, sir, and I'll say it again: to march against the siege lines now could stir—"

"Oh, damn you, Blaise-Willoughby, you don't appear to understand it's an *order*. An order from Her Majesty – the despatch is quite clear that the Queen inspired it, the Queen herself! Lakenham?"

"Sir?"

Fettleworth dabbed a pudgy hand at the despatch from Murree. "Sir Iain wishes no time to be lost, and no more do I. The sooner Peshawar's relieved, the sooner we can concentrate our strength on this blasted threat from Afghanistan and the tribes inside the Frontier. I'm putting the First Division in – all of it, except for one cavalry regiment for the provision of extended patrols. Kindly draft the orders, Lakenham. The attack will go in at three points: the battalions under Brigadier-General Shaw from the Peshawar cantonment, backed by artillery, will advance from the west ... our troops here in Nowshera will form two columns, one to attack from the north, the other from the east. The columns are to march so as to reach the perimeter at ten p.m. tonight, attack under cover of the darkness, and enter Peshawar after smashing the siege lines." He paused, swelling out his ample chest. "I shall accompany the eastern assault myself, I shall speak to all the men before the columns march out ... we have stout fellows, Lakenham, and we shall bring succour to Peshawar."

Brigadier-General Lakenham gave a stiff nod and excused himself. There was much to be done – too much, in a short

71

time. There was blunder in the air, in Lakenham's opinion. The situation along the Frontier was brittle, very brittle, and to denude Nowshera at this stage was dangerous in the extreme. Put bluntly, Peshawar was not worth the risk.

Seven

During the early hours, before the action orders had reached Fettleworth, the gunfire seemed to have ceased over the city, as though the besiegers felt that enough damage had been done. The burning went on here and there, and dawn had showed a pall of smoke hanging over the clustered buildings. The girl still led Ogilvie on, searching for the ancient who might know the whereabouts of the Star of Islam. All night they had walked the alleys: the old man lived on the other side of the city, and the destruction had led the girl to lose her way, and when at last they had reached the old man's abode he was not there. A wizened crone had given directions as to where he might be found, and they had set out again, weary now and hungry though the crone had provided them with some stale crusts, some nuts and a mouthful each of water that had smelt of drains.

In daylight, Peshawar was a terrible sight: the whole city seemed full of the dead and wounded, some of the latter being tended by their families where they lay in the streets and alleys, though mostly they had been left to moan and suffer while the scavenging pariah dogs pulled and bit at bloody wounds. Ogilvie, apart from chasing away the dogs whenever he came upon them, was forced to pass by. There was in any case nothing he could have done, and his mission

came first. Time was passing too quickly: he had found out
nothing, and Blaise-Willoughby would soon grow im-
patient. He might perhaps have done better to ferret around
on his own, rather than use time in a hunt for an old man who
might prove to have no knowledge of the Star of Islam's
whereabouts after all. On the other hand, he could prove to
be a short cut. Ogilvie and the girl moved on, along one alley
after another amid mixed smells of burning, of gunpowder,
of oils and spices, of sheer heat and incense, past shops
selling liquor, past the opium dens ... at least the girl
appeared to know where she was going now, and as they
passed a mosque, miraculously untouched amid an area of
otherwise total destruction, she pointed ahead to some
buildings left intact beyond the shattered sector.

"My kinsman will be found there," she said. "The shop of
the seller of brassware."

They went on towards the shop. Despite the state of the
city and the early hour, business appeared to be as usual.
Brass objects, both useful and decorative and many of them
beautifully enamelled, were on display outside. In the dark
interior a man sat cross-legged and watchful for custom; the
girl approached him and enquired after her kinsman, whose
name, as she had told Ogilvie earlier, was Amanullah
Zalmai.

"Amanullah Zalmai is here. Who wishes him?"

"His kinswoman, Homaira Sarabi. Also Abdul Satar
Dawar from Afghanistan."

The cross-legged man turned his head and called through
to the back. He was answered after some delay by the shrill
voice of a woman: the visitors would be received but they
must not stay long; Amanullah Zalmai was tired, and though
he had much love for his kinswoman, who was both
beautiful and devoted to the faith, he had important matters
to attend to when he was rested.

Thus bidden, Ogilvie and the girl went through the shop,
pushing aside a hanging bead curtain. They entered a
passage that led through to a small garden, brilliant with
flowers and with a shady tree in the centre. It was like an
oasis, though there was a layer of dust from the shattered

73

buildings, dust that had settled everywhere, even upon the frail figure that lay as if dead upon a ricketty *charpoy*. The head was small, skull-like under the turban; the beard was a river of white cascading to the waist. The body was thin, emaciated, the arms and legs seeming no thicker than pencils. The eyes, which swivelled towards Ogilvie and the girl, were bright, black and beady. When Amanullah Zalmai uttered, the voice was strong enough.

"Welcome, kinswoman."

"It is a happiness to see you again, Uncle Amanullah."

The eyes glittered towards Ogilvie, the head remaining still. "Why come you, and your companion?"

The girl looked quickly at Ogilvie, then turned back to the ancient bag of bones. "My companion is named Abdul Satar Dawar and he comes from Afghanistan seeking the all-powerful one, the Star of Islam, for whom he has word of gathering support for our people against the Raj."

"And I, beloved kinswoman? What does he want of me?"

"I told Abdul Satar Dawar that you would perhaps know where the Star of Islam is to be found, Uncle Amanullah."

"This I know."

"And you will help?"

There was a pause, then the old man gave a dry cackle of laughter. A sudden breeze shook the leaves of the tree, and more dust descended upon the thin body. Amanullah said, "The all-powerful one knows well that support is waiting in the hills and that our people are poised to march against the Raj and to take the military garrisons by fire and sword. It is not new. Why do you come, Abdul Satar Dawar, with old stories?"

Ogilvie bowed to the ancient, hiding his face as he spoke. "I come with word of the position of our force, of its strength, and—"

"Lift up your face, Abdul Satar Dawar." The tone was sharp, peremptory. Ogilvie looked straight at the old man. "The eyes are the mirrors of the soul, is this not so?"

"It is indeed so," Ogilvie answered, praying that on this occasion the mirror should be clouded. He continued with his story. "I bring word for the Star of Islam not only of the

74

positions of our rising people, but also of the British soldiers . . . I am able to report to him upon the preparedness of the Raj, upon what measures the British are likely to take when the rising starts and they can dally no longer, and to suggest how best these can be countered."

"You are a deserter from the Raj? You are a soldier, Abdul Satar Dawar?"

"You know well that our people do not serve the Raj, Amanullah Zalmai. I am not a soldier except in our own cause. But my ear is as long as your beard, and I have kept it to the ground." Ogilvie paused. "You will tell me where to find the Star of Islam?"

There was another dry cackle and again the aged eyes seemed to glitter like jet. A skinny arm was lifted, and skeletonic fingers pointed past Ogilvie and the young girl. Ogilvie turned; he had heard no sound, but behind him stood a man, immediately recogniseable from the description passed by Cunningham via Sergeant Cairns who had witnessed the attack on the RSM's wife: a big man, well over six feet, a hooked nose, no hair on the face, dressed in a white garment – and to settle it, the branded star. This man stood with his arms folded across his body, the left hand very close to the hilt of a curved sword, scabbarded and hooked to a belt around the waist. He said, "You shall come with me and tell me your story, Abdul Satar Dawar, and I shall test the truth of your words."

Very suddenly the arms moved and the sword was drawn. Its point, razor-sharp, was laid against Ogilvie's throat.

*　　*　　*

Throughout the area of Bloody Francis' command that afternoon there was much activity as the regiments and squadrons and batteries made ready for the assault. There was a coming and going of staff officers, of quartermasters and armourers, of medical details and field ambulance sections, farriers and veterinary officers, Supply and Transport, Ordnance, sappers, signal companies and all that went to make up a full Division of the British Army in India.

75

Despite Blaise-Willoughby, who had constantly reiterated the misgivings that had struck the whole chain of command, Fettleworth had convinced himself that everything was for the best. If it wasn't, well, it wouldn't be his fault anyway: he had his orders and they had come from unimpeachable authority and that was that. He strutted his headquarters, looking warrior-like. If he could successfully relieve Peshawar, much honour should accrue. His name, no doubt suitably embellished by a grateful sovereign, would become a household word in London, and throughout the Empire he would be linked with such illustrious names as Wellington, Havelock, Gordon, Kitchener, Roberts of Kandahar. By being present in person upon the field of battle, he would ensure that the victory was his, and already he could see the artists' impressions in the *Illustrated London News* and *Punch*. He would be in line for promotion, might even succeed Sir Iain Ogilvie in Her Majesty's good time. Even Sir George White: to be Commander-in-Chief, India, would be perfectly splendid, though it could not come yet. It was customary for the supreme appointment to be made alternately from the British and Indian Armies, but Fettleworth believed that, with the relief of Peshawar behind him like the relief of Lucknow, he could afford to wait Her Majesty's pleasure. As the day darkened into evening, Fettleworth took a *chota peg* with Brigadier-General Lakenham and his battalion and battery commanders; and later, when the First Division was ready to move out in its two columns, he addressed all ranks from a rostrum outside the great doorway into his headquarters. They were, he said, about to write yet one more page into the long and glorious history of the Raj, and Her Majesty the Queen-Empress was herself taking the most keen interest in each one of them.

"Do your duty," he bellowed solemnly from his rostrum. "You have stout hearts, and I shall be with you in person."

*   *   *

Ten miles away, westwards of the besieged city, the Royal Strathspeys had made ready, with their brigaded battalions, for the assault in conjunction with Nowshera. Watches had been synchronised by means of the telegraph from Nowshera, and the western assault was under orders to advance at twenty minutes past midnight, the objective being to strike hard at the enemy simultaneously with Fettleworth's two columns who had farther to march. Lord Brora was in fighting mood, and restless to be off. His eyes shone, and he spoke in forthright terms to Andrew Black.

"Muslim and Hindu, I don't give a fig for either. They're all the same to me. Cannon fodder." Striding the parade-ground as the regiment put the last touches to its preparedness, he drew his broadsword and gave it a flourish. The blade glittered in the moonlight. "The men will be driven tonight, Black. Driven hard, I say! How's MacTrease shaping up, as acting Sar'nt-Major?"

"Well enough, Major."

"Well enough is not good enough, Black. You must watch him, d'you understand?"

Black coughed. "Perhaps my choice of words was wrong, Major. MacTrease will be a fine substitute for—"

"For a deserter!"

Black seemed lost for words: he gaped. Then he found tongue. "Cunningham's no deserter. Absent he may be, but—"

"Any officer or man," Brora announced truculently, "who leaves his company in action without orders to do so, is a deserter."

"I think you'll not find the Colonel—"

"I dislike being *argued* with, my dear Black." Brora flourished his broadsword close to the Adjutant's face, and Black, grimacing, stepped hurriedly backwards. "When your precious Mr Cunningham is retrieved, assuming he's still alive, I shall press for a Court Martial and I give you my guarantee that no damn colonel in all of India is going to stick his neck out so far as to deny my representations, which if necessary will be made over Dornoch's head to Calcutta!"

"But surely in the circumstances—"

"I think you've said enough, Captain Black, so kindly hold your tongue." Brora pulled out his watch. "We have but

77

twenty minutes to go now. I shall expect your report of readiness in ten."

Black saluted stiffly, turned about and marched away. In ten minutes he returned to report to the Major, who stalked off to report in his turn to Lord Dornoch. Precisely on the appointed minute, the 114th Highlanders marched out from the cantonment, silently without benefit of the pipes and drums, to join the remainder of Brigadier-General Shaw's brigade for the advance through the night.

*   *   *

Once again, during the preceding morning, Ogilvie had been led through the ruins of Peshawar, this time by the man known as the Star of Islam, who was accompanied by an escort of four warlike but filthy Pathans. The *jezail* had been taken from him but there had been no personal search and he still retained his revolver. The girl, Homaira Sarabi, had been left behind with the old man, her kinsman. As Ogilvie moved through the wrecked streets, he began to feel as though he were part of a royal progress. As the Star of Islam was seen and the purport of the branded forehead recognised, men fell upon their knees as if called by some unheard *muezzin* to kneel before the Prophet or Allah himself. No word was uttered by the Pathans; the eyes were watchful and the hands steady on the *jezails* as the rusty bayonets were held towards Ogilvie, who had been left in no doubt that he was being regarded for the time being at any rate with a natural suspicion. It was by no means impossible for a British officer to pass as a native before natives, and indeed such had been done successfully very many times. When a Briton had been many years in India, as Ogilvie had been, he tended to take upon himself many of the attributes of the native; and a fine command of the dialect set the seal. Blaise-Willoughby, for one, had passed frequently and for long periods as a native of the sub-continent. But, naturally enough, it was always a good deal easier to pass as a native from another and distant part of India. This time, Ogilvie was attempting the more difficult task of representing

78

himself as a Pathan to a Pathan and it was not a very great consolation that the Star of Islam appeared to be, as were so many men of action and bravery, somewhat obtuse as to his mental powers: there was a similarity between the Pathan and Bloody Francis, up to a point. Ogilvie had noted the lowness of the star-branded forehead, the rather bulging eyes, and the expression which, though undoubtedly warrior-like and fanatical, spoke of a turgidity, a singleness of thought. Nevertheless, no leader could be entirely stupid and Ogilvie could feel the thump of his heart as he walked on between the hawk-faced men from Afghanistan. Around them there was still the smell and smoke of burning, but now the heavy gunfire had died altogether, at any rate for the time being. The sun was high now, and the heat was bringing out the stench of death and rotting flesh full blast. Here and there masonry fell, causing clouds of dry dust to rise suffocatingly. The escort pushed through the mob, and the mob pressed back deferentially as the Star of Islam passed by, and the air was filled with cries of support for him, laced with imprecations against the Raj. If the truth should shortly be revealed, and Ogilvie be left to the mercies of that mob, he knew he wouldn't have a chance. He would be rent limb from limb and his entrails scattered by the busy knives.

The trudge through the city continued, beneath a black flutter of wings as the vultures gathered overhead, circling, waiting their time for a safe meal. The word had spread through the ranks of prey that Peshawar offered meat in plenty so long as the street-bound dogs were not permitted too long a time in which to cheat them of it. Ogilvie watched them with loathing, though he had seen their revolting antics often enough when on the march through the Frontier lands, or on patrol out of cantonments. They seemed symbolic of the savage cruelty of the sub-continent where life was of little account. Sometimes it had seemed to him that the Indian masses had three choices: they could die by the sword, or by disease, or by starvation while the great princes, the maharajahs and rajahs, lived their lives of gluttony and splendour, bedecked with jewels and gold plate, secure in their palaces guaranteed by the power of the British Raj . . . he checked his thoughts. That way lay sedition, and the way was in any case wrong: too black and white a view should not be taken. The Raj was an immense power for good, and was served by dedicated men, and it was beyond imagination to conceive of what would fill the vacuum if men like the Star of Islam should undermine British rule.

The movement through the dust and the various smells ended at last: it ended in the rubble of a gun-shattered building, where half-a-dozen Pathans squatted round a cleared space in a courtyard behind. These men threw themselves forward, bending with outstretched arms, as the Star of Islam appeared. He gave them a brief command, and they got to their feet, one of them pulling at a ringbolt set into the paving of the courtyard; a slab rose a few inches and was manhandled aside. The high sun showed descending steps. Ogilvie was pushed by the bayonets towards the steps, and he went down, followed by the Star of Islam and the men of the escort. Before the paving-stone was replaced overhead, a tallow lamp was lit. The yellow beams flickered over ancient stone; there was a musty smell. The space they were in was small, but a passage led off, and Ogilvie was pushed along this ahead of the escort and the flaring lamp, bending his body from a low ceiling, also of stone. The place had the feeling of a one-time dungeon and here and there, as if in confirmation, heavy ring-bolts were set into the walls with handcuffs and leg-irons still dangling from them. From the passage they emerged into a fairly large apartment furnished with a long settee and a number of ornate, gilded chairs. There were rugs on the stone floor, and in one corner a *charpoy* with a veiled woman lying asleep upon it.

The Star of Islam gave an order. As two men advanced upon her, the woman awoke, got up, and made her obeisances. She was young and, Ogilvie believed, pretty behind the veil, with a supple body and long black hair. She was hustled from the apartment, through a door at the limit of the tallow lamp's range.

"Our business is not for women's ears," the Star of Islam said. "You would agree, Abdul Satar Dawar?"

"I would agree, O powerful one." Ogilvie, freed now by the escort, went down on his knees – not, he hoped, too clumsily. It seemed to pass; the Pathan told him to get to his feet again, then stood close, staring into his eyes.

"And what is our business, Abdul Satar Dawar?" he asked suddenly. "You may speak now, and reveal your heart's secrets to me."

"As you say, O powerful one, O Star of Islam." Ogilvie paused, marshalling Blaise-Willoughby's orders in his head. "I come with word from beyond the passes out of British India . . . word that twenty thousand men are marching from Kabul to join those of our people already under arms inside the Frontier."

"So many?"

Ogilvie nodded. "This surprises you, O Star of Islam?"

The Pathan made a gesture of negation, almost of irritation. "I am aware that our people will give full support. What else do you come to tell me, Abdul Satar Dawar?"

"Firstly that our army from Afghanistan is already crossing the mountains of the Frontier, singly and in groups, and will be ready to come together again and to fight—"

"When?"

Ogilvie said, "In two days from now, O powerful one."

"And secondly?"

"Secondly that the foolish British do not suspect the intentions of our people, and that the signs are good for us—"

"Then why do they not send soldiers to relieve Peshawar?"

Ogilvie shrugged. "It is in the nature of the Lieutenant-General sahib, commanding for the Raj in Nowshera . . . he is fat and lazy, given to pomposity and *chota pegs* and much food. His staff play polo and indulge in the sport of sticking the unspeakable pig with lances. The Lieutenant-General sahib prefers, so it is rumoured, to leave the Muslim to slaughter the Hindu, and that only after this has been done will the Raj march upon Peshawar." Once again Ogilvie paused, then asked innocently, "It is so, is it not, O Star of Islam, that we of the faith will slaughter all the Hindus when they have served their purpose?"

The Pathan laughed, his eyes narrowing to slits. "For a certainty this is so, Abdul Satar Dawar. The Hindus are as stupid as the British! And as wicked . . . and when their use is over, we shall fall upon them with the sword and with the help of Allah and Mohammed His Prophet. But in the meantime, is there not a difficulty, Abdul Satar Dawar?"

"A difficulty, O powerful one?"

"If the Raj does not commit its soldiers in the north to fight here in Peshawar, our advancing armies will be faced with their undiluted strength. Our plan was to strike them in the back, was it not, while they were engaged in fighting the Hindus along the siege lines?"

"This is true, but . . . "

"But what, Abdul Satar Dawar?"

"The Raj can perhaps be informed of the true facts, that there is an unholy alliance between those of the faith and those of the Hindu religion, and that it would be in the British interest to attack quickly and stamp out the fire. Can this not be done?"

"It can be," the Star of Islam said softly, "but it would prove difficult to make the British believe it! The British mind is a stupid thing, and is set like the Himalayas themselves. To the British, there is no common ground between Muslim and Hindu, not even the fact of hatred for the Raj."

"Yet there will be ways to make them believe. Of this I am certain."

"Then you shall tell me of these ways, Abdul Satar Dawar." The Pathan eyes scanned Ogilvie's face closely, seeming to bore right into his mind. "First you shall tell me how you gained your reported knowledge of the British lack of will to attack the siege lines?"

"I have kinsmen," Ogilvie said, returning the man's stare, "who are trusted and who serve the British in Nowshera – in the very headquarters of the Lieutenant-General sahib himself. These kinsmen overhear much that is useful."

"Including the counsels of the Lieutenant-General sahib?"

Ogilvie inclined his head. "Even so, O Star of Islam."

82

"And then they speak to you of these matters?"

"That is so." Ogilvie pressed upon an apparent advantage. "If I were to make my way back to Nowshera I could speak further to my kinsmen, and words could be let loose where the British would hear them – words to tell them of the alliance and to draw their teeth towards Peshawar as was intended."

The Pathan leader blew out a long breath to fan Ogilvie's nostrils and appeared to be brooding on the suggestion. Ogilvie spoke again, tentatively, feeling that the moment was reasonably propitious. He said, "First, O powerful one, it would be necessary for you to trust me—"

"Certainly!"

"And it would be necessary for me to know certain facts about the siege, and about your intentions, and the strength of our forces already inside the Frontier, and inside Peshawar itself—"

"And the purpose of this knowledge, Abdul Satar Dawar?"

Ogilvie said, "So that I may personally be armed with the truth, the better to instruct my kinsmen in what misleading statements should be dropped into the listening ears of the Raj. When a man makes misleading utterances, O Star of Islam, he can sometimes come close inadvertently to the truth – and thus it is better that he knows the truth so that he can avoid uttering it."

The Pathan gave a loud laugh. He clapped Ogilvie hard upon the shoulder in a friendly fashion, but there was a curious look in his eye as it reflected the yellow light from the tallow lamp. "You speak much truth, Abdul Satar Dawar," he said, "yet at the same time you ask much of me. Now it is my turn to ask many things of you – of Abdul Satar Dawar from Afghanistan which is also my country . . . of Abdul Satar Dawar who comes at risk of his life to help Allah and myself. You will answer truly?"

"I will answer truly," Ogilvie said. The thump of his heart seemed to strangle him as the questioning proceeded. What was his village, what was the name and family of the headman, how many people dwelt there, what had been his route into British India . . . what was the name of his father and of his mother, of his mother's father and his father's mother, what was his trade and for how many years had he plied it; and much more beside. Blaise-Willoughby's briefing had been thorough and painstaking, and Ogilvie's learning had been equally good: he passed the test and received the blessing of the Star of Islam, who would set him on his way for Nowshera and his trail of mendacity to provoke the Lieutenant-General sahib to attack and thus expose his rear to the Pathan hordes that would soon pour across the Afghan border.

It had been easy, perhaps much too easy . . .

"Come," the Pathan said, taking his arm in a friendly grip. "We shall take food together before you leave. First I shall show you my headquarters, which are both comfortable and well provisioned . . . and also safe against the British when they come."

He moved ahead of Ogilvie, towards the door through which the veiled young woman had gone earlier. They came into another passage which, when lit by the tallow lamp being borne by one of the escort, was seen to be higher and wider than the first passage with its hand-cuffs and leg-irons. Off this one, cells opened: stinking compartments with heavy doors into which were set bars so that any occupants could be watched. One, and one only, was occupied. In passing Ogilvie looked through the bars of the door at a wretched figure spreadeagled against the wall with its wrists tied above its head; a bulky figure in filthy native garments, but with close-cropped gingerish hair unlikely to be found upon a Muslim or a Hindu. Ahead of Ogilvie the Star of Islam turned and, noting his interest, stopped and called for the lamp to be held higher and shone through the bars. The agonised eyes of the Regimental Sergeant-Major stared back, and Ogilvie gave an involuntary exclamation which he covered in an attack of coughing.

The Star of Islam looked at him curiously. "You wish to know who this man is, Abdul Satar Dawar?"

Ogilvie nodded dumbly.

"He is a spy for the Raj, a soldier from those that wear

84

skirts and go to war behind the pipes. He sought me, and he found me." The native laughed. "It has not availed him . . . he will remain where he is until the British come, and then he will die, and his body will be flung to the British as an earnest of what will happen to the Raj along all the Frontier."

Eight

There was no reaction from Cunningham. Ogilvie had no idea whether or not the RSM had recognised him by face or voice; but was sure that, if recognition came, he would assess the situation quickly and say nothing that would give the game away. In the meantime Ogilvie was faced with a dilemma of his own: if he went ahead with his plan and made contact with Division, and reported to Blaise-Willoughby, then the British, obviously, would in fact *not* march upon Peshawar but would remain ready to repel the invasion from the Afghan hills, and contain the Star of Islam in Peshawar. Cunningham's life might last a while longer; on the other hand the non-appearance of the counter-attack from Nowshera might possibly arouse many suspicions in the breast of the all-powerful one, suspicions that might speak of British chicanery – Ogilvie could not even now be sure that the Pathan had not noted that exclamation he had given upon his first startling sight of the RSM – and such suspicions might lead him to take his revenge earlier on his snared victim.

Ogilvie played for time, and played dangerously. He said,

"It is often the case, O Star of Islam, that the British grow more savage when their soldiers are ill-treated."

"You criticise my action, Abdul Satar Dawar? It is not wise so to do, my friend." The voice was cold; the eyes flashed in the lamp's light. "Should you be so concerned about a pig of the Raj, an infidel, himself a torturer of our people?"

Ogilvie bowed his head meekly. "I crave your pardon, O Star of Islam. What you do is right, since it is done in the name of Allah. I have no reason to disagree."

"And yet have done so. To do so is not worthy of a Pathan. It is unusual, for a Pathan."

Ogilvie waited, his head still bowed. There was murder in his heart, a strong desire to bring out his still concealed British Army revolver and finish off the Star of Islam for good, and think about escape afterwards, escape from what would be a ravening mob when the word spread. But there were four men present beside the Star of Islam, four very watchful men now . . . suddenly, trust was no longer in the air and Ogilvie realised, with a heart that sank into his boots, that he had gone too far. A moment later the Pathan leader spoke again: "There will be a further test, a final one." He passed orders to his attendant tribesmen and, while two of them closed up behind Ogilvie and thrust their bayonets into his backbone, slightly penetrating the flesh as a warning, the other two stood by the door to Cunningham's cell. Their leader called out for the gaoler, and another Pathan entered the passage and unlocked the door with a large key that turned protestingly through rust and age-old dirt.

The door was swung open, creaking on its great iron hinges, and the two men entered. Ogilvie was pushed in behind them and held in a corner by the bayonets, now at his stomach. Another tallow lamp was brought by the gaoler, and while the first one was held so as to illuminate the dangling body of the RSM, the other was held aloft above Ogilvie's face; and then the Star of Islam turned and stared at him.

"I shall watch, Abdul Satar Dawar from Afghanistan, and

if I do not like what I see upon the face of a warrior, you shall die by my own hand."

Ogilvie swallowed, but met the Pathan's eye, managing to appear indifferent. The Star of Islam ordered the gaoler to carry out his duty. Ogilvie watched as the man bent. There was a metallic rattle, and leg-irons were placed about the RSM's ankles. After this came a pause. The gaoler moved across the cell and Ogilvie heard, a moment later, a curious grinding noise, a sound of protesting metal. Dimly he saw the outline of the gaoler, bent to his task, one arm and his body moving in a kind of circular motion as though he were winding in a bucket from a well.

But there was no bucket, and no well.

Slowly, very slowly, the top portion of the wall against which Cunningham was spread was moving away upwards, and behind the RSM's thighs a horizontal gap was starting to appear as the gaoler wound away at his handwheel. Ogilvie saw the leg-irons jerk and tighten, biting into flesh; higher up, the gripped wrists whitened and seemed to extend as the joints were pulled. A gasp, and then a groan, came from the RSM, and in the lamp-light great beads of sweat appeared on his forehead and rolled down his face. Ogilvie did all he could to keep his face expressionless, even to show a gloating at the agony suffered by a soldier of the Raj; but, judging from the look on the face of the Pathan leader, he was not doing well. Sweat, a give-away if ever there was one, started down his own face. He had to remember his duty: that must over-ride consideration for one man. He tried again to force indifference upon his features, and met the sardonic smile on the face of the Pathan. He had lost; and in losing knew that now there was no more to lose. As a cry was torn from Cunningham, Ogilvie reacted fast. He smashed a fist into the looming, grinning Pathan face and the Star of Islam lurched against the men with the *jezails* and then fell to the ground. As the guards recovered and closed in, Ogilvie brought the revolver out from the folds of his clothing and fired point blank. One of the men crashed down, clutching at his throat, and blood gushed. The others backed away; the gaoler, letting go of his handwheel, fled through the open

87

door of the cell, and Ogilvie ran for the wheel and spun it back. The gap in the wall grew smaller. Ogilvie kept the remaining tribesmen covered with his revolver while the wall slotted firmly back into place, then gestured to the keys, dropped on the stone floor by the departed gaoler.

In Pushtu he said, "One of you, release the man from the wall. Quickly!"

The leader was back on his feet now, rubbing his jaw. He stared at Ogilvie. "The revolver . . . it is of the British Army – of the Raj. And so, I think, are you who calls himself Abdul Satar Dawar—"

"Never mind what I am. Do as I say, or I'll kill you."

There was a pause, then the Star of Islam nodded to one of his tribesmen. The man moved across towards Cunningham, picking up the keys. He released the leg-irons, then the wrists were freed. Cunningham slid down the wall and collapsed in a heap on the ground. His face looked almost green in the flickers of the tallow lamp. He did his best to sit up, but there seemed to be little strength left in him. The sound of running footsteps came from the passage, and many *jezails* were thrust through the doorway. Ogilvie's revolver was already aimed at the Pathan leader. He squeezed the trigger; but just as he fired the butt of a reversed *jezail* smashed against his wrist, and the shot went wide. A moment later he was overwhelmed by a rush of Pathans and flattened to the ground. As he lay there beneath the foul-smelling bodies, he heard an excited voice reporting to the leader.

"A messenger, O Star of Islam, from beyond the lines of the Hindus. The British in Nowshera are thought to be making ready to march on Peshawar."

*　　*　　*

Ogilvie had been placed in a cell next to that still occupied by Cunningham. He was plagued by rats and smaller creatures that crawled and bit, and he lay shackled in total darkness. When the messenger had come with his report of preparations in Nowshera and also in the cantonment outside Peshawar, the Pathan leader had decided that the

88

erstwhile Abdul Satar Dawar, who was in all likelihood a British agent, would be of more use if kept alive. Bargaining counters could prove handy. The tribesmen had been ordered to let their prisoner get to his feet, but to hold him still until the Star of Islam had taken some preliminary revenge. A fist had then cracked against his jaw, and for a moment he had hung unconscious. Then the Star of Islam had left the cell, and Ogilvie had been removed. Lying in the darkness, he found much to ponder on: the messenger who had come from beyond the lines could have been let through by agreement with the besiegers – or the existence of the O'Kelly Drain was known to the Pathans and the cobras had once again been braved. On the other hand, this underground headquarters could conceivably connect, like the O'Kelly Drain, with the world beyond the city. If so, it would provide the Star of Islam with the perfect escape route when the First Division moved in; it gave the Pathan leader total freedom of movement, to come and go as he pleased after a British entry. And as to that, was the messenger's report an accurate one? Fettleworth had been adamant, by all accounts, that Peshawar was to be left alone. If fresh orders had come, then how had the situation changed and what was stirring now against the Raj – or had the high command come to believe that the Political Department had been wrong in their estimation of a full-scale attack from Afghanistan? From his conversation with the Star of Islam, Ogilvie knew that the threat was real, that the Political Department had been right in their reports; and his clear duty now, if only there was a way of carrying it out, was to make this known to the Divisional Commander before the troops moved out. There was no indication, so far as Ogilvie knew, as to when Fettleworth would march, if this was his intention. There might be plenty of time yet; but currently at all events there was a total lack of opportunity. . .

The darkness in the cell was intense, totally unrelieved, a darkness that seemed to grip and enfold and to invade even the senses so that in time thought itself became difficult. The silence was equally obliterating except when the rats scurried invisibly, or the dry crackle of the beetles was faintly heard.

Time was an unknown quantity; no one came near, no food or water was brought. There was no audible sound from the cell where Cunningham lay. The living world was a thing apart.

* * *

In that outside world, the Raj as represented by Bloody Francis Fettleworth was advancing ponderously through the night as the clock moved on. Fettleworth, mounted on his charger, was in the lead; behind him marched the massed infantry. The heavy artillery, the great limbers drawn by plodding elephants, came on behind. On the flanks the cavalry was as yet held down to the infantry step; in due time they would ride ahead to form the spear of the attack. Shortly before they did so, the long divisional column would split into its two component parts, with Fettleworth himself detaching to lead the eastern column in. Brigadier-General Lakenham would command the assault upon the north of the city, and was indeed much looking forward to action as some relief from his staff duties under a tiresome master.

Currently Fettleworth was being extremely tiresome, nagging and nit-picking. "Lakenham. . . "

"Sir?"

"The guns. I suppose they really do know their orders?"

"They do, sir."

"I don't want them blasting off . . . Peshawar's suffered enough by all accounts. They're not to do a damn thing till the order reaches them and it's likely it won't be given at all. I think guns are a bloody nuisance, frankly." Fettleworth lifted a silver flask, and took a swig of whisky. He sighed. "A necessary evil at times, no doubt, but I don't like 'em. Gunners are unreliable, always pooping off at shadows, don't you know." There was a pause. "Who was it who said that infantry was the queen of battles, Lakenham?"

"I fancy it may have been the Duke of Wellington, sir."

"Ah, yes, yes, probably was. A good man, Wellington, plenty of sound commonsense. Squares . . . you still can't beat 'em, what?"

Lakenham gave no answer, but reflected that it was fortunate God was on the side of the British – His help might be needed yet. Fettleworth went on to ask peevishly if the bullocks were ready if the damn guns should be needed – the elephants were no good in action, they panicked, Fettleworth said unnecessarily. Had the medical officers reiterated the instruction in the Field Service Pocket Book that the infantry was to shift the right sock to the left foot, and vice versa, each morning when on the march? They had not, since the actual march was a short one by military standards, the Chief of Staff said. Fettleworth started an angry argument about sweaty socks, and the southward advance continued. The night seemed filled by the marching sounds, the clink of rifles and equipment, the rattle of mess tins, the creak of the limbers and the harness as the patient cavalry moved on at a walk. Fettleworth had reached the subject of clean surplices for padres when his nagging was stilled by his ADC, riding close with a report sent forward by mounted runner from the rearguard company, extended half a mile behind the main body of the advance.

"Sir!"

"Well, now what is it, young man?"

"The rearguard's been overtaken by a mounted officer from Division—"

"Division's here," Fettleworth snapped. "I'm Division. How can I overtake myself with a mounted officer, pray?"

"I'm sorry, sir. I should have said, from Nowshera—"

"Yes. You'll not get far in the army if you make silly reports, will you? Well?"

"Sir, the Pathans are moving fast on Nowshera, a strong force – they've gathered well inside the Frontier—"

"What?" Fettleworth swung round on his Chief of Staff. "Lakenham, halt the column at once." As the Chief of Staff rode to the rear to pass the order back and the long column began to come to a somewhat ragged halt, Fettleworth barked at the ADC. "Who says so, may I ask?"

"Major Blaise-Willoughby, sir. Intelligence reports —"

"God damn and blast, I'm wide open!" Fettleworth's eyes bulged into the night. "So's Nowshera!"

91

"Yes, sir."

"Where's my Chief of Staff? Go and get him back."

The ADC rode away and found Lakenham. When the Chief of Staff returned Fettleworth rounded on him. "The attack must be called off, Lakenham, and we must march back to protect Nowshera and the rest of the garrisons—"

"The orders from Murree—"

"Bugger the orders from Murree, Lakenham, the situation's changed and it's likely Murree doesn't know yet. In the meantime, I'm the officer responsible and it's my first duty to protect Nowshera, is it not? One's always being faced with this sort of thing when one bears command."

"No doubt, sir. If you ask me, someone's blundered rather badly this time—"

"True. And I shall be having someone's balls for breakfast – damned if I won't!"

There was a grin on Lakenham's face as he said evenly, "I fancy you'll have some difficulty over that, sir."

"Why?"

"The order came initially from Her Majesty, sir, did it not?" Without waiting for the explosion, Brigadier-General Lakenham turned his horse sharply on its haunches, and rode away again to oversee the turning back of the long divisional column. They would go north at forced-march pace, hurrying to defend the northern garrisons; and before the order was given to move off, Lakenham, doing something that Fettleworth had omitted to do, detached two mounted runners from the cavalry with orders to skirt Peshawar to the north and then drop down upon the cantonments and warn Shaw's brigade to halt the western assault on the city.

*   *   *

Lord Dornoch, advancing, as senior of the colonels, at the side of the Brigade Commander, offered a suggestion. "It's time to move into the attack, sir, do you not think? We've not been spotted yet, but we'd do better not to push our luck too far and lose the advantage of surprise."

Brigadier-General Shaw looked ahead towards the siege lines and the dark mass that was Peshawar city. Here and there camp fires burned, here and there an isolated flare. The trumpeting of gun-elephants came, presumably from the compound where they would be tethered after their haulage duties were done. The sound of song and of weird, tinny native instruments floated back on a slight wind. "They're not especially alert, Colonel. Not even picquets posted, at any rate not extended this way."

"No."

The Brigadier-General turned to look back towards the nearer ranks of men just visible in the dark, then gave a brief nod. "Very well," he said. "We'll go in by battalions – now." He passed the word to his orderly officer, who rode back with the order, and the column began to deploy into its three battalions for separate penetration of the siege line.

Lord Dornoch, under orders to take the centre position with the Royal Strathspey, had one request to make of the Brigadier-General: "Have I permission for the pipes and drums, once we've been seen?" he asked.

"Most certainly – they give heart to the English as well as the Scots, Dornoch."

Separated laterally by three hundred yards between battalions, the advance, when the final order came from Brigade, moved in at the double with bayonets fixed. They were not seen until they were within little more than a hundred yards of the siege lines, and then there were shouts of alarm from the massed but unready Hindus and a ragged volley of shots took the running ranks. A few men dropped, and as the British soldiers opened a concentrated fire with rifles and Maxims, the *doolie-wallahs* moved in under fire with their stretchers. As the men doubled on grim-faced behind the bayonets, Pipe-Major Ross led the drummers and pipers on to the strains of *Cock o' the North,* action tune of the Royal Strathspey. Just before the van of the rapid advance hurled itself with wild Highland yells against the siege line, Lord Brora's horse was shot from under him and he crashed to the ground. As he crouched, swearing blasphemously, in the lee of the dead horse, the Scots leaped over him towards the enemy. When they had passed, the Major was able to get to his feet; and as he did so, he was approached by a rider in the uniform of the Guides, a *sowar* whose left arm hung bloodily by his side.

"Who're you?" Brora demanded in a savage temper "And where from?"

"Sahib, I am from the divisional column out of Nowshera—"

"What are you damn well doing here, then?"

"I come from the Lieutenant-General sahib, Major sahib, alone now because my lance-*duffardar* who was with me is now dead, with word that a native force is poised to attack Nowshera, and that the assault has been cancelled—"

"The devil it has! I think you lie. I think you are trying to weaken the attack, you black bugger!" Brora, furiously angry at having dropped behind the battalion, drew his broadsword and swept it savagely in the air in front of the *sowar's* horse. "What else have you to say?"

"Orders for your brigade, Major sahib. It is at once to withdraw into cantonments and be ready to defend them."

"Balls to that," Brora said flatly. "It's too damn late, as no doubt even a damn native can see for himself!"

"If you will please inform your Brigadier-General sahib, Major sahib—"

"I'll do no such damn thing! How do I know you aren't in the bloody Pathans' pocket?"

The *sowar* almost wept. "Major sahib, I come only to—"

"If you're loyal, you shall prove it." The broadsword swept round towards the embattled siege lines behind. "Go in and fight. That's an order, to be disobeyed at peril of your life. Kill some of the bastards. That's an order too."

The *sowar* said no more; he saluted stiffly, and at once rode his horse forward, charging for the Hindu rifles. Brora saw him fall; in the light of a flare he saw the limbs twitch and then lie still. He laughed aloud, and ran ahead, and seized the bridle of the dead man's horse, then mounted and galloped into action, waving his broadsword above his head. Retreat was not for any British officer or man and he would have none of it. His horse's hooves took the siege line and cracked

94

a few Hindu skulls, and his broadsword flailed to decapitate a few more, and he turned to ride along the siege line itself, hacking and yelling like a madman, the lust for blood very evident when his eyes shone in the light from the flares and camp fires.

*   *   *

Ogilvie's cell door creaked open and light came in. He blinked for a while. A voice from beyond the light said, "You will come."

"Where to?"

"To the presence of the all-powerful one, the Star of Islam."

Two men entered, and Ogilvie's arms were seized. One of the men bent and removed the leg-irons. He was taken from the cell and along the passage to the room he had been in earlier. The Star of Islam was seated on one of the gilded chairs, and before him, handcuffed, stood the Regimental Sergeant-Major looking murderous but somewhat recovered. Cunningham gave no sign of recognition. The Star of Islam said in a soft voice, "Events are stirring, Englishman whose name I do not yet know."

"What are these stirrings?" Ogilvie asked.

"The British – many of them being those in skirts – have attacked the city from their cantonment, but they are doomed . . . our armies are already massing in the north for the great assault. Now my presence in Peshawar is no longer necessary, and I shall leave for the hills while the people of Peshawar slaughter the soldiers in skirts – the soldiers of whom this man is one." The Pathan indicated Cunningham. "When I leave – soon now – both he and you shall accompany me."

Even as he spoke, events had begun their forward march: a man entered the apartment from the passage leading from the steps to the courtyard above. The entry was hasty, and the man's eyes were wild: his report was almost incoherent, but Ogilvie caught the gist: the white soldiers of the Raj had cut the siege line in three places, there had been much slaughter of the Hindus, and now the British were fighting their way into the heart of the city amid the beating of the drums and the fearful wailing of the pipes.

"How far are they from this place?" the Star of Islam asked.

"They are close—"

"But will not find us! Nevertheless, the time has come for us to leave, and—"

"Master, we must leave most speedily, for it is being said that there is treachery—"

"On the part of the accursed Hindus?"

"No, master, on the part of our people . . . they have grown angry that the Hindus should kill as they have been killing, and now they have turned upon the Hindus." The messenger paused, licking his lips, fearful of what he had yet to report. "Master, the weaker of our people are casting the blame on you – and there are those among them who know your whereabouts."

The Pathan leader's eyes blazed and he lifted a hand as though to strike the bearer of bad news. "You fear that they will come here, and dare to strike at me – is this what you say?"

"I say rather that the British soldiers will come. I say that they will be led to the courtyard by treachery."

There was a tense silence. The Star of Islam paced the room like a panther, his face working. Ogilvie kept his expression blank, glanced briefly across at Cunningham between the bayonets of his guards, saw the mounting excitement in the RSM's eyes. The Star of Islam, it seemed, had been most wonderfully hoist with his own petard: the Hindus had perhaps been too partisan in their interpretation of their own role in the unnatural alliance. The Pathan paced on; the order to vacate the underground headquarters did not come, perhaps would not. *Badal* – revenge – was a strong implant in the Pathan philosophy, and the leader, likely enough, wished to remain to root out the treachery . . . there was a struggle going on in his mind, so much was obvious. But the mental battle was to be resolved for him: from above came an almighty crash, as though the walls of the building overhead had come down, and close upon its heels a violent explosion came, rocking the apartment. A crack appeared in one wall, there was a rising, choking cloud of dust that swirled in from the passageway, and then the sound of rifle fire was clearly heard. Something had been breached, a penetration made. The Pathan leader reached his decision: retreat was called for now, and he lost no more time in giving the order for it. As more firing was heard closer at hand, Ogilvie took his chance in the general confusion. He threw himself bodily upon the Star of Islam and brought him crashing to the ground; at the same time Cunningham lashed out with his handcuffed wrists, tearing the face of one of his guards with the heavy, rusted metal. From the passage there came a long-drawn scream and the sound of desperate fighting. A heavy blow from the butt of a *jezail* took Ogilvie behind the ear, and the Star of Islam dragged himself clear and ran swiftly for the door and the passage at the other end of the room, pulling the door shut behind him and then noisily ramming home bolts at top and bottom. Only seconds after he had vanished from sight, the British bayonets, dripping blood, burst through from the direction of the courtyard entry. Cunningham called out, indicating the door through which the Pathan had gone. The door was of stout construction: explosives were brought, and the apartment was vacated, Ogilvie being carried out in a *doolie*. When the door was breached, the passage was blocked farther along, beyond the stinking dungeons, by what appeared at first sight a solid stone wall but was revealed on close inspection as a slab lowered by ancient machinery to block the way. The Star of Islam had gone.

*　　*　　*

In the fresh air Ogilvie came back to consciousness to find himself with a section from the Manchester Regiment. Cunningham, still in his handcuffs pending the attentions of the regimental blacksmith, was sitting on a pile of rubble. Ogilvie's head was splitting and there was a good deal of blood on his ragged native clothing. He caught the eye of the section commander, who, having been informed of his

97

identity by Cunningham, was giving orders for him to be removed in the *doolie* for medical attention. Ogilvie asked, "How did you find us?"

"Sheer luck," was the answer. "The Hindus started shelling again and one landed close here and opened up the passage. I saw natives below and decided to investigate, that's all."

Ogilvie nodded, then winced as waves of pain went through his head. "Where's my regiment, do you know?"

"In the thick of it, over there." The subaltern waved an arm. There was a good deal of rifle and Maxim fire, mostly distant. "Brigade's formed up again, all battalions together—"

"I must rejoin," Ogilvie said. He sat up, felt faint for a moment, then the mists cleared, leaving him with a sick feeling. He insisted on getting to his feet: his wound was not severe and all available *doolies* would be needed for the real casualties. The Manchesters' subaltern supported him and said he intended taking his section back to Brigade along with Ogilvie and the RSM. The section formed up as escort with the two Scots in their native rags in the centre. They marched off with the rifles and bayonets ready, through the dust and the rubble and the sound of the guns and the distant yelling of natives. Soon Ogilvie saw the Brigade standard fluttering bravely in a fresh breeze, lofting over a shattered building, then the embattled British regiments, formed – which would have delighted Bloody Francis Fettleworth – into square with the rifles pointing outwards, those on the far side of the square firing point blank into a screaming horde of natives. In the centre the large figure of Lord Brora stood foolishly upraised upon a chunk of masonry, brandishing a fist towards the enemy. As the section from the Manchesters marched in, Brora turned to stare at apparent prisoners under escort: he leaped down from his position and hurried to meet them, possibly hoping to find the Star of Islam. His eyebrows went up when he recognised Ogilvie; his face grew mottled when he recognised the Regimental Sergeant-Major and he seemed about to bellow when his attention was caught by an incident to the left of the square: a native was running

98

out at immense speed from between close-set buildings, waving a white handkerchief. Brora lifted his voice and shouted to the ranks to hold their fire. As the native dashed through the line of rifles and bayonets and panted up to Lord Brora, Ogilvie penetrated the disguise: Major Blaise-Willoughby from Division, minus Wolseley. The Political Officer was demanding to be taken at once to Brigadier-General Shaw.

Nine

Within half an hour of Blaise-Willoughby reporting in private to the Brigadier-General, a conference of commanding officers of battalions was called at Brigade. This was attended by Ogilvie and the RSM so that they could give first-hand accounts of their movements to the Brigadier-General and to Blaise-Willoughby. After disappearing disguised into Peshawar Cunningham, as he had already told Ogilvie, had had the luck, if such it could be called, to spot the Star of Islam holding himself aloof from the fighting – spectating, as it were, from an alley under strong guard of his henchmen. Seeing red, Cunningham, in his native clothing, had tried to fight through to the man, using his revolver, but had not unnaturally been overwhelmed and captured and after that his disguise had been seen through easily enough. Cunningham was no smooth-tongued Political. Blaise-Willoughby in particular seemed vastly disappointed at Ogilvie's and Cunningham's lack of any really useful information; they had gleaned nothing that had not already been overtaken by events. When Ogilvie had made his report, the Brigadier-General had solemn words to say. He informed

99

the colonels of Blaise-Willoughby's tidings – of Fettleworth's decision to withdraw his two assault columns, which now explained the total lack of support given to the brigade's attack during the night. He passed on the reason for the withdrawal and stressed that the situation was now grave in the extreme, with an apparently unstemmable river of Pathan tribesmen pouring across the Frontier. Already the Dargai Heights, near the Kholat Pass some fifty miles north-east of Peshawar, had been taken; and both Mardan and Nowshera were considered to be under imminent threat. Then he dropped his bombshell: the railway train from Nowshera to Kalka had not arrived at its destination. Patrols had been sent out to check the line right along its length and between Attock and Rawalpindi the train had been found halted, its military escort decimated along the track and in the coaches, and the families, the women and children from the Peshawar cantonment, nowhere to be seen. The bodies of three women had been found amongst the military dead. No native bodies had been found, and the hard ground had shown no tracks whatsoever.

"Division," the Brigadier-General said, "is heavily com-mitted to the north-east and General Fettleworth will not weaken his position. Major Blaise-Willoughby brings orders ... I am to extricate my brigade from Peshawar and force-march towards Rawalpindi to carry out a search of the hills north and east of the railway line. It appears that Rawalpindi is in no position to assist other than in their own immediate vicinity, since the garrison's depleted to a bare defence by the despatch of troops to the Nowshera and Mardan sectors."

*   *   *

Lord Brora was in a savage mood after the Colonel had passed on the orders. "I imagine Fettleworth gives not a damn fig for the women! If we fail to get out of Peshawar, he'll wash his hands of them!" He seethed. "Surely to God he has a freer brigade than ours available."

"Well, it seems he hasn't, Major. We have our orders. We

100

shall obey them – and we shall not fail to fight our way out of Peshawar," Dornoch said.

"In and out," Brora said scathingly, "like the man and woman in a damn weather-box!" He shook both fists in the air. "By the time we reach the hills it'll be a long way too late."

Dornoch said, "It seems we should not have entered the city at all. General Fettleworth sent mounted runners, who failed to reach us. If they had, it might have been a different story – but it's no use crying over spilt milk." He lifted an eyebrow at Brora. "What's the matter, Major?"

"Nothing." Brora, whose face had suddenly deepened in colour, controlled himself. Then he changed the subject. "You're no doubt aware that Cunningham's rejoined?"

"I am."

"I trust you intend placing him in arrest, Colonel?"

"I do not," Dornoch said evenly. "You've already—"

"If you do not, what's the effect upon discipline going to be, may I ask, Colonel?"

Dornoch's face hardened. "It's a matter for me – not for you. There will be no charges brought."

"As second-in-command—"

"As second-in-command, Major, you will obey my orders and accept my decisions without question. I wish to hear no more on the subject."

Brora gave an ironic bow from the waist. His face was livid now, the mouth a thin, tight line of compressed lips. He said, "I grant your wish, Colonel. A time will come when others more highly placed than you will listen." Rudely he turned about and marched away, the very swirl of his kilt seeming to display an arrogant disregard for his Colonel. Dornoch stared after him for a moment, then shrugged. Brora had to be accepted for what he was: a boor, but a first-class fighting officer when action came. But he would not be allowed his way in regard to Bosom Cunningham except over Dornoch's dead body.

* * *

101

There was no time to be lost and within an hour of Blaise-Willoughby's arrival, which had been through the cobra-inhabited O'Kelly Drain, the withdrawal to the south-east was under way. With the heavy guns and the Maxims clearing a path for them, the infantry broke out behind their rifles and bayonets, charging groups of natives who melted away like snow before the sun. The brigade was under fire from snipers on the roof-tops and from high windows, but there was no real confrontation as such until the siege line was reached, when the fight grew murderous as the Hindu hordes did their best to contain the soldiers inside the city. Knives and bayonets grew red together, and much work was done by the broadswords of the Scots officers as they hacked their way into the lines to the accompaniment of continual rifle and Maxim fire, the latter in particular cutting swathes through the native ranks. As usual, Brora seemed to be everywhere at once, busily whirling his broadsword and yelling out oaths as he cut, thrust, lunged and sliced. His exasperated hypothesis that the brigade might fail even to get out of Peshawar was given the lie, and not least by his own untiring efforts; and when they had cut their way through the lines, and re-formed towards the enemy for a farewell burst of fire, there was no pursuit by other than a few volleys that dwindled as the Brigadier-General passed the order to retire at the double to the south-east.

The brigade had carried out its dead and wounded, and when, later that day, the regiments in column of route were some ten miles beyond the city, the order came to halt and fall out and the dead were placed in their shallow, hastily-dug graves. The firing-parties discharged their salutes into the lonely, desolate air over the resting-places to be marked with cairns of stones. Ogilvie, his head bandaged, had a word with the Regimental Sergeant-Major before the column moved on again. Cunningham was in a morose mood; his hands itched to be laid upon the Star of Islam.

"He'll come into our sights again, Sar'nt-Major," Ogilvie said. "We have to concentrate on the families now."

"Aye, we have that, sir." Cunningham gave an involuntary sigh as his thoughts turned inwards. Then he stiffened like the ramrod he was. "Those of us who've already lost . . . maybe we understand the better what the others are going through."

"Perhaps," Ogilvie said, and changed the subject. Brora's niece was much in his mind; it did no good to dwell upon what might have happened, but there was no doubt that the whole brigade had been in a vicious frame of mind ever since the news had been passed and if and when the Pathans were caught up with there would be no mercy shown. The anxieties showed in the grim, bitter faces; the gnawing uncertainty and the eagerness to know the facts and to get to grips with the Pathans lent strength to men already tired from a long night's fighting. The voices of the section sergeants and colour-sergeants on the morning's march had given the step and nagged routinely, but in fact there had been no need at all for the nagging, no need to rasp. The forced march was a very willing one, and only the halts grated. Brora's face as he rode the column – he had been appointed Brigade Major in the room of an officer killed in the break-out that morning – was savage. He was far from unique in having womenfolk among those who had vanished, but he seemed to be taking matters very hard. Andrew Black, never one to miss an opportunity of ingratiating himself with his seniors, had presumed to offer sympathy.

"What do you know about such matters?" Brora snapped at him. "You've no family out here."

"No indeed, Major."

"Then save your breath for matters you understand, which I would take it includes the battalion's turn-out." Brora pointed to one of the marching Scots. "That man, take his name. His helmet lacks its chinstrap. As Adjutant, I expect you to keep your eyes open, Captain Black."

Brora's voice had been as usual loud, and the incident had provoked the only ripple of light-heartedness that day; Captain Black, that punctilious officer whose eagle eye for dress was so well known and, at any rate when on the march in difficult country, so much detested, had at last had his come-uppance and the fact cheered the men. The name duly taken by the culprit's section sergeant, Black had ridden up the column looking sulky and depressed, and Lord Brora had turned his sour attention to the other brigaded battalions. Ogilvie, in the lead of B Company of the 114th, was approached by Blaise-Willoughby, who was now, like Ogilvie himself and Cunningham, out of his native rags and dressed in bits and pieces of uniform unceremoniously taken from the dead. Blaise-Willoughby was not in fact accustomed to wear uniform as a Political Officer, but had put the point that since all columns on the march in hostile territory were usually under the watchful if hidden eyes of the Pathans along the heights above the passes, he preferred not to be seen dressed as a native. He might, he had said, compromise his own future usefulness by being recognised; Ogilvie's own view was that Blaise-Willoughby felt he might be particularly at risk from snipers' bullets if he should be thought a renegade for whom the British might have a use, but had let the point pass: Blaise-Willoughby was a touchy man. Coming up now, the Political Officer quizzed Ogilvie once again about his experiences in the Star of Islam's underground hide-out.

"We've been into all that, Major," Ogilvie said.

"Yes, I know. So often points came back to one in conversation, though . . . small points that would seem perhaps inappropriate in a formal report."

"I reported very fully. Really, there's nothing to add."

"Well, possibly not." Blaise-Willoughby paused, frowning, and reached up as if to pat the fur of the absent Wolseley; he scratched his ear instead. "I believe you said there was no mention of the families, of the attack on the railway train?"

"None."

"Yes. Funny, that. Very odd."

"Why odd, Major?"

"Well, when they rumbled the fact you were British – surely you follow what I mean, Ogilvie?"

"I'm not sure that I do."

Blaise-Willoughby made a sound of impatience. "Oh, come now. I doubt if the women and children will all have been killed. They'll have a better use as hostages, won't they—"

"You mean pressure on me?"

"Yes, of course. Just a thought, you know. You might have been useful to them if the families had been made use of, if you'd been made aware of what could happen to them if you didn't co-operate, wouldn't you agree?"

Ogilvie said, "The Pathan meant to take me and the RSM with him, only he didn't get the chance in the end. The pressure could have come later."

"Yes, quite. I take your point. It just occurred to me that the families might reasonably have been used against you from the start. It's still odd. Of course you may say that your Pathan simply didn't know . . . but he's the leader, Ogilvie, and we have to assume he has his tribesmen under full control – they usually have, you know. They're extremely autocratic and to disobey inevitably means death or at the least mutilation – eyes put out, that sort of thing. Oh, he'd have known, all right, and that's what worries me. The underlings wouldn't take the risk of acting without orders, and to attack a train full of women and children, and capture them . . . well, it's not small beer, is it?"

"Hardly."

"It could, and most probably will, have far-reaching consequences. The effect on our troops, and on the high command, you know. Massive retaliation. The Indian princes, too. Usually, as you know, they tend to sit on the fence as long as possible, keeping in with both sides . . . but they're very dependent on the Raj in the last resort, and though they're not noticeably chivalrous, they do know how we regard women and children. They may throw their weight actively behind us now." Blaise-Willoughby sounded excited at his own thoughts. "This Star of Islam could cook his goose by such an attack – if he was responsible."

"So you mean—"

"What I mean, my dear chap, is this: it might *not* have been the Muslims who attacked that train! We've been making the assumption it was, but I'm beginning to think it could have been the other side of the alliance – the Hindus."

105

"But they're under the Star of Islam's control too."

Blaise-Willoughby gave a hollow-sounding laugh. "I very much doubt that really. The whole thing's unnatural. The Star of Islam may be the all-powerful one to his own people, but to suggest he has complete control of any Hindu . . . it just won't wash. They may go so far with him, but not too far."

"D'you mean the alliance is cracking up already?"

"I wouldn't say quite that – not yet – but it's under strain. You said yourself – no, you didn't, the Brigadier-General did – that the signs were becoming evident in Peshawar. In my view, and I'm not inexperienced, the Star of Islam is dependent upon sheer speed. He must win quickly or he's lost. If he wins, which God forbid of course, he must then very speedily smash his Hindu allies. Then, and only then, is Islam supreme."

The Political Officer meandered on, thinking aloud and clearing his mind. It was strange that the Hindus had not seen through the Muslim ploy from the start, but the Muslims were clever and wily. Of course, numerically the scales were very heavily in the Hindus' favour: the subcontinent contained some two hundred and seven million of the Hindu religion as against a mere sixty-three million of the Islamic faith. Together they made up ninety-two percent of the population; the remainder consisted of a mixed bag of Buddhists, Christians, Sikhs, Jains, Parsees and a multitude of smaller sects banded together as Aboriginals. But never mind the Hindu preponderance, Blaise-Willoughby said, the Muslims and especially the Pathan element were warriors with a long fighting tradition behind them while the Hindus were mostly merchants and clerks and what-have-you, fat and comfortable and generally lethargic, and it would be comparatively easy, after victory over the Raj, for the Star of Islam's hordes, backed as they were by massive armies from Afghanistan, to drive the Hindus out of the north-western part of India. Quite clearly, Blaise-Willoughby said, the Pathan was not aiming to conquer the entire sub-continent. That would be beyond the wildest of dreams. No: the objective must be to establish an Islamic state contiguous to

106

Afghanistan, possibly with the hope of extending its boundaries eastward as the opportunity offered itself in the future.

"Where's his boundary to be at the start?" Ogilvie asked.

"Well, one can only estimate. Taking the geographical features into account, my guess would be the Indus and the Sutlej rivers. Possibly as far as the western edge of the Thar desert. Right up north to Kashmir. It's even possible that that's the *agreed* split, the division between them after the Raj is defeated. As I think I said to General Fettleworth in Nowshera, a running sore has started. We'll move in all we've got to defend the north-west sector. All other commands will be gradually depleted by the necessary reinforcements. Ootacamund will be weakened, and that'll give the Hindus their chance to attack Southern Army. It's clever. And it's an appalling prospect, Ogilvie, absolutely appalling."

* * *

The march to the south-east was appalling also: the day's heat was intense and the pace was gruelling. Dust settled on men's bodies and was turned to mud by the pouring sweat; thirsts grew intense, feet swelled in the heavy boots, rifles and equipment became lead weights. Nevertheless, with their particular objective in mind, the men slogged on without much complaint. By the time the light had gone from the sky, the brigade had reached the railway line running through to Rawalpindi, striking it at a point above the spot where the train had been ambushed. Marching on towards Rawalpindi, the van of the column found the coaches, guarded now by an infantry unit of the Indian Army, whose colonel confirmed to Brigade that patrols from Rawalpindi were searching to the south and west of the railway line. The Brigadier-General dismounted and with his orderly officer and Lord Brora, and the battalion commanders, made an inspection of the scene under the light of flares. A cleaning-up operation had been mounted by this time, and the dead had been buried. Blaise-Willoughby rooted about in a search for clues, finding nothing. As he had known earlier, the attackers had left none of their dead behind, a fact that had indicated to him that they had not wished the British to know their identity. Dornoch's eyes were misty as he surveyed the empty, broken coaches and thought of his wife in native hands. He turned away, shoulders bowed, to find Brora also staring at the wreckage.

"A terrible business, Major."

There was no answer from Brora, and Dornoch saw to his immense surprise that tears were running down the Major's cheeks. It was natural enough, yet embarrassing to see, and Dornoch moved on as though he had not noticed. In a way it was heartening to know that Brora had his human side, however carefully concealed. Possibly he had been fond of his niece and sister-in-law but, again, if he had been he had kept the fact hidden. A curious man, Dornoch thought, and an uncomfortable companion; hard to the point of ruthlessness yet able to cry like a woman. He moved on towards the trestle table that had been set up to represent Brigade. A map of the area had been withdrawn from its case and unrolled upon the table, and the Brigadier-General was studying it in the light of a guard lantern held by an orderly. Eerie shadows flickered, outlining the lean features of the Brigade Commander, reflecting golden light from the stars and crown on his shoulder. He looked up as Lord Dornoch approached. Dornoch asked, "What now, sir?"

"I don't know." Fingers drummed on the table. "This damned hard ground – the lack of any trail – it's the very devil! All we can do is comb our area, but in the meantime the men need rest. I've a mind to go into bivouacs till dawn. What d'you think, Colonel?"

"Not here, at all events." Dornoch gestured towards the silent railway train. "Too close to what's happened, I fancy."

"We must avoid fancy," the Brigadier-General said.

"I agree, sir. But it would be a hard job to hold the men. My married strength is fairly high amongst the NCOs and men."

The Brigadier-General looked up. "Relic hunting?"

"It would be natural."

"Yes, you're right. And we could conceivably come under

attack." The Brigadier-General looked up again as another officer joined the group. "Ah, Brigade Major. I intend to cross the railway line at once into our area of search, and then go into bivouacs three or four miles the other side, then—"

"Bivouacs, sir?" Brora had recovered; his tones were back to normal. "Did I hear you say *bivouacs?*"

"You did. Do I take it you have some objection, Lord Brora?"

"I have the strongest possible objections, my dear sir! We are under orders to find the women and children, are we not?"

"Certainly we are—"

"Then why the devil do we not go and find them? There's no time to be lost. Those murdering buggers—"

"Lord Brora, kindly moderate your tone. There is a need to rest the men and horses—"

"Oh, balls to the men, and who but a lunatic would worry his backside about a damn horse in the circumstances?" Brora shouted, his face a deep red in the guard lantern's light. "There's not a man in *my* regiment, I can't speak for the others, who'd not march till Kingdom Come to bring out the women and children!"

The Brigadier-General stared back at Brora's furious face. He said evenly, "You've suffered with many of us . . . I shall disregard what you've said but it will not be said again. You know very well that men cannot fight without rest, and the transport is dependent upon the animals, who also cannot go on for ever." He took the map and rolled it up, and handed it to his orderly officer to be replaced in its case. "My orders stand and you, Brigade Major, will see to it that they are passed on."

Brora seemed to be beside himself. He said, "And I, sir, shall see to something else as well. I shall see to it that the decision of a damn *madman* is properly brought to the notice of the Commander-in-Chief!" He turned away abruptly, and strode off beyond the rim of the guard lantern's light. Dornoch met the incredulous eye of the Brigadier-General.

He said, "I apologise for my second-in-command, sir.

Whatever you may now think to the contrary, he has his good points." He smiled somewhat thinly. "Though I have to confess that I, too, am under threat of report to higher authority over a regimental matter. I remain unworried."

"But you'll deal with it?"

"I shall deal with it, I promise you."

The Brigadier-General nodded. "I'll leave Brora to you, then – and by God I wish you luck!"

* * *

The railway line was crossed and when it was well behind a suitable spot was chosen by the orderly officer riding ahead of the advance and the brigade went into their night bivouacs, the shelter-tents being pegged out in neat lines with proper spaces in between as laid down in the regulations. In the Royal Strathspey's lines the Regimental Sergeant-Major carried out his inspection as closely as ever: he had put his personal loss behind him so far as the surface was concerned; though there was strain in his eyes and his face seemed to have grown thinner and more lined, his movements were as brisk as ever and his attention to detail had not slackened. The men watched him as he marched past the shelter-tents; he had already suffered what many of them might yet have to face, and because he knew what was in their thoughts he marched the smarter and criticised the more, and found fault where an eye less eagle would find none. He left mutterings behind him and was pleased to do so. He was still the Regimental Sergeant-Major . . . and if the old bastard could carry on never mind what had happened, and still be every inch a soldier, then the men would find it hard not to act similarly if and when their own turn should come. Example was still what was needed in the British Army, and come what may, the British Army would get it. . .

But that night, when for the first time in the field since Bessie's death the Pipe-Major followed regimental tradition by playing the battalion into their tents to the tune of *The Flowers of the Forest*, Cunningham almost broke down. He recovered quickly when he heard footsteps behind him, and turned a firm face.

110

"Mr Cunninham, to be sure." It was Lord Brora.

"Sir!" Cunningham's right arm flashed in salute.

"What, precisely, are you doing?" Brora asked.

Cunningham stared. "I was listening to the Pipe Major, sir, prior to—"

"Are you not still the Regimental Sar'nt-Major, Mr Cunningham?"

"I am, sir."

Brora sneered. "Very sar'nt-majorly, to be ears acock-bill to the music, like a damn recruit. I take it you'll soon return to your duties?"

"As I was about to say, sir. I was listening prior to carrying out a full patrol of the 114th's sector of the bivouacs, sir, and as a precaution, a patrol of the whole perimeter as well. I do not ever neglect my duties. Sir!"

"I think you sound impertinent, Mr Cunningham—"

"And I think I do as well, sir. I am unaccustomed to be compared with a recruit, sir. If you have complaints about the way I carry out my duties, I would be obliged if you would refer the matter properly to the Colonel." Cunningham gave another salute and turned away, shaking with anger. In his view Brora gave every sign of incipient insanity and could scarcely be tolerated much longer. From some distance off, Cunningham halted and turned: the Major was where he had left him, staring so far as could be told at nothing. Cunningham shrugged and walked on. He carried out his solitary patrol, making contact with the guard commander and the posted sentries along the perimeter, close sentries who with the bivouaced brigade itself were under the cover of the outlying picquets posted as soon as the night halt had been ordered. As Cunningham made his rounds the moon stole out brightly from cloud cover and shone in silver on the bare, lonely hills lying starkly to the north. Those hills would hold their usual quota of bandits and possibly also the men who were currently disturbing the Pax Britannica under which the Raj was ruled; but the hills were nicely distant and any attack would need to come openly across the plain. Good warning must needs be given. The moon shone on, bringing up the white lines of tents starkly and very visibly. In India there was never any possibility of concealing a large body of troops, and they must always take their chance, and be ready.

All was well for now, anyway; satisfied, Cunningham marched back towards his own tent, set up and prepared by his bearer. He found little sleep: the past returned, and this would be the first time he would march back eventually into cantonments and not find Bessie waiting. His heart ached and it seemed as though its break must bleed him to death. India had turned upon him savagely, and rent him with a tiger's claws. The Major had not helped. Cunningham shifted restlessly. He felt constricted, confined in the small shelter-tent. If only he could get his hands on the black-hearted murderers . . . soldiers were soldiers and knew what they faced, but you didn't expect women and bairns to be wantonly attacked for no reason. . .

It was no use: sleep was not going to come. Cunningham pulled himself from the tent and stood up outside, sniffing the cold air of the night. There was a strongish breeze now, coming down from the north and bringing a touch of the Himalayan snow-caps along with it, and the moon had been swept back behind the heavy clouds. The night was black as pitch by contrast with the earlier silver brilliance. Cunningham, picking his way between the lighter shapes of the tents, walked somewhat aimlessly towards the perimeter, thinking his own thoughts. He pulled out his watch: he might just as well not have bothered, he was unable to see the face, let alone read the hands, but by his reckoning he had been in his tent for some three hours and it was now around one a.m.. Dawn would not be too far off, then they could get on the move again. Rumour had come down from Brigade that the Brigadier-General intended to split his force into independent companies with orders to tooth-comb their allocated sectors. There was risk in this, but Cunningham understood the dilemma: a brigade was unwieldy, slow-moving, and could not cover so much ground as a number of small units. . .

Cunningham's thoughts broke off, suddenly. He kept very still and used his eyes to rake the ground towards the northern hills. Something moving . . . he was almost sure. But not quite: eyes could play tricks at night. Yet there *was* something moving . . . a darker shadow against the night's blackness, coming closer. None of the picquets appeared to have noticed, nor the sentries, but Cunningham was convinced. He moved a little closer to the perimeter and brought out his revolver.

Now there was no doubt at all: the shadow was not far off – and in the morning, or sooner in fact, the sentries would account for their criminal lack of vigilance in no uncertain fashion. There was no time now to call out the guard, more shadows could be closing behind the first one, and the fastest way was a bullet and the resulting noise to wake the camp.

Cunningham took aim and when the shadow was within range he fired. The explosion shattered the peace and quiet and a cry was heard and the shadow vanished. The bivouacs came alive, men turned out from the tents with rifles ready; the guard commander and a corporal ran for the spot where the revolver fire had come from, and found Cunningham bending over a cursing figure on the ground: Lord Brora, with a bullet mark scored across his buttocks.

Ten

The Surgeon-Major was quickly upon the scene: he pronounced the wound to be superficial and very far from serious. In the light from a guard lantern shrouded by a canvas screen, Lord Brora's buttocks were bandaged, an undignified proceeding. When the word spread, as it did remarkably quickly, there was laughter from the rank and file of the Royal Strathspeys. Brora himself, at first speechless, soon found vociferous tongue and, duly repaired, made for the Colonel's bivouac.

"The man attempted to murder me, Colonel," he stormed.

"Nonsense—"

"It is not nonsense, it is fact. I am Lord Brora, and I know what I am talking about. Shortly before the shooting took place, I had had words with Cunningham. I had occasion to draw his attention to his duties, and he was insubordinate." Brora seethed. "I demand that he be placed in close arrest immediately, to face Court Martial when we return to cantonments. That I demand, and that I shall have."

"I think you'd do better to calm down," Dornoch said. "I shall go into this after first light, and not before." He turned away into his tent, leaving Brora to stamp the ground like a stallion. Dornoch's mood was sombre and anxious: already he had received reports from the Subaltern of the Day and the sentries in the sector where the incident had occurred: they were not reassuring. Major Lord Brora had in fact intimated to the guard commander and sentries that he intended leaving the bivouacs to reconnoitre towards the hills and that they should keep their eyes skinned for his return. What Brora had done had been colossally stupid and had Dornoch's approval been sought he would have vetoed the move. But Brora was not the man to ask anyone's approval and he would have smacked down any demurring on the part of the guard commander, using his rank and his bombast . . . nevertheless, Brora had a right to expect a safe return within the perimeter and this could not be denied. Cunningham, when spoken to, had been genuinely shocked at his own act. It had been unfortunate to say the least, but in Dornoch's view Brora had brought it upon himself. To speak of attempted murder was insane, and perhaps by the dawn Brora would have come to his senses. That, at any rate, was the Colonel's hope in delaying any further probing of the matter, and already he had intimated such to the Brigadier-General. But this was not to be. After the bugles had blown Reveille next morning and the men began turning out, Brora came again to Dornoch's bivouac, his physical movements a trifle stiff.

114

"With regard to last night, Colonel," he said.

"I consider it better left alone, Major—"

"You do, and I do not. Therefore Solomon must be judge. I shall take the matter to the Brigadier-General." Brora turned on his heel and stalked away towards the Brigade tent. Five minutes later he was seen to leave, and shortly after this a runner came to Lord Dornoch with the Brigadier-General's compliments: he was to attend upon Brigade before breakfast. As the smells of cooking wafted across from the field kitchens and the sun came splendidly over the eastern hills, Dornoch approached Brigade. Brigadier-General Shaw, attended by his orderly officer, was once again busy with the maps, but pushed them aside as the Colonel of the 114th Highlanders entered.

"Ah, Dornoch." The Brigadier-General indicated a camp stool, and Dornoch sat. "A nasty business."

"I prefer to call it a stupid one, sir."

The Brigadier-General gave a short laugh. "On both their parts, what? I'm not sure you aren't right. However, your fellow peer's had his dignity hurt as well as his backside. Both may soon subside, don't you think?"

"I begin to doubt it. Lord Brora's a difficult man, as you know yourself. I believe now he'll press charges."

"Well, certainly he seems inclined to at the moment, I agree. You said last night that you refused to accept the attempted murder theory. You still feel the same?"

"I do, even more so. It's utter rubbish, sir. Cunningham's a first-class sar'nt-major, the very best there is—"

"Not to be swayed by his wife's death, Dornoch?"

Dornoch stared. "I fail to understand, sir."

"Thrown off balance . . . mind disturbed?"

"Mind disturbed, sir? I really don't understand the term. Do you?"

The Brigadier-General shrugged. "Frankly, no. Soldiers are soldiers, warrant officers even more so! Yet there are new theories around these days, Dornoch, promulgated by the medicos - the younger ones mainly. They talk of the stress of war and long campaigns and what the result can be upon the mind. Your Mr Cunningham's been a long time in India,

115

perhaps too long. Now he's under the strain of losing his wife in a particularly vicious way, and almost under his very eyes. It could have curious and uncharacteristic repercussions for all I know."

"I think not in Cunningham's case, sir. Indeed I am sure not!"

"Ah, but you're not a leech, Dornoch – no more am I, of course, but I've read papers lately, the sort of stuff that's always being showered on one from Calcutta. These new ideas – they're worth taking seriously up to a point, I believe."

"I'm afraid I can't agree, sir. Many officers and men have served years in India, and wives have been lost before now. I don't deny it's cruel, but it's not the kind of thing that makes any man, let alone a sar'nt-major, take pot shots at his officers – whatever the medical papers have to say about it!"

"It's been known," the Brigadier-General said mildly. "Officers, unpopular officers, have been shot by their own men in action before now." He paused and stuffed tobacco into a pipe. "I believe Brora is, in fact, a very unpopular officer, is he not?"

"He is," Dornoch answered shortly, "and I can't deny it. But we were not in action, and Cunningham's no fool. It would take the biggest of all fools . . . and he's not the sort in any case."

"Not when normal, Colonel. That's what we must bear in mind. I entirely take your point that he's been a first-class warrant officer and I'm not saying I haven't an open mind – what I *am* saying is that Brora's statement stands and unless he retracts it must be placed on record and will in due course be reported to Division for attention by General Fettleworth."

"Are you suggesting a Court Martial, sir?" Dornoch asked, his voice incredulous.

The Brigadier-General shook his head. "No, not in the first instance, certainly. And there'll be no question of an arrest in the meantime. Subject to my full investigation at a more suitable time, I may decide to ask for a medical board, Dornoch, to ascertain the state of Mr Cunningham's mind.

After that, no doubt, he'll be at the disposal of the War Office at home, who will make their own recommendations and decisions as to his future."

"And you've told Lord Brora this?" Dornoch was shocked.

"Yes. I believe it's likely to satisfy him. As to Mr Cunningham himself, I shall leave his movements to you with a suggestion that when the brigade splits into its small units, he be sent as far as possible from the vicinity of your Major."

*   *   *

Upon the return two days earlier of the main divisional columns to Nowshera, Fettleworth had been greeted with the direst of reports, the reports brought by Blaise-Willoughby subsequently to Brigade in Peshawar of the Pathan advance towards the garrison at Mardan and the seizure of the Dargai Heights. Not long after this Mardan had reported that the garrison was under strong attack and the casualties had been heavy; and after that Mardan had fallen silent and it was assumed that the field telegraph lines had been cut. Parties of sappers had been sent out with field signal companies in an effort to restore communication, but when these too had failed to report in, it was assumed that they had come under attack and may have been annihilated with their infantry escort. Fresh patrols were ordered and in the meantime Fettleworth floundered in a sea of urgent orders and requests for information coming in by the minute, as it seemed, from Murree and Calcutta. Not only this: patrols reporting in from the regions to the north and west spoke of more and more wild Pathans, apparently well-armed, pouring in hordes from the Afghan hills to form what could become, if it had not already become, an irresistible flood tide rising against the Raj.

"What the hell more can I do, Lakenham?" Fettleworth asked with a touch of desperation: Cheltenham, that awful place, was looming very close indeed now. "I've committed all the men I possibly can, short of leaving Nowshera defenceless. I can't do more, can I?"

"I think—"

"Except perhaps make further representations to Sir Iain and get him to speed the reinforcements from Ootacamund."

"They can come no faster than the railway train can bring them, sir, and the despatches indicate that they have entrained already. Meanwhile, you have troops—"

"Yes, yes." Fettleworth pushed irritably at a mountain of paper on his desk. "Nevertheless, ask Sir Iain again – that'll show I'm not sitting back. I wish we could get some word about the families, Lakenham." Fettleworth paused and mopped at his streaming face: it was all too bad, he should shortly be going in peace and comfort to the lovely cool of the Simla hills, where all was *chota pegs* and horse racing. There would be no chance of that now. He said, "Something's worrying me. Our men."

"Yes, sir?"

"When I addressed them, I promised I would lead them in person."

"Which you did, sir, until you turned back from Peshawar."

"I'm aware of that, thank you, Lakenham. The point is, I'm not with them now. I hope it'll make no difference to their fighting spirit. What d'you think?" He peered up anxiously.

The Chief of Staff breathed hard down his nose as he met the questioning stare from the bulging blue eyes of his General: he was thinking many things. In his mind's eye he saw Bloody Francis like a sack of potatoes astride his charger, which looked like a beast of mettle but in fact was, by veterinary connivance, the slowest horse in all India and one from which even Bloody Francis could scarcely fall; he saw the swelling scarlet chest and the eyes that could grow misty at mere mention of the Queen; he saw the apoplectic face of Bloody Francis above the outstretched foot kicking at the backside of his cringing bearer; and he heard in his ears the unkind comment uttered *sotto voce* by the rank and file about their incredible General. Gently he said, "I believe they'll understand, sir."

"Good. They're not unintelligent, of course. They'll realise how I'm tied to my blasted desk at times like this." For a moment Bloody Francis pondered, a hand playing idly with his silver-mounted blotter. Then he said, "Send a despatch, Lakenham, to all units: Your General is with you all in spirit and commends you for your gallant and selfless conduct in the field of battle. I think that'll do."

"Yes, sir." Lakenham coughed. "The field telegraph lines and the signal companies are much stretched—"

"Yes, yes, yes, don't always dredge up the difficulties, Lakenham, it can be sent out as convenient."

* * *

The brigade had split up as ordered, and as soon as the bivouacs had been dismantled and the shelter-tents loaded onto the pack mules and camels, and the field kitchens had been cleared away and stowed, they marched out for their separate areas to start the long search. Mindful of the Brigadier-General's advice, Lord Dornoch had sent the Regimental Sergeant-Major to march with the company that he knew would be most appreciated: B Company, commanded by James Ogilvie. The RSM would in fact provide some needed stiffening; casualties sustained by the brigade in Peshawar had led to a re-allocation of junior subalterns to other companies and Ogilvie was to march with his senior subaltern Alastair Faulkner as the only other commissioned officer. Brora was to ride with D Company, Dornoch with E Company, and Andrew Black with A Company. The Brigadier-General, dispensing with the ser- vices of his Brigade Major, rode in company with his orderly officer and a detachment from the Manchester Regiment, taking with his brigade standard the central position in the extended search, a position in which he would be more or less equally available to all the units when necessary. With him went the heavy artillery, the small formations taking either Maxims or mountain guns, dismantled and strapped to the transport mules. Before they had all marched out, the Colonel had had a word with Ogilvie in regard to the RSM, telling him in confidence of the Brigadier-General's proposals.

"It's lunacy," he said, "but there we are, James. I'm not particularly worried – no medical board's going to find anything wrong with Cunningham's mind." He smiled. "The boot may be found on the other foot – but that's between you and me, d'you understand?"

"Yes, Colonel."

"Right – you know the orders. Carry on, and the best of luck." They exchanged salutes and Ogilvie marched back to his company. The orders were to look for any spoor left by what was bound to be a considerable body of men and horses and then, if any leads were picked up, to follow. In the meantime the finding unit would despatch runners to cross the line of Brigade's plotted and mapped advance, contact the Brigadier-General and report. Thereafter the remaining independent units would be contacted by mounted runners and the brigade would be brought together on a line of march towards the enemy and re-formed to advance with all possible speed, picking up the spoor that would have been deliberately left behind by the finding unit. The plan was a ramshackle one with obvious faults and limitations but was the best possible in the circumstances. Hanging over all their heads was the likelihood of the Pathan hordes advancing south and east from the Frontier and overwhelming them long before they had managed to make contact with the women and children. In Ogilvie's view it was possibly a first priority, even above the families, to lay hands on the Star of Islam; he remarked as much to the Regimental Sergeant-Major as they headed into the hills.

"He's the king-pin," Ogilvie said. "Get him, and the steam goes out of the rebellion."

"It may, sir." Cunningham added with feeling, "There's nothing I'd like better."

"I know that, Sar'nt-Major, but remember he'll be wanted alive if possible."

"Aye, Captain Ogilvie, sir, I'll remember that." The RSM paused. "If we find him, that is. I'd not give much for our chances in this area. He'll be away to join the main armies in the north-west."

"Well, someone may pick him up."

"Aye, well, we must hope for that. It's the worst situation we've known yet, is this one, sir. I'm not hopeful of the outcome."

Ogilvie lifted an eyebrow. "Rather unusual pessimism for you, isn't it, Sar'nt-Major?"

"Maybe it is, aye. It's the way I see it. You can't hold the Raj when all the buggers combine against you, sir."

"But their strength is their weakness at the same time, isn't it? Combinations can break apart, then the Raj steps back in again. It's bound to come, you know."

"Then it must come fast, Captain Ogilvie, or we're sunk, that's my view." Ogilvie made no response; they marched on in silence, keeping a watch on the hills as they came below their shadow, making for a pass that according to the map led north-easterly in the direction of Murree. Ogilvie wondered how matters stood in his father's headquarters. It was certain that the garrison would have been reduced by the need to reinforce the First Division and stem the Pathan advance before it reached Nowshera; his father would no doubt have borne in mind, however, that the armies out of Afghanistan could outflank towards the east and drop down upon Murree itself. If Northern Command should be overwhelmed, then the battle would be already more than half lost for the Raj. It scarcely bore thinking about, with all its implications of pillage and plunder, murder and rape, of burning and laying waste, of the dismantling of the British institutions that had done so much to bring the sub-continent out of the Dark Ages of princely oppression and to set a standard of conduct worthy to be followed by the oncoming native administrators. It must not be allowed to happen, but in all conscience the RSM's sentiment had been not far wrong: the total number of men available to the Raj was a drop in the ocean when set against the combined native millions, and nothing spread so fast as the ravaging forest-fire of rebellion. . .

At his side, Cunningham spoke again, hesitantly and with some apparent reluctance. "A word if I may, Captain Ogilvie. A private matter."

"Of course."

121

"Between you and me alone, sir."

"It'll go no further, I promise you, Sar'nt-Major. And it's about last night, isn't it?"

"It is, sir, aye." Cunningham blew out a breath of relief and gratitude. He marched on for a while in silence, then said, "I'll not ask what's to happen as the result of the view the Major took, for it's not my place to ask that, and not your place to answer if I did. I understand well, none better." He cleared his throat. "I'd like just to talk it out, sir, if you follow me?"

Ogilvie nodded.

"I don't know why I did it, and that's the honest truth."

"You saw what you took to be the approach of the enemy, Sar'nt-Major. That's clear enough."

"Aye, that's what I did think! But it may not have been just that. The buggers have been on my mind, Captain Ogilvie, since Bessie went. I had murder in my heart, sir, and that's a fact. I acted on a mad impulse to kill one of them."

"As any soldier should."

"Aye, but there was a difference. Murder is not battle. It was in my mind, Captain Ogilvie, do you not see? It disturbs me to think of it now."

"Only, I believe, because it turned out to be Lord Brora, Sar'nt-Major!"

"Aye, well, that may be I suppose, but I don't think it is all the same, sir." Cunningham marched on; the heat of the day was mounting now and the sun shone down from a clear blue sky with not a cloud in sight. There was no wind to bring any touch of cool and soon the advance would become gruelling; meanwhile as the soldiers neared the entry to the pass there was no sign of any enemy, not even a sight of the usual peak-top watchers, dodging between the boulders and bearing *jezails*. But there was a feeling of oppression in the air, as though the very absence of potential snipers brought foreboding of worse to come. Suddenly Cunningham said, "Speaking of the Major, sir. I think he was at fault to go beyond the perimeter last night. That could have brought danger to the whole brigade, sir, insofar as the sentries' guard was down, expecting to see the return of one of their own officers, if you follow me?"

Ogilvie said, "You may be right, Sar'nt-Major, but it's not for me to pass judgment."

"I understand that, Captain Ogilvie."

"But if you should ever need a friend, an officer to represent you, you've only to ask." Ogilvie brought up his field glasses and closely studied the hills ahead of their track. The pass was deep, the sides sheer; there would be no possibility of extending picquets on the flanks until, perhaps farther along, those precipitous sides took a gentler slope. In the meantime B Company would be wholly at the mercy of any *jezails* that might be concealed above. Ogilvie turned back down the line of marching men, and had words with his subalterns and Colour-Sergeant MacTrease, and shortly after this the Scots, with their rifles ready and bayonets fixed, moved into the head of the pass.

Eleven

The women and children of Brigade had not been ill-treated, though they were tired and hungry. They were bunched together under a strong and well-armed body of natives; although no one had said as much to them, it was obvious they were to be held as hostages and used against Northern Army. From the railway line they had been taken, across the pommels of Pathan riders – Blaise-Willoughby's notion of a Hindu attack had been given the lie – in a northerly direction and as the next day's dawn had come the Pathans had halted at the entry to a cave system in the high side of a pass. The hostages had been set on their feet and herded into the cave, being made to walk a long way into the hillside until, at the end of the winding entry passage, they entered a large rock-

123

sided chamber where they were told to sit. A Pathan had harangued them in English, threatening them with death if they should attempt to get away. When he had left, a strong guard remained, staring at the women and children over the bayonetted *jezails* in the light of a number of flares set in holders around the walls of the chamber.

All the women and children being of the British Army, they were naturally enough imbued with protocol: here, in enemy hands, they were virtually a replica of their brigaded regiments. Mrs Major Gaskin, lady of the Supply and Transport officer on the brigade staff, assumed a natural seniority to and precedence over Mrs Lieutenant MacCrum, lady of the 114th's quartermaster; and the small daughter of Colour-Sergeant Collins of the Manchesters knew very well that she could rule the roost over the son of Corporal Matthews of the same regiment. Command was important in a threatening situation, and all the ladies, wives and women knew their stations to within a hair's-breadth. Since the Brigadier-General was a widower with no dependants on the station, command devolved upon Lady Dornoch as the senior Colonel's lady; and she found staunch support from Lord Brora's niece Fiona Elliott, whose standing as a mere niece was somewhat nebulous and therefore allowed her to act as a kind of liaison between officers' mess, sergeants' mess, and barrackroom. It was perhaps natural that the women and children had so far as possible segregated themselves along battalion lines; habits died hard, and one wished to be with one's own particular friends. Lady Dornoch, however, considered this to be a mistake: captivity was, she said to Fiona and Lady Mary, no time for stand-offishness and in any case the 114th had never been a stuffy regiment. As the senior battalion it was up to them to set an example of comradeship so that when and if the chance should come, they would all act together as their menfolk would have done. So Fiona was given her orders: provided there was no violent reaction from their guards, she was to circulate and encourage and try her very hardest to jolly the women and children along, get them all talking so that their ordeal would be made the easier to bear.

124

"Generate the party spirit, Lady Dornoch?" Fiona asked sardonically.

"I don't see why not," the Colonel's lady answered, smiling. "Surely it's better than moping, isn't it? We have to keep the children's minds off danger, Fiona. Go and see what you can do, won't you?"

Fiona got to her feet and took a few preliminary steps towards a group of NCOs' wives. There was no interference from the guarding Pathans, and she continued on her way. Lady Dornoch watched her with a somewhat whimsical smile: Lord Brora's niece was young and vivacious and friendly; one day she would make a good wife to a regimental officer. There was courage in her bearing; that counted, in India especially. And her very youth was in her favour now: she would be mentally resilient, and would be better with the wives and children than a middle-aged colonel's lady whose back was already stiffening with rheumatic twinges . . . and who had been long enough in India to feel old and tired and sun-withered and no longer much help to those half her age.

*   *   *

Far across the seas, Lord Salisbury had once again made the journey north to Balmoral in response to a peremptory summons from the Queen. The interview had been far from pleasant; Her Majesty had been much sorrowed and angered by the dreadful news from India and had suggested to her Prime Minister that every available soldier should immediately be embarked aboard a fleet of troopships from Portsmouth and sailed to Bombay. Lord .Salisbury had countered this by insisting that they could not arrive in time and, although more regiments and corps would indeed be trooped forthwith to India as reinforcements – one could scarcely do less even if they did arrive too late – it would be most undesirable to denude the British Isles of their proper defence and thus lay the kingdom wide open to persons overseas who might harbour nefarious designs upon the heart of the Empire. This reference to her German grandson was not lost upon the Queen, who grew angrier; when Lord

125

Salisbury was adamant that under no circumstances would he permit the whole of the home-based British Army to be trooped to India, even if there happened to be ships enough which there were not, he was driven from the castle drawing-room with upraised walking-stick and a series of screams of anger that brought attendants hastening to Her Majesty's presence. Lord Salisbury, his colour high, had made an undignified exit to the waiting carriage, eventually arriving at Kings Cross station still in a certain degree of hurt dudgeon. Once again he had opened his conservative heart to liberal Mr Gladstone, whose aged eyes had gleamed with somewhat spiteful pleasure that someone else was getting it now. Mr Gladstone had not proved very helpful and Lord Salisbury had soothed his own ruffled feelings by sending, via the cable links, harshly worded despatches to the Earl of Elgin in Calcutta; and speedily the result sped onward from Calcutta and reached the First Division's headquarters in Nowshera, by way of Northern Army Command in Murree.

"Sir Iain's gone mad," Fettleworth announced flatly. He poked at the GOC's despatch that reflected the royal anger from Scotland. "I must defend Nowshera whatever happens, must I not?"

"But perhaps not too cautiously, sir," Lakenham said.

"What the devil d'you mean by that?"

"I have said before now, sir – attack is often the best means of defence. It would appear that the GOC is now suggesting that you think along similar lines."

"Similar lines be buggered. He's virtually suggesting I *evacuate* Nowshera, that I *abandon* the town and my own headquarters—"

"Oh, come, sir, a slight exaggeration I fancy—"

"Exaggeration my arse!" Once again Bloody Francis prodded a pudgy hand at the offending despatch. "How the devil do I comply with all this rubbish without – without putting sweepers and *punkah-wallahs* and God knows what into the firing line? I'm doing all I can already! I see no reason why I should be tormented by Murree."

"Not by Murree alone, sir." Lakenham gave a discreet cough.

"Calcutta, then. His Excellency. Elgin doesn't know the first thing about handling armies in the field – that's quite evident. Nor about the need to hold bases, which any fool ought to know the importance of."

Lakenham said, "I quite agree, sir, but it seems to me that Her Majesty—"

"Her Majesty? What d'you mean, Lakenham, Her Majesty?" Fettleworth's eyes bulged towards his Chief of Staff, who merely lifted his shoulders slightly and pursed his lips. "D'you mean to say," Fettleworth went on after a few moments, "that the Queen behind all this? The Queen herself?"

"It bears her stamp, sir."

"Stamp?"

"Style, sir."

"Yes. . ." Bloody Francis pulled at his walrus moustache. "You may be right, Lakenham. You may be."

"The Queen's taken a personal interest already, if you remember."

"Yes, I do." Fettleworth sat back with arms outstretched against his desk, and his face took on a loyally pugnacious aspect. He released one scarlet arm and pulled again at his walrus moustache. "The Queen . . . yes. Well, perhaps she feels. . ." His voice trailed away as he searched for the appropriate words; Lakenham assisted him.

"No doubt the Queen feels that a personal appeal to her commander on the spot will not go unheard, sir."

"Yes, it's possible. She's an astute enough woman . . . I was presented to her once as I dare say you know—"

"You've mentioned it before, sir."

"Yes, well. I was impressed with her as a person as well as a monarch – much impressed. I dare say she remembers the meeting."

"No doubt, sir." Lakenham pressed gently and discreetly. "And her wishes . . . they can in fact be complied with—"

"Can they?"

"I assure you of it, sir. You have provided amply for Nowshera's defence, and many men can be spared for the sector above Mardan, as the orders say they should." The

Chief of Staff went on to itemise the regiments and corps that could be despatched with a minimum of delay. It was a lengthy list; Bloody Francis had provided only too amply for Nowshera's defence in the stubborn notion of keeping his own base intact come what might. Lakenham, as he saw the dawning compliance in the Divisional Commander's face, piously thanked God for the Queen. Last time she had been wrong; this time her strategy was beyond reproach. It took the Chief of Staff a little longer to extract the orders; but at the end of the conference the word was passed that the Pathans were to be held at the Mardan perimeter at the expense if necessary of Nowshera, and that the Dargai Heights were to be retaken for the Raj. Bloody Francis called for *chota pegs* and while quaffing his said portentously as though the whole thing had been his own idea, "Of course, my dear Lakenham, it's always better to use troops to *hold off* the enemy and block his thrust, rather than allow him a deep penetration – at any rate, unless you can be sure of moving across his rear and cutting his lines of communication and support, which currently we can't. A time may come when we can, however."

"It's possible, sir."

"Yes." Fettleworth rubbed his hands together. "I wonder what's for lunch. Damn and blast all this wretched business, there's a damn meat shortage now. . ."

* * *

Long since, the man known as the Star of Islam, emerging from the tunnel leading from his Peshawar hideout into the countryside beyond the perimeter of the city, had by devious but safe routes reached his supporting armies beyond Mardan. He had found no sign of British patrols: luck had been with him, which was surely a sign of Allah's esteem, for Allah controlled all men's fortunes. With his armed escort he had outflanked the embattled Mardan garrison and made contact, still unseen, with the scouts of his gathering army from Afghanistan. Soon after this he was closeted on a hillside with the commander of the force, a Pathan by name Ghulam

128

Khan. To this man he reported on events in Peshawar and outlined his plans for the advance upon the Raj. With the Dargai Heights in Pathan hands they held a commanding position; and the Star of Islam now wished an assault upon Fort Jamrud so that the eastern end of the Khyber Pass should be secured.

Ghulam Khan spread his hands wide. "To do this is without point. The British will not attack Afghanistan through the Khyber, while for us, we can bring support into India without need of the Khyber."

"Nevertheless it is to be done. I wish to rule from the Khyber eastwards," the Star of Islam said with all Fettleworth's obstinacy. "We have men enough—"

"Not so. Never are there men enough."

The Pathan leader bared white teeth in a savage smile. "I say there are men enough, Ghulam Khan. Now you will listen and not interrupt." He paused. "Our armies will move down past Mardan while men are detached for the assault upon Fort Jamrud. They will then sweep down upon Nowshera, where is the headquarters of the First Division, and then move east to destroy Murree and its defenders. When this is accomplished a force will be sent to attack and take Rawalpindi and then, with more support entering from Afghanistan, I shall form our victorious army along the western bank of the Indus, where they will stand to repel any counter-assault that the Raj may mount with the help of soldiers from the south – from Ootacamund." He smiled again, triumphantly. "Our Hindu friends—"

Ghulam Khan spat contemptuously.

The Star of Islam said in a soft voice, "Soon I, too, shall spit upon the Hindus, but for now they are to be useful. They are about to take advantage of the northward movement of the British and attack the Southern Army of the Raj, and soon all the garrisons in the south will be in their hands—"

"You should not make the mistake, O Star of Islam, of believing in too easy a victory. The British are worthy warriors who will fight stoutly."

"But less stoutly without their leaders, Ghulam Khan – but more of that soon." The Pathan swept an arm in the

129

direction of Mardan. "When the British garrison falls, the effect upon the Raj must be great and will echo throughout all India. You have done well for our cause, Ghulam Khan. I am much pleased."

"And Peshawar?"

"Peshawar has served its purpose, Ghulam Khan. Battle is now joined, is it not, with the Raj, and there is no further need to lay siege to Peshawar. You will send messengers with orders to our allies the Hindus . . . they are to withdraw and make their way to the south to join their brother Hindus." The Pathan's eyes gleamed. "The more Hindus that cross the Indus, the better for Islam – and for themselves!"

*　　*　　*

B Company of the Queen's Own Royal Strathspey marched through the narrow pass in semi-darkness: they were too far below the rearing peaks of the hills for the sun to reach them, and only pale light filtered down. The going was terrible: the floor of the pass was strewn with boulders of all shapes and sizes and there was a tangle of scrubby growth that had somehow managed to survive the poor light. Flesh and clothing became torn and heavy equipment, rations and water grew heavier. There was a feeling in the air that they were upon a wild goose chase and that time was wasting: clearly, no one had travelled this pass for many months, even years. Colour-Sergeant MacTrease spoke of mutters from the men.

"The pass won't go on for ever, Colour," Ogilvie said.

"No, sir."

"It may be leading us in the right direction, or it may not." Ogilvie was conscious of the triteness of his words, but what else was there to say? Of all the small units into which the brigade had been split, only one, presumably, was going to find the captured families; all the others were going to march pointlessly. Nevertheless, he understood the feelings of his Scots well enough: they were in a vast territory and surely luck alone could bring success. In the meantime the personal anxieties multiplied and fancies ran riot as they pressed on through the gloom of the pass. After another two hours' marching, that gloom lightened ahead as the sides took on an angle of slope away from the sheer, and they came out into sunlight that streamed down upon the protecting Wolseley helmets and was reflected dully from the metal of the rifles and bayonets.

Ogilvie passed the word for the picquets to take post, and men detailed by MacTrease doubled ahead and climbed the sides of the pass on a diagonal line of advance to give protection to the men below against any hostile tribesman who might fancy using his *jezail*. But all was peaceful. Ogilvie scanned the ground ahead and on the flanks through his field glasses, and then passed the order to halt and fall out for a ten-minute rest and smoke. He dropped to the ground himself beside Cunningham and asked, "What d'you make of it, Sar'nt-Major?"

"Of what, sir?"

"The emptiness." Ogilvie waved his hand around. "The total lack of tribesmen. It's unusual."

"It is that, Captain Ogilvie, sir. To me, it speaks of a total effort – all the tribesmen gathered into an army against us."

"An army that isn't in these parts, wherever else it may be!"

"Aye. One that may be gathering to attack Murree." There was almost indifference in the RSM's voice, and Ogilvie looked at him sharply. All the heart had gone out of Bosom Cunningham; he was merely plodding on, his mind fixed upon getting Bessie's killer in his sights or in the strong grip of his hands. The Raj, Ogilvie believed, came a poor second to that, but it was a state of mind that Cunningham would pull himself out of eventually. Brora had a lot to answer for as well. That business the night before was weighing heavily and had knocked the RSM sideways. . .

Ogilvie said in a low voice, "Don't give up, Bosom."

"Sir?"

"You know what I mean. You're the regiment! We're not going to lose you. The Colonel's a good friend in need—"

"I know that, sir." Cunningham seemed about to say more when a shout came down from ahead and as Ogilvie scrambled to his feet a picquet was seen to be running down the hillside towards the resting men, still shouting. As MacTrease and the section sergeants fell the company in, Ogilvie ran forward to meet the picquet.

"What is it?" he called out.

"Tribesmen, sir – a bloody great mass o'them, sir, like an army, advancing across our track ahead from the west."

"I'll go with you and take a look," Ogilvie said. He turned to the runner who had accompanied him, and passed back orders to his senior subaltern for the men to stand-to and await his return, keeping as concealed as possible in the pass. Then he ran with the picquet up the hillside to the crest. Some three miles ahead by his reckoning, moving across a flat plain into which the pass widened and vanished, was a massive dust-cloud. Through this could be seen a great concourse of men. Gaudy uniforms broke the dust cover, and standards and banners streamed. There was a heavy rumble, distantly heralding limber wheels, and through a thicker pall of dust the great grey sides of the gun-elephants were glimpsed, lumbering like a tide into the east.

*   *   *

Nowshera was beginning to resemble a ghost town, at any rate so far as the cantonments were concerned. Fettleworth's battalions and batteries and squadrons had marched or ridden towards the battle zone, going to the assistance of the beleaguered Mardan garrison, leaving Bloody Francis to feel uneasily naked in his headquarters. As from the Peshawar cantonment, the British families in Nowshera had now been evacuated to Simla and its friendly hills, this time successfully and safely. The town patrol was maintained, and this was the only remaining manifestation of the might and glory of the Raj apart from the sentries posted outside Divisional HQ, and the standard flaunting from Bloody Francis's flagstaff. The town patrol, found currently from a mixed and unusual bag of Supply and Transport, ordnance, and infantrymen officially on the Sick List but not so sick that they could not be made use of in emergency, tramped the streets under a corporal of the 1st Hampshires ex Sick List and gloomily bore the shouted insults of a mob that was beginning to flex its muscles as the word came through the grapevine of Pathan successes at Dargai and Mardan.

"Bastards," the corporal said phlegmatically as filth impacted against his immaculate khaki-drill tunic. "Much more of this and I'll start a bloody war of my own, I don't think." He raised his voice. "Watch it, you men. Don't let the buggers get you rattled. If we start anything, we'll be torn into little strips of skin, right?"

The patrol marched on, eyes flickering from side to side along the alleys. Left, right, left . . . the rifles always ready, the minds and hearts wishing to use them but praying that the need might not be forced upon them in the narrow confines of the dirty, stinking streets. As always, the British Army, that long-suffering agent of the Pax Britannica, had the rotten end of the stick and had to slog it out and look smart and indifferent and keep its bloody temper. Not an easy job. It was small wonder that when they returned to cantonments their native bearers got the heavy end of their ammunition-boots up their backsides, and not always in a friendly spirit. Maybe the domestic natives were loyal to the Raj, and undoubtedly many in fact were. But there were the others, the time-servers who would turn and bite the moment they saw the chance coming. The men moved on, feeling their backs immensely vulnerable, but they would not turn their heads: to do that might show unease, even fear, and the Raj was not fearful. Even animals could smell fear in a man, and that was when they pounced. Through the mob went the Wolseley helmets and the starched tunics, the shining regimental badges and buttons, the polished boots. Polish still shone in patches through muck. Sweat darkened the starch around armpits and shoulder-blades. From the rear as the men passed by a hand darted out from the mob and impaled something on the last bayonet, that of the corporal of the Hampshires. He felt the slight tug, and he brought his rifle and bayonet to the vertical, and looked up: a piece of goatskin, cut to a square, a large piece, disfigured the steel. Clicking his tongue, the corporal removed it and was about to cast it away when he saw words burned into it by a red-hot iron, an old Pathan habit . . . he clenched the skin in his fist and marched on. There would be no telling who had stuck the bloody thing on his bayonet and it would be foolish to attempt to find out. When he returned, at the end of the patrol, to the town guardroom he read the words, whistled in astonishment and concern, and handed it, with his report, to the officer of the patrol. No time was lost in rushing the goatskin through to Division, where it was brought to the immediate attention of Lieutenant-General Fettleworth. The message was very pointed: the commander of the British soldiers in Nowshera, together with the Northern Army Commander in Murree and, to crown them all, the British Commander-in-Chief in Calcutta, was to be handed over to the forces of Islam. If this was not done within forty-eight hours, the families from the Peshawar cantonment would die by the sword.

Fettleworth's face lacked all colour when he had read, and his hands shook. He rose from behind his desk, then slumped back into his chair again. This, Her Majesty could never have visualised.

"It's the end, Lakenham," Fettleworth said.

"The end, sir? I fail to follow you. You don't intend to collapse your command like a pack of cards, do you?"

Fettleworth seemed broken; there was no reaction to rudeness. He said, "It's unthinkable to hand over the high command. It's also unthinkable to desert the women and children. They have us in a cleft stick, Lakenham."

"Then we must uncleft their damn stick, sir! We must cut the women and children out, and we have forty-eight hours in which to do it." The Chief of Staff paused, face grim. "If we fail, you must face the hand-over, because—"

"No, that's not to be thought of—"

"I disagree, sir." Lakenham's voice was hard and as cold as ice. "That message will by now be known to every man in the town patrol, and it will spread like wildfire. The grapevine of the rank and file is just as effective as that of the Pathan, and it cannot be said throughout the British Army in India that the generals of the high command hid behind the skirts of their women and children!"

134

Twelve

On the lip of the pass Ogilvie brought down his field glasses. "They're not Pathans," he said to the picquet who had reported.

"Not, sir?"

"Far from it! It's a private native army on the march – God knows where to and why. The nearest prince round here is the Rajah of whatsit, Kohat. He happens to be a Hindu, for what the knowledge is worth in the current situation. In the past he's blown hot and cold as regards the Raj."

"You think it could be his army, sir?"

"It's possible. Whoever it is, we lie low." Ogilvie thrust his field glasses back into their leather case and started down the hillside, leaving the picquet still posted with the others. Reaching the pass, he doubled back towards his company. Rejoining, he briefed his subaltern together with Cunningham and the NCOs as to the sighting and its possible implications. Cunningham was about to speak when another warning shout came down from the picquets on the heights. Ogilvie swung round and saw the distant dust-cloud approaching from the direction of the native army's advance, riding from the plain into the low hills where the pass flattened out. Then from out of the dust-cloud he saw riders coming on at the gallop with native guidons streaming from the lances. He was about to give the order to stand by to open fire when Cunningham grasped his arm.

"White flag, sir! Flag of truce!"

* * *

The goatskin message was considered most urgently by His Excellency the Viceroy, acting now in his capacity of Governor-General in Council. He conferred, after a full meeting with the members of council, with Sir George White, one of the highly-placed officers personally concerned. White made the point that he personally would never sacrifice the women and children, but that to hand over all the military commanders appeared on the face of it to be out of the question.

Lord Elgin's reply to that was startlingly pointed. "Why?" he asked. "I'm sorry to be frank, but you're all replaceable. The women and children – to their husbands and parents – are not."

"I take your point, Your Excellency. I have no answer to that, except that to bargain with the Pathan is always bad practice. Once threat is given in to, the rot has set in. The rest follows as the night the day."

"Then it's impasse, as General Fettleworth has also said."

"Hardly that, sir. As General Fettleworth has further said in his despatch, we have to cut out the hostages and throw this Star of Islam's threat back in his face."

"In forty-eight hours – less, now? With all our forces committed, or about to be committed, against the Afghan invasion? It's impossible, Sir George! Quite impossible, as I see it."

The Commander-in-Chief stroked his chin, his eyes grave. "The territory's huge I have to admit. I understand from Murree that Shaw's brigade is searching currently, but there's been nothing further reported."

"Nor will there be, I'm convinced. Those poor wretches could be anywhere and they'll not be found except by sheer chance." The Viceroy rose to his feet and stalked across to a wide window looking out over the splendid gardens of Government House and the profusion of colour from oleanders and euphorbias, English roses and Cape jessamine backed by thick screens of palm and bamboo. On the courtyard away to the left the Viceregal Bodyguard was parading, a brilliant splash of Empire in their scarlet and gold jackets, thigh boots and striped puggarees . . . the greatest Empire the world had ever known – far-flung, immensely rich, immensely powerful – seemed epitomised in the splendour of the Viceroy's residence, yet all could be shaken to the core by a smelly, uneducated Pathan tribesman from the lonely Afghan passes, acting in the name of his religion, and bringing together a rag-clad army with virtually self-explosive rifles of doubtful age and parentage but arrayed in such potentially overwhelming numbers that they could in fact defeat the best disciplined and armed soldiers in the civilised world. It was nothing short of tragedy; and though Lord Elgin would never have put his own position above his consideration for India and the Raj, and his duty to the Queen, it could prove a very personal tragedy and of this he was naturally acutely aware. Viceroys, no less than generals, could fall and the crash would be immense. To return home from a broken, war-torn India, to return as a failed Viceroy, was as unthinkable as to leave the women and children from Peshawar to their fate. The message had spoken of the sword: Elgin knew that that was intended as a statement of fact. The slaughter would be horrible and bloody. It was less than forty years since babies had been spitted on the native bayonets in the Mutiny, and in the interval incipiently rebellious minds had not grown more tender.

Elgin turned again and faced the Commander-in-Chief. He said, "We need time, Sir George. Time to find the hostages, time to allow the reinforcements from Ootaca-mund to reach Northern Army – you'd agree with that?"

White nodded.

"Then we must make time for ourselves," Elgin said energetically, "since no one else is going to!" He strode across to his desk and sat down. "We must *buy* time," he went on. "The message from the Star of Islam must be used in our favour – it must be used to buy that time, do you see?" He leaned forward. "I shall accede as to one third. One general – to buy time, Sir George. Now then: the Pathan asks for you, for Sir Iain Ogilvie, and for General Fettleworth. You I cannot spare. It's up to you to recommend a name to me: Ogilvie or Fettleworth. Who can be the more easily spared in your opinion, until such time as he can be cut out again by force of arms?"

*　　*　　*

White had been frigidly antagonistic to the orders, but Lord Elgin had proved adamant. The choice, when it had to

137

be made, had not been a difficult one; as a matter of form White had pondered and judicially considered the merits of each case, but it had still not been difficult and Lieutenant-General Fettleworth had as it were lost the toss even though he was the officer whose forces were those most immediately involved in the fighting. Sir Iain Ogilvie's was the larger command and his absence would be felt more keenly; while the absence of Fettleworth, though the Commander-in-Chief would not have dreamed of saying so, would be felt very little. Fettleworth's Chief of Staff, Brigadier-General Lakenham, was an able fellow and would deputise most admirably. . .

The dreadful news was duly delivered via the telegraph to the First Division in Nowshera and brought by Lakenham to Bloody Francis, who refused to believe it.

"Oh, nonsense, His Excellency would never give in!"

Lakenham tapped the despatch. "Black and white, sir."

"Confusion along the wire, Lakenham. You know the old soldier's story: send reinforcements, we are going to advance . . . rendered upon receipt as send three-and-fourpence, we're going to a dance. Either that, or some fool's idea of a joke."

Lakenham sighed impatiently. "Perhaps you'd like me to ask for confirmation, sir?" he asked with his tongue in his cheek.

"Yes, a good idea. Do that, if you please, Lakenham."

Lakenham gaped. "Are you serious, sir? The despatch is perfectly clear—"

"Of course I'm serious!" Bloody Francis snapped. "Kindly inform Calcutta that the despatch was received garbled and I must have it repeated and clarified."

*   *   *

Along the pass above Rawalpindi, the advance of the native horsemen had halted as it met Ogilvie and the Regimental Sergeant-Major. Hawklike faces looked down from above the dirty but colourful uniforms, which Ogilvie had by now positively identified as those of the Rajah of

138

Kohat's private army. The lance-points were lowered to the ground, honouring the flag of truce that floated from the leader's lance.

"Who are you, Captain sahib?"

"I am the officer commanding a British company of infantry," Ogilvie answered, "as no doubt you can see for yourself. I am not permitted to tell you more. Do you come in peace – does your army march in peace as regards the Raj?"

"My master's army," the leader answered loftily, "marches for Her Majesty Queen Victoria the Queen-Empress, and thus marches not in peace, but in war for the Raj."

"His Highness is loyal today, then?" Ogilvie asked with a grin. "That's good news! What do you want of me?"

"A parley with His Highness, Captain sahib."

"For what purpose?"

The native officer said, "Your picquets were seen distantly and known to be British, and His Highness wishes advice as to where he should march his army most usefully."

Ogilvie caught the RSM's eye, which gave a fractional wink: their thoughts were similar – an army marching aimlessly to war held overtones of sheer hilarity. Ogilvie asked, "Where is His Highness heading at this moment?"

"Towards Murree, Captain sahib. Not to attack, but to offer his loyal services to the Lieutenant-General sahib, for his disposal."

"A good idea! I suggest he carries on."

"First His Highness wishes words. I am sent to take you to him, Captain sahib." The tone had hardened: orders were in the air now rather than a request. "You may bring also your Sergeant-Major sahib if you wish."

Ogilvie shrugged: a parley could be useful so long as it didn't waste too much time. "I'll come alone." He turned to the RSM, telling him to inform the senior subaltern that he was to take over the command. He added, "If anything goes wrong, Mr Faulkner's to carry on as ordered by Brigade. He's to give me one hour, that's all."

"I shall see you safely back first, sir."

Ogilvie smiled, and took the RSM's arm for a moment. He

said, "Women and children first, Bosom, and that's an order." He turned back to the Rajah's squadron, and the commander gave him a hand up to sit behind him on his mount. They swung round at once and rode away, leaving the Regimental Sergeant-Major to stare after them. Ahead, the Rajah's army had taken the opportunity to halt and fall out, and the party of horsemen soon joined them. They were a rag, tag and bobtail outfit, Ogilvie thought, but currently all would be grist to the mill of the Raj and his father would be glad enough of any reinforcements. Besides, loyalty was never to be sneezed at so long as it endured, but the Rajah of Kohat's loyalty was a brittle thing. Ogilvie was taken towards one of the elephants at the head of the column, an elephant with a gaudy gold-canopied *howdah* on its back. In this *howdah* Ogilvie recognized His Highness of Kohat: obese, black bearded, clad in robes of gold thread – real gold most probably – and with an emerald green turban on his head. Rings loaded with rubies, emeralds and diamonds weighed down the fingers that were lifted in greeting to the representative of the Raj; and in the *howdah* with His Highness sat four concubines, making going to war a pleasant business.

The Rajah gave an oily smile. "Greetings, Captain sahib."

"Greetings, Your Highness." Dismounting from behind the cavalry officer, Ogilvie came to attention and saluted smartly.

The Rajah said, "Greetings to the great Queen Victoria, to whom I am immensely loyal, oh, none more so! The sun lives in her navel."

India was India and the sentiment was intended to be unexceptionable and perhaps Her Majesty would have understood, but Ogilvie was unable to conceal a grin, finding it impossible to equate the Queen with anything so mundane as the possession of a navel. He gave a formal bow of acceptance of the compliment on the Queen's behalf. Without more ado the Rajah gave an order and the *mahout* bade the elephant kneel. The young women tipped and dipped, the elephant brought the *howdah* to embarkation level and Ogilvie was invited aboard. It was, he found, a tight squeeze and the air was heavy with body sweat that the various perfumes failed to subdue entirely. Upon the face of His Highness sat a wide and friendly smile. The elephant rose again, lumberingly, and Ogilvie clutched at the *howdah's* sides.

The Rajah said amiably, "I march to fight for the British Raj. May it live a thousand years."

"You also, Your Highness. Also the state of Kohat."

"And Queen Victoria."

"Yes, indeed." Ogilvie could think of no precise equivalent of Queen Victoria in native India and let it pass. He brought the Rajah to consideration of more immediate matters by saying, "I am told you intend marching to Murree. This I commend."

"I will be appreciated, Captain sahib?"

"Yes, very much, Your Highness."

"I will receive honour?"

"It is possible—"

"Knighthood of Most Exalted Order of Star of India . . . Knight Grand Commander of same order?"

Ogilvie gave a sigh; conversations in India tended to be long-winded, and time was pressing upon him. "It is possible, Your Highness," he said again. "My father may be in a position to recommend this, if—"

"Your father, Captain sahib? Who is he, your father?"

"The General Officer Commanding in Murree, Your Highness."

"Oh, such a man!" The Rajah clasped his hands and jiggled dangerously in his seat with hopeful pleasure. "The General sahib of the Northern Army, oh, what a fortunate meeting with his son! He will arrange for Star of India?"

Ogilvie said with a straight face, "If you ask, Your Highness, perhaps you will receive. Especially if I am able to tell my father that you've helped me—"

"I shall help, yes, oh, indeed yes." The jewelled hands were still reverentially clasped.

"Then first, Your Highness, the Star of Islam – then the Star of India. Do you know, perhaps, where this man is, the one who calls himself the Star of Islam?"

"This I do not know unfortunately, or I would have found him and had him killed."

Ogilvie nodded, and shifted himself a little away from the somewhat unhygienic body of one of the Rajah's concubines. He asked, "Have you had dealings with this man, Your Highness?"

The answer came a shade too quickly. "No dealings."

"I understood there was an alliance of Hindu and Muslim—"

"Against Queen Victoria, yes. I am loyal to Queen Victoria, as I have stated."

"Of course, Your Highness, and I apologise." Ogilvie bowed his head. He would have wagered a pound to a penny that dealings had in fact taken place and that the Rajah's price had not been met by the Star of Islam. The Rajah of Kohat was in a powerful enough position to be able to say yea or nay. He was a man of much wealth as well as strength, and it was just as well he had thrown in his lot with the Raj. He must not be offended now. In the meantime further utterances indicated a consuming obsession with the notion of being made a Knight Grand Commander of the Most Exalted Order of the Star of India ... the native mind, especially the princely native mind, moved in most mysterious ways and it was possible that since the Rajah had everything else that riches could buy, he had become imbued with the value of bestowed honour that was beyond the reach of his moneybags. Ogilvie probed discreetly about the march of his army: had the movement of rebellious forces been seen, and if so, what were their dispositions and strength?

Nothing had been seen; the armies of the Star of Islam, the Rajah believed, lay to the north of Peshawar rather than to the south. Nevertheless, a find of some importance had been made.

"May I know its nature, Your Highness?" Ogilvie asked.

"A cave, Captain sahib. A cave guarded by Muslims, Pathans from Afghanistan from whom may Heaven offer us protection."

"Yes, Your Highness?"

"In this cave, women and children. British women and

142

children belonging to the soldiers of the Raj."

Ogilvie stared, a tremendous relief flooding through him. He wiped sweat from his face, unceremoniously, with his sleeve. "You freed them, Your Highness?"

"My brave army killed all the Pathans, Captain sahib, chopping them up with swords and lances. The women and children were unharmed."

"And now, Your Highness? I saw no women and children in your column when I was brought in."

The Rajah smiled widely and waved his arms in the air. "Where they are, they are safe. They are out of the war to come, and they are well guarded by soldiers whom I left behind in much, much strength."

"I believe they would be safer returned to the Raj, Your Highness. If perhaps you had brought them on to Murree—"

"No, no. I keep them safe – I, the Rajah of Kohat who is very, very loyal to Queen Victoria and the Raj over which she so benignly rules. When they come safe to the Raj again, perhaps to me the Star of India will come from Queen Victoria?"

"I think it would come faster, Your Highness, if the women and children were to be returned at once to British hands."

"My hands are safe and comforting, Captain sahib."

"Of course, Your Highness, but—"

"I shall travel to Great Britain, to Queen Victoria's immense palace of Buckingham in London, bringing presents to gladden her heart and assure her of my love and loyalty. . ."

It was no use; His Highness would not budge an inch from his position, would not reveal the whereabouts of the families. Ogilvie cajoled and pleaded but knew he must not threaten or the wily ruler might undergo a sudden shift in his loyalties. He held the cards; and the families were still under threat, no less than before. When it came to their own interests, there was little to choose between Muslim and Hindu and the latter could kill as bloodily as the former. There was just one favourable decision forthcoming: the Captain sahib was free to return to his soldiers and to march

143

ahead of the native army for Murree, where he was to inform his father the GOC that His Highness of Kohat was loyally coming to his assistance and that he held the families safe. The native army would halt when within five miles of Murree; after that further decisions would be made, the Rajah said enigmatically. The situation was not good; that army could be considered, should loyalty be no more than skin deep, to constitute a serious threat to Murree, denuded as it must be of its garrison sent to reinforce Bloody Francis Fettleworth's stand at Mardan.

Filled with misgivings, Ogilvie was ridden back to his company. Cunningham was relieved to see him, but shared his anxieties for the women and children.

"They can be put to the sword yet, sir. Will you tell the men?"

"I've no option," Ogilvie said. "I'm calling off the search in our sector and marching for Murree. They'll have to be told why."

"Aye, sir. I'll do the telling – and I'll make it plain that if the situation's no better, it's no worse either. There's hope in that." Cunningham saluted and marched away. Within minutes B Company was on the move again, this time swinging off towards Murree, which they should reach by the time the sun went down. They went at forced-march pace with the bare minimum of halts and they met no opposition. The Rajah had no doubt been right: the Star of Islam was still concentrated in the north-west, not yet ready perhaps to extend his attack beyond Mardan. By nightfall the Scots, well in advance of the more cumbersome Kohat force, picked up the lights of Murree ahead and shortly after this were halted by the extended scouts from the garrison. Duly identified, the company marched in and Ogilvie sought audience of his father.

When the report had been made, Sir Iain's glum face indicated his reaction to the loyal Rajah's move. He glowered. "That artful bugger's not coming here to help," he said.

"The Star of India, sir—"

"Oh, balls to the Star of India!" The GOC waved his arms

144

in the face of his son. "He can dangle it from his arse for all I care – no, he's placing his army where it'll be most advantageous to himself! The bargaining will start upon his arrival, and it won't be just for the Star of India, my lad, but for who's going to produce the bigger carrot." Suddenly a most curious expression spread itself across the face of the GOC, the anxieties of command mixed with an irrepressible impishness. He said, "Those families, James. The Hindus have them . . . and by now we'll already have delivered poor Fettleworth to the Muslims, by order of Calcutta!"

*　　*　　*

The despatch, when repeated, had been proved correct and authentic: Fettleworth's face had been a picture. He was a pricked balloon, one that called down the vengeance of God upon all who dwelt in Calcutta. They were, he said, bloody clerks and pimps, none of them fit to lick a private soldier's boots, yet they issued stupid orders to the military command as though they came from the Lord God Himself. He strode up and down his office, beside himself. He demanded *chota pegs* and drank them fast. Lakenham was patient and referred to Fettleworth's personal bravery – which in fact was not lacking – and that an awareness of this in high places had doubtless led to his selection for the honour. Fettleworth liked the word honour and repeated it once or twice. By degrees his mind swung round and Lakenham was able eventually to get his master to read the remainder of the despatch, which added detail not present in the original message. These further instructions were concerned with the method by which the Divisional Commander was to be made available to the Pathans. A message was to be sent from Division to the Star of Islam by way of his military commander outside Mardan to the effect that Lieutenant-General Fettleworth would leave Nowshera at 6 p.m. that evening and ride, with no escort other than a *sowar* of the Guides bearing a flag of truce, to a rendezvous on the southern side of Mardan. When brought before the Star of Islam Fettleworth was to indicate that he was surrendering himself as an act of goodwill and in the interest of the captured women and children. He was not to implicate the Viceroy nor the Commander-in-Chief but was to state that his action had been taken by his own decision alone and that, since he was not privy to the decisions of the Governor-General in Council, he was unable to indicate whether or not the remainder of the Star of Islam's demands would be met. He was merely to advise the Pathan leader that it would be in his own best interests not to cause any harm to the women and children in the meantime.

"It won't wash!" Fettleworth said in despair. "It's utter balderdash! Am I likely to surrender myself without reference to Murree or Calcutta?"

Lakenham shrugged. "It might be considered in character, sir."

"What the devil d'you mean by that?" Fettleworth stared belligerently.

There was another shrug from the Chief of Staff. "A man of independent mind, sir. I dare say the Pathans know this." His tongue was firmly in his cheek. "Such independence of thought marks a man out from his more sycophantic fellows, and becomes widely known . . . and the Pathans, who are themselves independent and individualistic, come to regard that man as someone after their own hearts."

"Yes, I see what you mean," Fettleworth said, sounding sage. "I suppose it's possible His Excellency had that in mind, but I still don't like it and I think it's full of holes. What happens to me when the others aren't handed over? And come to that – why me rather than them?"

"The junior general, sir," Lakenham answered promptly. "I see it as inevitable, the decision having once been taken."

"I thought you said a few minutes ago that I'd been selected for the honour, didn't you?" Fettleworth glared.

"Indeed I did, and I meant it. I apologise for the word inevitable, sir. It is an honour, especially for the junior general, to go as Her Majesty's personal emissary into the hands of the enemy." Lakenham paused. "Within the Empire, bravery never goes unremarked or unrewarded, and selfless heroism—"

"Oh, come, come, my dear fellow!"

146

"It is bound to be brought to the personal attention of the Queen, sir."

"Well – yes." For a moment Fettleworth closed his eyes and saw heartening sights of cheering crowds and a London bedecked with flags, and the normally down-turned lips of his sovereign relaxing into a smile. There was a hint of blue somewhere, a broad ribbon . . . if ever he lived to wear it! But of course he would; he would never be left to rot, he was a Lieutenant-General of the Queen and as such would merit the relieving attentions of a whole Army Corps if His Excellency thought those buggers were threatening his life.

Fettleworth looked at the clock; he had not much longer left. More *chota pegs* were brought by his native bearer, and Bloody Francis, with an eye to the immediate future, took them politely from the silver salver, one after the other, intoning thank yous. One never could tell; that bloody bearer could be in league with the enemy! A word speeding from Nowshera to the Mardan perimeter that the Lieutenant-General sahib was a considerate master might be of some help. Fettleworth hiccupped a little and caught the sour look in Lakenham's eye and pointedly took another *chota peg* and balls to Lakenham. . . Lakenham was an old woman, a blasted nanny in his outlook. Her Majesty was not especially averse to a little tipple on the part of her soldiers; she rated the sin of smoking to be very much more heinous, as His Royal Highness the Prince of Wales knew to his cost. Blurp. When within the next hour Lieutenant-General Fettleworth mounted his horse for his lonely ride out of Nowshera into the desperate hands of the Queen's enemies he rode more sack-like than usual and swayed alarmingly about in the saddle. He was still inebriated when he came within sound of the guns firing into Mardan and saw a troop of horsemen riding towards him, some of them with *jezails*, some with huge curved scimitars, all of them with alarming expressions. Not a word was said; he had evidently been recognised. The horsemen surrounded him and one of them prodded at his bulky body with a rusty bayonet, and he was urged on to skirt the Mardan perimeter while his escorting *sowar* turned and rode rapidly back to the safety of

Nowshera. Loneliness was complete. The Raj was behind him, a thing apart. Around him the sounds of fighting continued, and from Mardan and its garrison came the flicker of fires to redden the sky, and the stench of gunsmoke along the breeze.

"Where are you taking me?" Fettleworth asked in a haughty tone.

"You will see."

"I demand to know."

There was a laugh, an insulting sound. "You will demand nothing. For you, the Raj has ceased to exist."

Fettleworth decided that he must begin his captivity in the way he intended to continue it. He said loudly, "I am Her Majesty's Divisional Commander in Nowshera, and—"

"You are a fat pig."

"Her Majesty will—"

"And worse than a fat pig – a fat sow whose belly swells with its litter."

Fettleworth gave up. It was pointless to argue with the uneducated.

Thirteen

Within minutes of James Ogilvie's full report being made Sir Iain had ordered mounted runners out to contact Brigadier-General Shaw and his scattered units. "It'll take time," he said, "but we have the map references of their lines of advance. They'll be told to close Murree and reinforce the garrison until I have a particular use for them."

"And the families, sir?" James asked.

148

"They're better left," his father said briefly.

"May I ask why, sir?"

Sir Iain gave a gruff laugh. "It's damned cheek, but I'll answer you: subject to Calcutta's agreement, I shall deal with the Rajah of Kohat and get 'em out that way. If I attempt to cut them out, they'll be done for."

"And if the Rajah won't deal, sir?"

"Then I'll have to think again, won't I?" The GOC paused, eyeing his son. "Well? There's something else on your mind, is there not? To me, it's as open as a damn book."

"There is, sir. The Regimental Sergeant-Major." James explained fully. His father's reaction was angry.

"Let us have one thing straight, my boy. Mr Cunningham's not your sar'nt-major, he's your Colonel's. This is no affair of yours, d'you hear me? You've spoken out of turn in referring the matter to me behind your Colonel's back."

"But—"

"There are no buts. You have taken advantage . . . when serving under my command, Captain Ogilvie, you are not my son but a damned captain of infantry addressing his General Officer Commanding. Do I make myself clear?"

"Yes, sir. But you allowed me to finish my report."

A mixture of emotions chased each other across the General's florid face, then he gave a short laugh. "Damn me if I didn't! Unofficially, I'm glad enough to know, but I shall not allow foreknowledge to affect my judgment if and when the matter's referred to me. In the meantime, be assured of what you already know well enough – that Lord Dornoch's a just officer. And one thing more, then be about your duties."

"Sir?"

"A wink's as good as a nod to a blind horse." Sir Iain stared at his son. "If you're blind, send in your papers and get out of the army!"

*   *   *

During the following day the orders reached the independent units of the brigade and the convergence upon Murree began; by evening Brigadier-General Shaw, with his force

149

almost complete, halted outside the city to wait until the last of his command had reported back. Some four miles distant to the north-west could be seen the camp fires of the native army from Kohat. Lord Brora, back to his temporary duties as Brigade Major, was loud in his contempt for the orders that had withdrawn the brigade from the search for the women and children. He waved an arm towards the native encampment.

"We should attack, sir. I'm astonished that General Ogilvie has not already done so."

"The overall strategy is his concern, not ours," Shaw said.

"Certainly it is and I've not suggested otherwise, my dear sir. I merely say it's wrong." Brora's voice grew louder. "Take that damn heathen princeling, teach him what's what, and the families will be brought to Murree and handed over in a twinkling!"

"Easier said than done, Major."

Brora gave a scornful laugh. "Simply because the bugger's in the centre of his army? I know one thing: all Ogilvies appear tarred with the same damn brush if you ask me!" Without waiting for a reaction, he turned his horse and rode away arrogantly. The Brigadier-General stared after him, lips compressed. Lord Brora was an impossible man, a man with enough money and influence behind him to make it easy for him to display contempt for his superiors. He would not always get away with it, but he had sufficient common sense not to overstep the mark insofar as his military duties were concerned, thus there was no way in which he could be brought to book: on past occasions, when in effect he had gone beyond his orders, the result had been success for the arms of the Raj and it had thus been inexpedient to discipline the man. Meanwhile there was the matter of the 114th's sergeant-major yet to be properly considered. The facts appeared plain enough and indeed were not disputed: Cunningham had shot at an officer with whom he had had a recent bandying of words, and warrant officers did not bandy words with holders of Her Majesty's Commission. Nevertheless, the Brigadier-General's sympathies lay with Cunningham and he found it hard to extinguish the wish

150

that Cunningham's aim had been better...

When the last of the scattered units marched in after nightfall, weary and hungry and needing rest, the Brigadier-General took his force into Murree. The General Officer Commanding had, in the interval since his son's arrival, been in touch with Calcutta, and now a conference of brigade and battalion commanders was called. Sir Iain summed up the overall situation concisely.

"Mardan's still under heavy attack and the Dargai Heights remain in Pathan hands, gentlemen. Division from Nowshera's heavily engaged and all I can report is that they're holding on. But there are indications from our patrols that the Pathans have outflanked with a strong force and are likely to advance on Nowshera and Murree. I assess their intentions as being to advance farther and besiege Rawalpindi, and then consolidate before extending farther to the Indus. In the meantime we have other urgent problems to consider, one of them being of course the families now in the Rajah of Kohat's hands—"

"I suggest we cut them out, General, as was the original order," Brora interrupted.

"You do, do you?" Sir Iain said icily. "In my view that would bring them into greater danger—"

"Then, as I've already said to Brigadier-General Shaw, why not seize the damn Rajah himself?"

"Because to do that would be to bring in his army against us, would it not?"

"But look here—"

"With that you must be content, Lord Brora, and if you wish to continue arguing, you'll do it from outside in the corridor – with a native sentry to prevent you coming in again. I trust that's clear?" Sir Iain stared with raised eyebrows, coldly, at Brora, who muttered to himself but subsided. The GOC went on, "The other problem concerns General Fettleworth, who is currently, and as it happens uselessly, consorting as a prisoner with the Star of Islam himself." He explained the unfortunate circumstances, then went on: "Calcutta has agreed that I should parley with his Highness of Kohat and try to obtain the release of the families as well as his declaration to fight with us. Much hinges upon the outcome of the parley."

"And General Fettleworth?" Lord Dornoch asked.

Sir Iain, a grin lurking around his mouth, said, "I have been given no orders in regard to General Fettleworth, Colonel. It crosses my mind that Calcutta is looking upon him as our resident Trojan horse behind the Pathan lines, though I fail to see what the devil he can achieve, I must say."

* * *

Fettleworth had been escorted beyond Mardan, being passed on the way by hordes of the native levies pouring south-eastward out of Afghanistan towards Peshawar and Nowshera. After a long ride he was told to dismount, and stiffly did so, feeling ill now that the *chota pegs* had drained away to leave tormenting dregs of headache that had not been helped by his dreadful ride across rough terrain such as he had not experienced since his days as a regimental officer. Keenly now he felt the terrible indignity of his position and the dreadful unfairness with which he had been ordered to sacrifice his person. Now he was on foot and climbing, which was worse in many ways than the ride. He puffed up a hillside, protesting that he could move no faster when the rusty bayonets pricked cruelly into his behind.

"I am no longer young," he said plaintively. "Have the Pathan people lost their respect for age?"

"You are a fat pig."

Fettleworth groaned and clenched his fists with rage. Each time he had uttered the response had been the same, and in his view it boded ill for him. Fat pigs would scarcely be treated with the respect due to rank, and it came to him that pigs were not beloved of the Muslims whatever the Hindus might think of them. Or was it the other way round? Fettleworth's mind was in a whirl: Hindus certainly respected the cow, which was holy and much honoured. There could be all manner of sinister implications in his being a pig. He faced the truth: never in all his Indian service had be bothered to acquaint himself with barbaric – no, he

152

mustn't think along those lines – *native* customs or the likes and dislikes of those over whom he held sway. Tiresome really, and dangerous: a full knowledge of one's captors' ways could be useful, but it was too late now. He sweated in spite of the cold of what was now night, and puffed, and groaned aloud and jerked his bottom away from the wretched bayonets whose rust and filth might bring him the Lord knew what plague or misfortune. He fell on his face and got up with scratches and bruises and with his scarlet tunic torn on a blasted prickly bush . . . on and on and on until at last he reached the peaks like some damn picquet. Then he was propelled a little way down the other side, but not before he had had a bird's-eye view of the fighting in and around Mardan, the fires, the burst of shells, the enemy flares in terrible profusion and all the accoutrements of war massed so vengefully – an alarming sight to be sure. On the other side loomed the great dark humps and jags of the Afghan hills. He was led like an animal to a flat ledge of rock some way down from the summit, then pushed into a cave opening off this ledge, a cave lit by a nasty smoking flare. The space being confined, the smoke was concentrated and made Fettleworth cough and splutter and choke.

Beyond the flare he saw a man and recognised him, from the branded forehead, as the Star of Islam. The Pathan spoke. "You are the Lieutenant-General sahib from Nowshera?"

"Yes," Fettleworth answered sourly.

"You are welcome."

"What do you want of me?"

There was a laugh. "Of you I want nothing. You are my prisoner. That is all."

Fettleworth asked, "Will you now return the women and children as agreed?"

The Pathan moved forward, past the smoking flare, and stood in front of Fettleworth. "The agreement was for three British generals. You are but one. Why is this?"

Fettleworth followed his orders. "I'm unable to speak for the others, or for His Excellency the Viceroy of India. I had no orders to come, but I came."

"You are a brave man, General sahib."

"I came to take the place of the women and children. Now I ask for their release. As a man of honour, you cannot refuse."

"I say again, my demand was for three generals. We must now await the other two . . . and I think the wait will be a very long one, General sahib!"

"No doubt," Fettleworth said stiffly.

"For reasons different from what I believe you are thinking," the Pathan said. His gaze swept Fettleworth's sweating face. "Word has come to me that the women and children have been taken from me and are now in the hands of Gundra Singh, Rajah of Kohat—"

"A Hindu, and friendly to the Raj!"

The Pathan smiled. "At a price, General sahib. But that is not what must now concern you. You have come most opportunely, and I shall find you useful as a replacement for lost hostages."

The implication penetrated and smote: Fettleworth felt quite faint. His dreadful journey had been totally unnecessary and he had needlessly been delivered up to the enemy who would now torture him, most likely. His knees wobbled and unholy thoughts came into his mind in regard to His Excellency. Licking his lips, he glanced round at the deplorably filthy men who had addressed him so many times as a fat pig. He looked at the hard faces, at the bayonets and *jezails* and knives. There was a horrible watery feeling in his stomach . . . but, after all was said and done, he remained the Commander of Her Majesty's First Division in Nowshera and Peshawar. It was a most sustaining thought. Fettleworth straightened his body and pulled down his torn and rumpled tunic and settled his sash in a more soldierly fashion. Damn natives! Fettleworth did what he had so often advised his juniors to do in times of danger and difficulty: he thought of the Queen-Empress, conjured up a vision that became, for him, not far short of reality. Over the distant, night-shrouded peaks of wild and lonely Afghanistan rose Queen Victoria in splendid regal array, spreading her ample skirts over the mountains of the Hindu Kush which for Bloody Francis

Fettleworth had for the moment of the vision become the Grampians around distant Balmoral. Fettleworth's eyes misted: she was a most gracious old lady and a strengthening one. Fettleworth, feeling her presence like a *chota peg* to bring fire to the belly, turned upon the Star of Islam.

"I am to be treated with the respect due to my rank. I insist upon that, in the name of Her Majesty the Queen, Empress of India." Then he gave a startled jump as once again the bayonets prodded his bottom and he was led away protesting, deeper into the cave, by the wretched natives.

* * *

The Rajah of Kohat, who was well aware of the value of keeping the other side waiting and guessing, sent back the staff captain who had been despatched through the darkness from Army Headquarters to arrange the parley: he would not, His Highness said, be available until the morning sun broke through; and when the officers of the Raj came to him, only two must come: the General sahib commanding the Northern Army, and his son the Captain sahib with whom excellent relations had already been established.

Shortly after dawn, Sir Iain and James rode out from Murree towards the encamped native army.

"Higgledy-piggledy," Sir Iain said, sounding moody. He lifted his riding-crop and pointed it at the jumbled array of tents. "Make any sar'nt-major or RQMS feel quite ill. You can almost smell 'em from here, too."

"They're strong nevertheless," James said.

"Damn it, I'm aware of that! We can well do with their help, more's the pity, but I doubt if a Star of India's going to be enough to guarantee it."

"A picture of the Queen, sir?" James asked with his tongue in his cheek.

Sir Iain blew through his moustache. "His Highness isn't General Fettleworth." They rode on in silence for a while, enjoying the fresh morning air, so welcome in India before the appalling heat of encroaching day, and enjoying the striking colours of sunrise over the hills beyond the native

155

camp. Colour was everywhere: green and purple, red and orange, crimson, a whole prismatic effect overlying the land and dappling the sprawl of tents and pennons and standards of Kohat. The General spoke again. "Those poor wretched families, James. They concern us all – I needn't stress it. So many of them from my own regiment as I regard it still – damn it, I know most of them from Corriecraig, and so do you." He paused, a hand pulling at his moustache. "Word travels fast in India, as you're aware. It's not really my concern . . . but I'm speaking now of one in particular. Brora's niece."

"Yes, sir."

"Forget the sir for now, I'm speaking as your father," Sir Iain said with a touch of irritation. "Nice young filly . . . damn good looking."

James was surprised. "You've met her, then?"

"In Simla, yes. Not met her precisely – seen her. She was pointed out to me – the connection with the 114th, don't you know."

"And mother?"

Sir Iain grinned. "You may well ask, my boy! Yes, your mother too. She liked the look of her, and she's well-connected which counts. Could be too like her uncle, though."

"Is that a warning, Father?"

"Take it whatever way you like, and I'll not say a word against your Major. But in a general way you'd do well to bear in mind that a tempestuous wife can be an uncomfortable bedfellow in a marriage, so can a tempestuous father-in-law."

"Father-in-law?"

Sir Iain laughed and said, "Uncle-in-law in her case. She's very like Brora in looks, James." He said no more, but left a conflict of thoughts and emotions in his son's mind. James Ogilvie's intentions in regard to Fiona Elliott were as yet unclear in his head. As the heir to Corriecraig Castle and the baronetcy, marriage sooner or later was virtually a must, but he felt that the time had not yet come. A married officer always left a hostage behind in a sense, and tragedy could come in India as it had come to Cunningham, though the

156

regiment would not always be in India. Marriage could tie a man down in detail and housekeeping concerns, however indirectly. Bills, larger than those of a single officer in quarters, had to be met; and the Ogilvies, though far from poor, were not as wealthy as some. Yet Fiona was intriguing . . . and it seemed as though one hurdle, at least, had been overcome already: his parents, the message appeared to be, would approve the match. Whether or not Lord Brora would be as approving was open to much question, and he was the girl's guardian. James Ogilvie's mind went back to Mary Archdale, widow of Tom Archdale killed in action some years earlier: that had been a fairly passionate affair and one that had found no favour with the Ogilvies, for besides being older than James, Mary had had a certain reputation for dalliance among the officers in garrison at Peshawar and Nowshera, and rumour had said that, had it not been for the death of Tom Archdale, there might have been the appalling scandal of a divorce . . . but all that was water under the bridge now, a part of his education.

James's thoughts were interrupted by his father: "They're coming out to meet us."

"Yes, sir." It was back to duty now; James looked ahead at four riders with lances, led by an officer.

"Unsoldierly-looking buggers," Sir Iain said. "Might be more of a liability than a help!" He laughed. "His Highness dissipates all his energies in bed – not surprising, with all those wives. Possibly he deserves his Star of India, though I doubt if Her Majesty would consider his efforts relevant to the bestowing of it."

They rode on, closing the approaching riders. Salutes were exchanged; the native officer appeared friendly, full of smiles. The horsemen formed around the two British officers as an escort and they rode into the heart of the camp, through a babble of voices and a smell of cooking-pots and burning wood, to halt outside a splendid tent, almost a marquee, from which flew the standard of the Rajah. Here they dismounted, and were ushered ceremoniously into the tent. They stepped into luxury and a noxious reek of garlic, the latter growing stronger as they approached its source –

157

the Rajah himself, grinning and nodding like a marionette from a richly-decorated cushion upon which he sat cross-legged with a number of women reclining beside him.

Sir Iain bowed. "Your Highness."

"Peace be unto you, General sahib, and to the great Queen Victoria." Coal-black eyes glittered towards James Ogilvie. "Already I have met your honourable son the Captain sahib, and he knows my wishes, General sahib."

"Yes, yes. The Star of India."

"Knight Grand Commander of this. Queen Victoria will grant this wish, General sahib?"

"Under certain conditions," Sir Iain said stiffly, "it is very possible Her Majesty would be most pleased to confer the honour – yes."

The Rajah smiled. "Please be seated, General sahib and Captain sahib." He indicated some cushions, and the two officers lowered themselves to the ground, watched intently by the concubines from behind veils. "You are now comfortable?"

"Very, Your Highness." Sir Iain sounded irritable. "May I remind Your Highness that time presses? The armies of the Pathans from Afghanistan are close and may shortly be upon us, and if the Raj should cease to exist then so will the Star of India. I ask your help, Your Highness, and that of your army, and I—"

"I have a very excellent army, General sahib. You will have seen this for yourself?"

"Yes. A fine body of men. None better." This was said through slightly clenched teeth. "I ask also—"

"Very, very good fighters."

"Quite. I agree."

"Loyal to me as I am loyal to the Raj."

"I'm relieved to hear it. Now, time—"

"Time is a man-made thing, it is not of heaven."

"Indeed," Sir Iain said shortly. "Neither are the damn Pathans of heaven, and they're coming if I may repeat myself." His voice grew louder, subduing further interruption. "If you promise me your military help against them, I'll promise you a GCSI. That makes you Sir whatsit – Sir

Gundra, I believe. What d'you say, Your Highness?"

The Rajah smiled again and picked his nose; then asked, "You are able to speak for Queen Victoria, General sahib?"

"Yes. But there is one further condition – request, I should say. A vital one. The women and children. They must be handed over to the Raj unharmed – and at once."

"Must?"

"Must."

"At once?"

"At once."

"They are not near, General sahib—"

"As soon as possible, then." There was a snap in Sir Iain's voice now, an end to patience. "No handing over, no GCSI."

"Not?"

"Oh, for God's sake," Sir Iain said. "Not!"

"No GCSI, no handing over, which places the boot upon the other foot, General sahib." He added, "At once."

Sir Iain seethed. "Even Her Majesty cannot possibly confer a GCSI from Balmoral all the way to Murree, it takes time. But if you agree, then you have my promise, and I consider that should be good enough."

The Rajah nodded. "Perhaps. The Raj is honourable, and I am loyal. I do not wish the Raj to fall." He gazed around at the luxurious trapping of his tent, at the women, at the wealth of precious stones upon their bodies, a mere fragment of what lay stored in his palace at Kohat; if the Raj went, so would all that, and into the laps of the thrice-accursed Muslims. It must not be. The Rajah arrived at a mental decision but the bargaining was not over yet, and there was no reason for the General sahib to know that the decision had been made. His Highness smiled again, oilily, and said, "I have other needs, General sahib, beside the most honourable Star of India."

"What needs, Your Highness?"

"Material to sustain the great honour to be given to me by Queen Victoria. Queen Victoria will expect no less of her loyal princely subjects." The Rajah paused. "I need guns and shells."

"You appear to have plenty already." Entering the camp,

159

Sir Iain had noted the presence of much heavy artillery and mountain guns, many of them no doubt filched from the arsenals of the Raj over the years.

"They are old," the Rajah said with some truth. "I need such guns and equipment as is used now by the Raj, and without it, I am most sorry, I cannot support the Raj, loyal as I am. In addition to the big guns, I need also rifles and bayonets and bullets."

Sir Iain breathed hard down his nose. "Like the GCSI, guns and rifles can't be produced on the spot, Your Highness, but—"

"But you give Queen Victoria's promise that they will come?"

"The promise may be made if you will first tell me what you will do to earn it, Your Highness."

"Most certainly, yes. I shall place my armies at the disposal of the Raj as you ask, General sahib—"

"I'm grateful. And the women and children?"

"I will send my soldiers to bring them here to my camp, and this I will do immediately your promise is given in the name of Queen Victoria and written down on goatskin with your seal of agreement."

"That," Sir Iain said, "will be done. Now—"

"One thousand pieces of the big artillery with limbers, ten thousand rifles with bayonets—"

"I'll send a staff officer to discuss the details, Your Highness. Now, as to the women and children. I wish to send men to accompany your soldiers. I suggest my son goes with them."

"That is agreeable," the Rajah said after some thought.

"But not my son alone. Others, too. You agree?"

The Rajah stroked his chin. "How many others, General sahib?"

"A suitable escort, whose composition must be left to me. I shall return to my headquarters now, Your Highness, and make arrangements with my ordnance staff for your artillery requirements. My son will return shortly with the escort for the women and children."

*   *   *

Riding back the General said, "Her Majesty's a generous woman, if only by proxy! The Rajah's demands will need to be scaled down fairly heavily, however. There's not a thousand heavy guns in all India! As to your escort, James, I'll send your own company, if your Colonel agrees. Those buggers will need watching closely."

"They will be, sir."

"Good! It'll be up to you to bring all the women and children back safely, then." Sir Iain gave a short laugh. "By God, it's amazing what a decoration can achieve! I suppose it's too soon to say that all's well that ends well – but it'll be a tremendous relief to have those families back. After that, the Star of Islam."

The mood of optimism, however, was not to last: urgent messages had reached Sir Iain's headquarters during his absence. A probe by a patrol out of Nowshera had reported a strong Pathan force moving south and east from Mardan, and it was believed that the Star of Islam was with this force in person. It appeared likely that the Pathan leader was moving on Murree and that soon the garrison would be under fierce attack.

Fourteen

"If the Pathans are coming, I'll have the Rajah's army inside the perimeter," Sir Iain said. "I'd not trust His Highness to maintain his loyalties once he gets a better offer!" He ordered his Chief of Staff to ride to the native camp with the escort for the women and children, and to make it plain to the

Rajah that his force was to enter Murree immediately or all question of armaments and orders of chivalry would be in abeyance. There was much coming and going at Army Headquarters as the garrison made the final preparations to repel the invading Afghan hordes; the addition of Shaw's brigade to the defence was very welcome, and although Sir Iain would have wished in the new circumstances to increase the escort that would accompany his son to the cave where the families were being held, he felt unable to do so. It was vital to hold Murree and that had to take priority.

"You may have to run through the Pathan advance," Sir Iain told James. "You'll have to lie low and avoid action if you can. Your orders are strictly to take over the women and children and not to engage the enemy en route, is that clear?"

"Yes, sir. And when I've taken them over?"

"You must decide in the light of the circumstances as you find them, but it would be inadvisable to think of bringing them here to Murree now."

"Nowshera, sir?"

"Doubtful. My signals officer reports that Nowshera's out of communication since they telegraphed that patrol's report. Peshawar's out too, of course. I can only suggest you hold them in the cave and await relief, which'll be sent as soon as possible, but I repeat, you must decide as matters develop." Sir Iain paused and looked shrewdly at his son. "You'll cope, I know. It's a big task for a single company, but you're not inexperienced in the ways of the Frontier, James."

"No, sir."

Sir Iain held out his hand. "Then the best of luck."

"Thank you, sir." James hesitated. "I have a request to make, sir. May I take Mr Cunningham with me?"

"Not up to me." The GOC lifted his eyebrows at Lord Dornoch, who nodded his approval. "Very well then, since your Colonel agrees. Off you go, now."

*　　*　　*

B Company of the Royal Strathspeys marched out from Murree accompanied as far as the native camp by the Chief

162

of Staff. They went with two drummers and two pipers, who played them out from the city beneath the domes and minarets lofting to a bright, metallic blue sky. They were speeded on their way by cheers from the rest of the brigade and from the remaining troops of the original garrison: their orders were known and every man wished them well in the execution of them. Ogilvie felt his responsibility keenly: so many of those cheering men had families held in the cave and he knew that all their hopes rested upon himself and his company. The pipes and drums played the Scots all the way to the native army's ramshackle lines, moving towards the Rajah's tent through the squalor and much chatter, to the strains of *Highland Laddie*. Once again Ogilvie, with the GOC's Chief of Staff, was admitted to audience of His Highness who lost no time in accepting the order to move: it seemed he had no wish for a pitched battle and had a touching faith in the ability of the Raj and Queen Victoria to provide protection inside the city against an artillery barrage, a faith in which the Chief of Staff unkindly encouraged him. It would, he said, be a good deal safer and His Highness must hurry. His Highness, who as it happened had received his own reports from native sources that the Star of Islam's hordes were sweeping towards the area, hurried. The orders went forth without delay and a degree of bedlam ensued as the native army milled about, its soldiers shouting and gesticulating for all the world like a bunch of camp followers. The concubines were loaded aboard the elephants, chattering ceaselessly, while a native guard, who would reinforce the Scots and guide them to the cave, mustered outside His Highness's tent. The cave was some thirty-five miles east of Peshawar city, which put it approximately, if the native reckoning was correct, within a day's march a little north of west from Murree. Leaving the Chief of Staff to cope with the movement of His Highness, Ogilvie marched his now mixed force out from the camp with the pipes and drums beating a fast step. There was no time to lose and there would be little rest for anyone until the cave was reached.

* * *

163

In that cave, spirits were at a low ebb despite the best efforts of Lady Dornoch. There was a mounting feeling of abandonment, a feeling that had increased after the terrifying experience of a change of captors. There had been slaughter, very bloody slaughter of the Muslim guard by the Hindus from Kohat, and though none of the prisoners had been in fact harmed, the effect upon the children had been devastating. Some of the tougher spirits among the wives had tended the few Muslims who had not been killed outright, but the wounds had been mortal and painful death had not been pleasant to watch. Lady Dornoch had secured permission from the Kohat guards to gather the children together in a side tunnel running off the main chamber and though a number of them cried ceaselessly for their mothers a kind of nursery atmosphere had been created after a while and the children had been coerced, unwillingly to begin with, into playing such games as Lady Dornoch and Fiona Elliott could devise. Their minds thus occupied, they quietened; Lady Dornoch had insisted upon strict routine: bedtime was bedtime even though there were no beds, and they got up in the morning at the usual time to eat such food as the guards provided, which was little enough: wild berries, fruit, a coarse black bread, and suspect water. What with the poor feeding, the lack of fresh air and daylight, and the overall anxiety, Lady Dornoch feared demoralization amongst the adult women. The only way to combat it, or try to, was to keep all minds busy, and this she did. While Fiona kept the children occupied, Lady Dornoch, with the assistance of other older wives, organised guessing games and discussions and even a sing-song. It was all very forced, but it helped to pass the time more quickly towards release, which Lady Dornoch insisted with an attempt at cheerfulness would certainly come. Few, she thought, believed her; and by degrees her own certainty began to flag. It was clear enough that they were being used as pawns between the two opposing sides, and it was unlikely that their whereabouts would be known to the army. And the army was no doubt very heavily engaged and under pressure.

She admitted as much to Fiona, sheer lowness of spirit

filling her eyes with tears. "We British are so short of numbers, compared with the natives," she said. "Every man will be needed to defend the garrisons."

"They'll come, Lady Dornoch." Fiona reached out impulsively and squeezed the older woman's hand. "Don't lose heart now . . . you've been simply splendid and everyone appreciates it, you know." She paused, frowning. "I wish mother had your guts."

"Fiona!" Lady Dornoch was shocked. "That's not a nice word, is it—"

"No." The girl laughed. "I picked it up from Uncle David, actually."

"And to speak of your mother like that—"

"Mother's a drip," Fiona interrupted, her eyes flashing in the light of the guard flares. "It's not her fault, though. She's terrified of Uncle David. He's a bit of a pig, isn't he?"

"Well, *really*—!"

"Oh, I know you can't comment, Lady Dornoch, and I shouldn't be saying it to you, I realise that, but often I think he's quite insane." She laughed again, but on a subdued note. "I hope it's not been handed down to me – after all, he was my father's brother. What does Lord Dornoch think of him, I mean *really* think of him?"

Lady Dornoch smiled and laid a hand on the girl's. "We must not discuss my husband's officers like this, Fiona, it's not done. I'm quite sure Lord Brora's an excellent second-in-command, and I have *no intention* of saying more than that." She closed her eyes and lay back against the hard rock wall. Fiona, she thought, was only too right; whoever had sent Lord Brora to join the battalion in India rather than retain him in the regimental depot at Invermore had no doubt wanted to get rid of him for a while, but a colossal mistake had been made. It was men like Lord Brora, she believed, who were giving the Raj a bad name, and were in some degree responsible for what was happening now. Lady Dornoch was just old enough to have heard her father's contemporaries yarning of India in the old days, and of how different had been the attitude then of the British officers towards the Indians. There had been mutual respect and

165

understanding and officers had made friends of the natives in a way that seemed no longer possible. Now, there were too many Broras whose noses were constantly in the air and who treated the natives as scum. Disloyal thoughts entered her unlikely head: while nowhere near so bad as Lord Brora, Generals Fettleworth and Ogilvie both high-handed the Indians from time to time, regarding them basically as inferior beings. It was not good for the Raj.

With a heartfelt sigh, Lady Dornoch got to her feet and tried to bring a smile to her face as she moved amongst the women. Regimentally things were changing too; she was not sure the women didn't rather resent her assumption of leadership just because she was the Colonel's Lady. Not the older ones, but a few of the youngsters. Nevertheless, she carried on.

*　　*　　*

General Fettleworth was currently in no position to treat the natives high-handedly: life had been dreadful and was becoming worse by the hour. He had not been permitted to shave and his face was covered with stubble, a patina of white; and his uniform was filthy. He was hungry and thirsty and was desperate for a *chota peg*. During the night he had fallen asleep upon the rocky ground and had dreamed of bearers and *chota pegs*, and believed he had uttered aloud in his distress, for he had been brought cruelly and suddenly awake by a thrust from a rifle-butt in his stomach and an angry native voice had said that fat pigs and pregnant sows did not have bearers to command. After that, sleep had not come again and in the morning he was very tired and had a splitting headache. Not long after the dawn, movement had started; below the hills Mardan appeared quiet, ominously so, and the Star of Islam had come to him to confirm that the British garrison had been overcome. Mardan was now in the hands of the Pathans and the British had been put to the sword, and the victorious sons of the Prophet were now about to penetrate deeper into the Raj.

"You will come with us," the Star of Islam said.

166

"I'm not fit. I'm no longer young, I suppose you realise? Even mounted—"

There was a scornful laugh. "You will not be mounted, General sahib, you will be cart-borne, then you will neither delay my advance nor have the opportunity to-escape."

And now, rumbling along in a south-easterly direction as he was able to deduce from the sun's position, General Fettleworth was indeed cart-borne and bedded down in smelly straw, his hands tied together behind his back and fastened by a loose length of rope to a cleat on the side of the cart. Behind him rode two armed desperadoes and in front his view was obscured by the huge undulant backside of a bullock which, after a while, had the effrontery to defecate virtually in his face. His scarlet tunic rose round his stomach, emerging from the straw surround like the back of his wretched conveyance's normal occupant – which he understood to be a pig. He seethed impotently. Damn natives!

* * *

B Company's advance was fast; every man was aware of the urgency. It was obvious that as he swept south the Star of Islam, who in fact had little farther to march from Mardan to the cave than had Ogilvie, would attempt to seize back his hostages if he knew what had taken place. Ogilvie's small force could not hope to beat off an attack by the Pathans in their strength; the one hope lay in getting there first.

"And then, sir?" the Regimental Sergeant-Major asked.

"Either we accept a siege, or we try to move out before the Star of Islam gets there."

"Aye, sir. Would you be thinking of making down into Waziristan?"

Ogilvie laughed. "Not too close to Kohat, anyway! The trouble is, we have no information as to where the Pathans might have penetrated."

"That's true, sir." Cunningham wiped sweat from his face. "There could have been other crossings from Afghanistan, into the Waziris' territory, I suppose."

"Exactly. It doesn't leave us many safe areas, does it?"

They marched on, the pipes and drums silent now as they traversed the passes behind the native guides. Ogilvie was having a careful watch maintained on those guides, who, when questioned, had professed total ignorance as to any possible Pathan penetrations to the south of the Khyber. They could well be speaking the truth, but Ogilvie was keeping an open mind as to their loyalties and their possible reaction should any Pathans be encountered. At the very least he suspected flight on their part, which would leave him without precise directions to the cave. He watched the fresh picquets as they doubled up the sides of the pass to relieve their fellows; no reports of sightings had come down and there had been no sniping. This was the second march in recent days when a total absence of snipers and watchers had been noted; the whole of the Frontier lands seemed as it were out of joint, the normal habits in suspense pending the coming of the Star of Islam.

"There's a queer feeling in the air," Cunningham said suddenly, as though he had sensed the officer's thoughts. "I don't like it, sir, I don't like it at all."

"Nor do I. I can't interpret it, though. Can you?"

Cunningham pursed his lips. "Not precisely, sir, no."

"A trap, an ambush?"

"Well, there's always the possibility, of course. Do you think that Rajah's to be trusted, Captain Ogilvie?"

"Not with a bent ha'penny! But are you suggesting he's deliberately heading us into a trap, Mr Cunningham?"

The RSM blew out a long breath. "Well, I don't know. There would not be much point in it for himself, sir, I imagine. Afterwards he'd find it hard to explain away to the GOC, who has him safely in Murree!"

Ogilvie nodded abstractedly: there were so many nuances, so many interwoven patterns, so many points where loyalty could cross with treachery, so many fine lines of distinction between the two in the princely native mind. His father would have been aware of all this, naturally, but had had to follow a soldier's line of reasoning and take a chance: the hostages had to be cut out and the Rajah's word accepted until it was proved false, and if in the process of proof a

British company had to be sacrificed, then such had to be accepted. That was all. If there should be treachery, then in fact there *was* point in it for His Highness of Kohat and never mind what the RSM had just said: the hostages could still be useful to the Rajah, and His Highness's army inside Kohat could swiftly turn against the Raj if changing fortunes made it appear to be to its advantage to do so. . .

The advance continued stolidly and sweatily throughout a long day; the pace was punishing but it was manfully kept up. Not a man dropped out to be sent to the ammunition mules. Still there was an absence of snipers and scrutineers along the heights. As the sun went down the sky to bring a promise of cooler air, Ogilvie drew his map from its case and studied it: they should not be far off now, in fact they must be almost there; and he had a feeling that they were going to get away with it and reach the hostages before the Star of Islam moved in; the difficult decisions would come afterwards.

The kilts swung on, the pipes remaining silent. The sound would give heart to the families once they came within range but could be a dangerous give-away to other listening ears. By the map, confirmed now by word from the native guides, the Scots were little more than half a mile from the cave, and the shadows were lengthening, when the brooding peace was sharply shattered by a burst of rifle fire from the rear. Ogilvie swung round on his heel to find a mass of Pathans streaming down from both sides of the pass, yelling like maniacs and loosing off their *jezails*.

Fifteen

"Fall out and take cover!" Cunningham's voice roared along the pass. Men went flat, flinging themselves behind the boulders and scrub and dragging the transport mules behind what cover was available. Fire from the *jezails* swept the pass, and was returned by the Scots' rifles. Quickly the Maxim gun was assembled and stuttered into action. The native attackers, slowed by the concentrated and accurate rifle fire, halted their advance and followed the Scots' example by diving for cover as the Maxim opened upon them. Many dead and wounded littered the hillsides and the floor of the pass. Alongside Ogilvie behind a boulder, the RSM said, "There's too many of them for plain bandits, sir."

Ogilvie nodded.

"I wonder if the Star of Islam's with them," Cunningham said meaningly, moving sideways as a bullet nicked rock from the boulder.

"Don't go risking your neck," Ogilvie warned.

Cunningham said, "I'll put the regiment first, Captain Ogilvie, don't fret." He paused. "If he's there, then this will be the main force, the advance on Murree. And I'm bearing in mind that we're not far off the cave."

"You mean the Pathans are going in to recover the hostages?"

Cunningham nodded. "I would say so, sir. Once they over-run us, that is. And with all the men they must have behind the peaks, it'll not take them long to do that." He lifted his head a fraction, then brought it down again quickly as more rock fragments flew. "On the other hand, this could be a small force detached from the main advance to bring out the hostages, sir."

"We'll find out which it is soon enough," Ogilvie said. He looked round as he heard someone moving up behind coming on at a crouching run. It was his senior subaltern, Alastair Faulkner. Ogilvie asked, as Faulkner flattened beside him, "How's it going?"

"Not so badly—"

"Casualties?"

"Nothing much," the subaltern said. "A few grazes, two men with flesh wounds, one of the Rajah's guides dead." He paused. "We seem to have the measure of them, don't we, James?"

"How?"

"They're not closing. We've pinned 'em down!"

Ogilvie said, "And they're pinning us down too – and for a purpose. It could be that the cave's under separate attack for all we know." He listened for a moment to the continuing fire from both sides – in point of fact it had lessened now, as both British and Pathan conserved their ammunition and opened only when heads were seen rising from behind the boulders. No more men appeared to be coming over the hillside, but that could not be taken as proof that no more were there. This could turn into a localised war of attrition, and a profitless one for the Scots. Ogilvie came to a decision. He said, "We're going to withdraw, Alastair."

"Withdraw? How?"

"I'm going to pull out along our original line of advance, and get to the cave. Sar'nt-Major?"

"Sir?"

"I want you to contact all NCOs and pass the word that when the bugle sounds a G, all sections except Sar'nt Davison's and the Maxim detachment will move out westwards at the double. I'll give you covering fire while you're on the move."

"Sir!"

"Sar'nt Davison's section will move to face the enemy, and remain here under Mr Faulkner to hold the natives where they are, on the hillsides. They're to give me an hour, by which time I should have reached the cave and taken over the women and children. Then they're to pull out and rejoin the rest of the company in the cave. All right, Sar'nt-Major?"

"Aye, sir."

"Off you go, then!"

Slithering on his stomach, Cunningham moved away down the line of cover. The moment his movement was seen, the fire from the *jezails* increased and was at once answered from the Scots. As the Pathans showed themselves a number of them were hit: arms were flung into the air, and the bodies fell, bouncing off the rocky sides of the pass to lie still at the bottom. From then on the fire was kept up at a high rate, but there were no more apparent casualties on either side. Ogilvie was joined by the bugler, who crouched by his side with the bugle ready, his boyish face tense. Then Cunningham was seen returning, with blood running from his left wrist: it was nothing at all, he said, just a slice from a bullet. He reported all sections ready and waiting the order, and Sergeant Davison's section already moving into position to hold the pass. A moment later Davison himself reported, approaching on his stomach as Cunningham had done. His face was grim and strained: sixteen rifles plus the Maxim against what might, if luck was against them, prove to be the main army of the Pathans, was little enough in all conscience, although the terrain was in their favour insofar as they could command the way through the pass from their cover.

"Good luck, Sar'nt Davison," Ogilvie said.

"I'll be needing it, sir."

"Do your best, that's all. I know what I'm asking of you."

"It's for the women and the bairns, sir."

"Yes." Ogilvie clapped the section sergeant on the shoulder, then nodded at the bugler. A single G was blown; at once the pass came alive with the movement of the khaki-drill tunics and the Wolseley helmets as the remaining sections came out from cover and ran, crouching and weaving to the west. Sustained fire came from the holding section, covering the dash to the rear. Bullets sped like bees from the *jezails,* ricocheting from the boulders, finding a target here and there. A lance-corporal fell alongside Ogilvie; in front, a private went down with a bullet splitting his head in half. There were many flesh wounds, but the company dashed on before the bullets, yelling out wild highland oaths and cries. Behind them, as the native force attempted a pursuit, the rifles of Davison's section pumped into Pathan bodies, picking off each man who tried to break through. Those who evaded the rifles fell to the swathe of the Maxim as its barrel swung from side to side. The slaughter was bloody in the extreme, but more and more natives came over the lip of the pass to replace the casualties, and Davison reckoned that he was indeed facing the main thrust of the Star of Islam's army. The rifle-barrels grew hot with the sustained firing, and more and more of the Pathans, coming over the hillsides in bunches, fell to the floor of the pass. Within a matter of minutes Ogilvie's company was clear and out of range, with the pursuit neatly if bloodily pinned down behind. Shortly after this the entrance to the cave system was in their view, still guarded by men wearing the colourful uniforms of the Rajah of Kohat, men who, if all went to plan, would prove friendly.

A breathless cheer went up spontaneously from the running Scots, but it was somewhat premature: as they closed towards the cave mouth the southern flank of the pass, which sloped away opposite the cave so that it was virtually flat with the surrounding terrain, was seen to be filling with Pathans also advancing on the entry. Ogilvie shouted to his Scots, urging them on faster yet: once they entered the cave, it should be possible to hold on in the hope that a relieving column could be fought through from Murree. In rear of Ogilvie, the Regimental Sergeant-Major and Colour-Sergeant MacTrease with his section sergeants ran furiously, shouting the men on. The Scots were firing point-blank into the Pathans as the opposing forces began to close each other. Not far to go now ... and then, as the leading files, with Ogilvie, stormed into the mouth of the cave and turned to form the defence alongside the Rajah's soldiers, something curious occurred: through the Pathan ranks burst a commissariat cart, running out of control, its bullock-traces apparently having parted company with its shafts, possibly under the impact of bullets. To the consternation of the bullock, which lifted its tail high in the air and stared with open nostrils, the cart careered down the gentle slope, bounding and lurching, towards the cave. There it overturned, discharging a mass of filthy straw and something scarlet.

Cunningham stopped, shouted, "I'll be damned!" and turned for the cart. He dashed for it, firing his revolver, charging straight for the oncoming enemy. Bullets spattered around him but he kept on. At the cave mouth Ogilvie waved the Scots on and saw them safe inside as the Pathan bullets sang and buzzed about the entry, smashing slivers of rock from the hillside above. The last to enter was the Regimental Sergeant-Major with his helmet shot away, propelling before him, with some difficulty, a quivering bundle wrapped in a dirty Pathan sheepskin and showing patches of scarlet in places and a face covered with white stubble. This bundle was pushed unceremoniously through the firing line at the entrance and then the RSM, saluting formally, made his astonishing report to Ogilvie.

"Sir! General Fettleworth, recovered from the enemy, sir, ex bullock-cart."

*   *   *

There were tears and smiles: the families, some of them now reunited with their menfolk, clearly believed at first that all was over. It was Ogilvie's job to disillusion them on that point without alarming them too much. They would, he said, be under siege until a relief column came through, and the availability of such a column must depend upon the movements of the Star of Islam's army. All the same, the effect of the Scots' arrival was immensely heartening, and no one was more heartened than Bloody Francis Fettleworth when he had pulled himself together and had his straw brushed away by a lance-corporal.

"Your sar'nt-major, Ogilvie," he said. "Stout fellow! He saved my life, don't you know. I shall not forget that. He shall be recommended to Her Majesty for a decoration."

"I'm glad, sir. Mr Cunningham's deserved it many times."

"I've had a terrible experience, Ogilvie, really terrible. Damn natives! Such indignities. I don't know what things are coming to, there was a time when a general would have been accorded the utmost respect by the enemy, but I fear that no longer pertains. What?"

"Evidently not, sir."

"Well, anyway, here I am back thanks to your Mr Cunningham. I shall now assume command." Fettleworth rubbed his hands together briskly. From outside came the sound of firing; at the entry a party of men was working feverishly, erecting a barricade of stones and boulders and earth that would be firmed down hard by the rifle-butts. "I am presently in the dark as to events. Kindly make your report, Ogilvie, and then I can decide what should be done."

"Very good, sir." Concisely Ogilvie reported upon recent happenings including his and the RSM's incarceration by the Star of Islam in Peshawar, and upon the state of Murree's defences, indicating that Brigadier-General Shaw's battalions had been held there as reinforcements.

"Ah, yes, Brigadier-General Shaw. His brigade in Peshawar . . . all a mistake, of course – I sent runners to cancel the orders, I suppose you know that?"

"Yes, sir. Brigade was informed after they'd entered Peshawar."

Fettleworth nodded. "Runners were killed, no doubt. I sent a lance-*duffardar* and a *sowar* from the Guides, you know. I would have expected one at least to get through, considering there was then no enemy activity north of Peshawar – however, there we are, it's water under the bridge, is it not? What are your proposals, Captain Ogilvie, for the future?"

"To hold on and await relief, sir."

"Yes, sensible. Food and water?"

"Very little of either came in with my company, sir. I'll have a report shortly as to how much was already in the cave."

"Quite. I trust we'll not be starved out, Ogilvie. As to food, I've not eaten for some time, except native muck, but it goes without saying that I shall not take a crumb from the women and children. I—" Fettleworth broke off, his unshaven face whitening in the light of the flares. An alarming sound had come, a noise like close thunder, followed almost immediately by an explosion that shook the entry passage, brought chunks of rock down dangerously, and made the flares

175

gutter as though blown by a strong wind. "Good God! What was that?"

"Artillery, I believe, sir." Ogilvie said. "We must move farther in, sir, quickly."

"Oh, rubbish! Artillery against solid rock? The guns are over-rated things at the best of times, and I can't see them making any impression now, Captain Ogilvie."

"The entrance, sir!"

"What? Oh. Yes, I take your point. I think we should perhaps clear the passage." Fettleworth turned and moved heavily along behind a flare borne by a private, making deeper into the mountainside. Since heavy artillery was being used, there was little point in continuing with the makeshift barricade, and Ogilvie withdrew the working party and ordered the passage to be cleared of all men. A guard would be drawn up at the entrance to the central chamber and the line was to be held to the last man. The cave entry had been wide enough to bring in the transport mules and the ammunition and commissariat carts, and these had now been safely lodged in side passages. There was a fighting chance yet: the entry passage itself was narrow, and invaders coming along it could be picked off with the greatest of ease. In addition, it took a sharp bend half way along, and this should mitigate the effects of artillery fire. At least, any shell entering would as it were meet its Waterloo at the bend. The blast was still an immense danger, however, and Ogilvie considered with Cunningham and MacTrease the possibility of constructing some kind of blast shield across the entry to the central chamber.

"There's rubble enough," he said, "if we can make it hold together."

Cunningham was doubtful. "It would be a better way, sir, to try to go deeper. I'll make a survey, with your permission?"

Ogilvie nodded. "Yes, by all means, Mr Cunningham, and the sooner the better." They went along to the chamber and found General Fettleworth munching a hunk of black bread whilst talking to Lady Dornoch. Outside, the artillery went into action again; Ogilvie believed that this time the explo-

176

sion was closer to the entry; given time, the native gunners would hit their target. There was stark fear in the faces of the women and children as the noise reverberated through the rock-walled chamber. Ogilvie, catching Fiona's eye upon him as he went, moved through to the tunnel used by Lady Dornoch as the nursery area, now empty of children. With him went a soldier carrying one of the flares, guttering and flickering. Ogilvie examined the walls: two more passages led off, and along one of them he saw another flare. Cunningham, making his survey . . . Ogilvie was about to tell his flare-bearer to go ahead along the passage when the man coughed and spoke.

"Captain Ogilvie, sir. Would it be in order to speak to you, sir?"

"By all means, but quickly."

"Aye, sir." The man hesitated. "I overheard what the General said, sir."

"Well?"

"Sir, he said a lance-*duffardar* and a *sowar* had been sent from the Guides, sir, to withdraw the Brigade—"

"Yes."

"Well, sir, of course, you see, sir, I was with the Brigade when we entered Peshawar – you were not, sir—"

"No. I was a captive of the Star of Islam then! What d'you want to say to me?"

"Sir, I slipped and fell as we took the siege line, and I dropped behind a wee while. I saw a *sowar* of the Guides, sir, riding to the perimeter. Then he was killed."

Ogilvie stared. "The General's runner, obviously. But that's history now, isn't it?"

"No, sir. At least I don't believe so, sir. Before he was killed, he had spoken to the Major, sir. To Lord Brora, sir, at some length, and to me it appeared as though he were making a report."

Sixteen

The implications of what the man had said in regard to Brora were disturbing, but there was no time to consider the matter now. Ogilvie told the private to keep his own counsel in the meantime and went on along the tunnel towards the Regimental Sergeant-Major as the native artillery continued its bombardment outside. He had reached Cunningham when a tremendous concussion came. The whole cave system seemed to shudder, and a blast of hot air swept through the tunnels.

"They've put a shell through the entrance, Captain Ogilvie," Cunningham said.

"So it appears. We'll have to get everyone deeper in." Ogilvie's ears were ringing still, and there was a stench of cordite. He ran back to the central chamber and found scenes of near hysteria. Children were crying loudly and clinging to their mothers. Between the chamber and the bend in the entry passage there had been a considerable fall of rock. Two men lay dead just outside the chamber, and the legs of a third protruded from beneath tons of shattered rock. Carrying a flare, Ogilvie ran along towards the rock fall, and caught his breath at what he saw in the guttering flame: the shell had done its work well; the passage was effectively blocked from floor to ceiling. After an inspection, Ogilvie went back to report to Fettleworth.

Fettleworth blew through his moustache. "How badly blocked, Captain Ogilvie?"

"It would take explosives to clear the way quickly, sir."

"Have we explosives?"

"No, sir."

"Cut open the cartridges, bag the powder to make charges?"

"It wouldn't be enough, sir, and besides, if we did that we'd have no ammunition to hold off the Pathans when we broke through."

"Yes, quite. I see that. Also an explosion could be dangerous. Cannot the men tear at it with their hands?"

"They may have to, sir, but they'd be sitting ducks for the

178

Pathans and we could expect another shell through the entry the moment the men were visible."

"So we could if we used explosives," Fettleworth said disagreeably. He pondered, then came up with his solution. "We must look on the bright side, Captain Ogilvie, must we not? If we can't get out, the heathen can't get in!"

"The food and water won't last for long, sir."

"True." Fettleworth glowered. "I wonder why the buggers did it! They must know our situation, must they not? One would have presumed they'd not wish to risk killing their hostages while they're still negotiable. This damned Star of Islam's no fool – he'd surely have known the risks attendant upon using artillery against the entrance, wouldn't he, especially if he meant to enter and attack us?"

"I imagine so, sir." Ogilvie hesitated. "It's possible there's another way in and out, sir."

"Ha! Yes! Yes, very likely. You shall find it, my dear fellow, and when you've found it I shall decide the next step." General Fettleworth lowered his rump to the floor of the chamber, and sat, mopping his streaming stubble and looking unwell. Ogilvie saluted and turned about to organise a tooth-combing of the passages. Even if they did find an outlet to the fresh air, it would be at best a fifty-fifty hope of escape: if the Star of Islam knew of an alternative exit, he would presumably have it covered. Meanwhile, the shelling had ceased; with the entry firmly blocked, the Pathans would be conserving their ammunition.

* * *

Reports reached Murree in the early hours of next morning via a returning patrol that had spotted distantly the advance of the Pathan army from the north-west; and had reported also that the native hordes appeared to have halted eastward of Peshawar and some twenty miles from Murree.

"Show me on the map," Sir Iain said.

The officer of the reporting patrol indicated a spot. "There was some action there, sir."

"British troops?"

"I assume so, sir. I didn't close—"

179

"Quite right. Your report was needed here. The spot you point out corresponds more or less with the position of the hostages as indicated by the Rajah. This halt in the advance ... were the Pathans making camp, d'you suppose?"

"There was no sign of that, sir."

"Just a temporary halt ... h'm. We assume, then, that they'll continue to advance on Murree." Deep in thought, the GOC strode across the room and back again. The moment of action could not be far off now, might indeed come by nightfall, and if Murree went, then all the north would go with it, and the Pathans could head clear for the Indus, with unending reinforcements coming in from the Afghan hills to mop us behind them. Somehow their impetus had to be checked, the advance slowed. One victory – just one victory, if it was on the grand scale, and the tide would surely turn. The Pathans did not stand up well to a war of attrition; they were not a professional army and after a while of stalemate they tended to grow bored and to drift away to their own concerns and livelihoods.

Murree was the supreme chance for both sides, the hammer that stood fair to break one or the other. And Sir Iain Ogilvie had no liking for sieges: the advantage always lay with the besiegers, especially when they had good lines of communication and a massive reserve in rear. So often in the past history of British arms, attack had proved the best method of defence: that was virtually an article of faith, an axiom of warfare. And shortly before the patrol had ridden into garrison with its report of the native advance, a stroke of most excellent fortune had come to the General Officer Commanding: three troop trains had puffed steamily into Murree at the end of their long journey from Ootacamund, bringing an infantry brigade to reinforce Northern Army, under the personal command of Major-General Sir Clarence Farrar-Drumm, an officer of advanced years. Farrar-Drumm, Sir Iain's opposite number in Southern Command, had deserted his headquarters in order to see action, and had wheezily declared as much upon his meeting with the Northern Army Commander.

"Shouldn't have done it, of course, but I've a damn good

stomach for a fight. Time I saw action again."

"When," Sir Iain had enquired politely, "was the last time, General?"

"Not sure now." There was a long pause. "Zululand . . . that was it. Only about fifteen years ago." Farrar-Drumm underwent a fit of coughing. "One tends to forget things, or the sequence of things."

Sir Iain's searching gaze took in the leathery old face with its frame of white hair that grew like wild bushes in every direction – head, ears, nostrils, trailing moustache, side-whiskers – and the heavy walking-stick upon which Farrar-Drumm leant as if his life depended on its support. He said, "You don't think you're a trifle *senior* to go into action again, my dear sir?"

"Oh, good gracious me, of course I'm not! Touch of the blasted rheumatics, that's all."

Sir Iain had given an involuntary sigh. Sir Clarence appeared well overdue for a bath chair, but he had brought a brigade with him and that was not to be sneezed at: more than 3000 men with their attached transport and machine guns, field ambulances, supply column and signal companies – it was manna from heaven, even if accompanied by Methuselah, and it could be put to good use. . .

The GOC dismissed the officer of the inward patrol, and ordered his Chief of Staff to assemble all battalion commanders and their equivalents in the artillery and cavalry formations for an immediate briefing. When the brass was present, Sir Iain's orders were short and to the point: the garrison would not remain as sitting ducks in Murree, but would march and engage the enemy in the field.

* * *

The search throughout the cave system seemed unending: beyond the two passages leading from the chamber occupied by the women and children, the whole thing was an underground sprawl of criss-cross tunnels in which men could very easily become lost, possibly for ever. Ogilvie's instructions were precise: no man was to lose contact with his next in front in the line. His company was added to by some of

181

the women, who volunteered to assist, and by the natives of the Rajah's army. But after many hours of searching and of climbing hopefully tunnels that rose towards the surface only to decline again, no way out had been found. Ogilvie's anxieties multiplied: never mind the food and water – the air was getting thicker and thicker, and in order to conserve oxygen flares were being used only when essential. The women and children sat now in darkness mostly, and spirits sank lower. Bloody Francis Fettleworth was in a poor way; he had, he announced, a fever of origin unknown except that it must have come from the damn natives whilst he was in their hands. He sat on the rough floor and moaned at Lady Dornoch. After some while, Lady Dornoch left him and made her way with difficulty through the darkness of the inner chamber towards light in the side tunnel, where she found Cunningham detailing a rested squad for another probe into the network of passages.

"Mr Cunningham," she said.

"Ma'am!"

"It's General Fettleworth. He's ill with a fever. Do you know where Captain Ogilvie is?"

"At this moment, ma'am, I do not. But when I see him, I'll tell him you want him, if you wish."

The Colonel's wife nodded. "Yes, please, Mr Cunningham." She hesitated. "I don't know what's wrong with the General, but it could be catching. I believe he should be isolated, just in case, but he disagrees."

"A problem, ma'am."

"He's been very forthright. Perhaps Captain Ogilvie will think of a way."

"Aye, perhaps," Cunningham said drily. Lady Dornoch went back to the Divisional Commander, who took up his complaints again. The chamber was damned uncomfortable and he was shivering like the plague, and a plague upon the Pathans. After he had uttered the word plague twice his shivering grew very much worse, while at the same time he felt sweat upon his skin, a bad sign he felt certain. Lady Dornoch's hand was comforting . . . but he was going to die, and he was damned if he wanted to die in a cave, like a rat.

When at last Ogilvie arrived, Bloody Francis' condition had deteriorated and he was almost incoherent. There were references to the Queen, and duty done, and Blaise-Willoughby's blasted monkey, and buggered if he was going to hand over to a bloody captain. Ogilvie caught the eye of Colour-Sergeant MacTrease in the flare's light, and nodded, and four Scots bent and lifted the Divisional Commander and bore him to a small section hollowed out from the side of one of the tunnels, a place like a ready-made tomb. Here Fettleworth was made as comfortable as possible; and Lady Dornoch insisted upon remaining with him. She had, she said, been the closest to him since his arrival. She was looking far from well herself, but Ogilvie knew her mind was made up and she would not be shifted.

* * *

Within an hour of the briefing by the General Officer Commanding, the reinforced garrison was formed up for the advance. Taking a risk, Sir Iain was moving out virtually every man and piece of artillery and every horse and mule that was capable of motion. The guns rumbled in the lead, then came the cavalry. Behind the cavalry and sandwiched between the two brigades of infantry was placed the army of His Highness of Kohat, safely contained in the middle of British arms, His Highness himself riding in his *howdah*, stripped now of concubines who had been left in Murree by order of Sir Iain Ogilvie himself. Sir Iain found war unfitting for women, and they just might prove useful as levers to ensure the loyalty of His Highness, though this was doubtful. Concubines were two a penny. Mounted scouts had been extended ahead of the long column, and more cavalry provided the rearguard. Leading his infantry brigade from Southern Army in rear of the Kohat soldiers rode Sir Clarence Farrar-Drumm, who had been lifted into the saddle by four of his *sepoys* in order to take his place and never mind objections by Sir Iain Ogilvie.

"I'm perfectly fit, General," he had said when taxed once again with his age. "It's true I don't ride as much as I used to, but I keep my body exercised with my machine, doncher know.

183

"Ah?"

"Vigor's Horse-Action Saddle. Mechanical contrivance, splendid thing. You should try it yourself, General. It's used by Her Royal Highness the Princess of Wales."

"Did you bring it north from Ootacamund?" Sir Iain asked.

"No, no." Farrar-Drumm coughed violently for a few moments. "I thought the damn railway train might shake it up, doncher know, and I couldn't risk that."

"I hope its effects will be found beneficial today, then, and you'll not fall off your horse. You'll be good enough to remember that I'm in overall command, General, and that your brigade's not to be used independently." So saying, Sir Iain had ridden away. Farrar-Drumm's face had reddened with anger, the effect being that of Father Christmas, and he had had trouble with his teeth when trying to frame an answer. Sir Iain admired the old gentleman and his courage but wished him far, far away . . . Waterloo was over, and so was the Zulu War, and it was high time the army shed its senile officers before they disintegrated and their commands with them. Long experience was not always a very valuable thing in a changing world. Sir Iain, as his column moved off, dismissed Farrar-Drumm from his mind and listened to the pipes and drums of his old regiment sounding from the van behind the cavalry. He was delighted and heartened to have the Royal Strathspeys with him: they were the very best there was.

*   *   *

"He's sleeping," Lady Dornoch said. "He's in a bath of perspiration, poor man."

"Will he sweat it out, do you think?" Ogilvie asked.

"I really don't know. . ."

"You should get some sleep yourself, Lady Dornoch." Ogilvie looked down at Fettleworth, still in his scarlet tunic, which was unbuttoned all the way down. His shirt was soaked, the high starched collar as limp as a rag. The woolly cummerbund customarily worn against the chills of evening was visible where the shirt rose and was also sweat-soaked and would no doubt bring prickly heat. Fettleworth looked almost like a baby. There was very heavy breathing, or snoring, and the limbs trembled. In the absence of a medical officer, Fettleworth might well die, but there was nothing anyone could do other than what Lady Dornoch was doing: water had been spared from the meagre supplies, and she was wiping Fettleworth's face from time to time with a soaked handkerchief. She looked ghastly herself; all the lines of her face had deepened, and her colour was bad, but she would accept no relief.

She said quietly, "I've been in contact, the others haven't. It's my duty."

There was no more to be said. Ogilvie turned away, sick at heart at what he might have to report to Lord Dornoch if ever they made contact again with the regiment. Moving down the tunnel, he met Fiona Elliott coming the other way, stumbling through the darkness until Ogilvie's flare gave her some light. He smiled at her, wearily: she didn't look too bright either, he noted. He asked where she was going.

"To Lady Dornoch," she answered.

"To take over? She won't have it, Fiona. I've tried."

"It's not fair on her . . . that wretched old man!"

"He's ill, Fiona."

"Yes, I know. I'm sorry." Her voice sounded brittle, as though she was on the point of breaking down in tears. She said, "This hell . . . let's talk, James. Please?"

He was about to say he hadn't the time, that he must get back with his company and rejoin the continuing search; but he changed his mind. Fiona, too, was his responsibility at the moment and she obviously had a need of him. He said, "All right, then. Let's get off our feet." They sat on the floor of the tunnel, backs against the wall. "What is it, Fiona?"

She laughed, a tense, nervy sound. "What is it? Oh, God, have you to ask that? I'll go mad if we stay here much longer. I'll scream and scream and scream!"

"I don't believe that," Ogilvie said. "You're not the sort. You've got more guts."

"Don't bank on it. *Are* we going to get out?"

"Yes. Never doubt it! If not by our own efforts, then by troops from—"

"No one's going to find us here," she interrupted dismally.

"That's not true. The whereabouts of the cave is known both to my father and the Rajah of Kohat. They'll get here, Fiona. The Raj isn't going to collapse, you know!"

"Isn't it?"

"Look here," he said irritably, "you've got to have faith in someone, even if not in me. What happens to all of us here is of immense concern to the people at home as well as the high command out here. People such as the Major, too – they'll raise heaven—"

"Uncle David thinks of no one but himself, James."

Ogilvie felt the wind taken out of his sails: the girl was right as to ninety per cent, but there was the remaining ten per cent and he made reference ot it. "He's concerned about you at all events. You can't deny that."

"No. And I wish," she said defiantly, "he'd *dis*concern himself . . . when things are normal, anyway. I'd be glad enough to see him now, I suppose!"

"We all would."

She gave a high laugh. "Even you, James?"

"Even me!"

"You absolutely detest him, don't you? Oh, don't bother to answer that, I shouldn't have asked. I know the answer anyway. And you needn't worry – he'll never have the command of the battalion. Uncle David's gone as far as he's going, and I believe he knows it. Which could explain quite a lot, don't you think, James?"

Ogilvie made no comment on that, but asked, "What makes you think he won't get command after the Colonel, then?"

"Oh," she said vaguely, "this and that. Men like Uncle David don't get command in regiments like yours, they upset too many people en route and they get known. Anyway, I'm really not so concerned about the regiment. It's – other things."

"Such as?"

"You and me," she answered, then added quickly, as though she felt she had gone too far for a gentlewoman not yet bespoken, "I'm not really forward, James, nor fast either. I don't suppose you understand." She began to cry and he put an arm about her body and felt it tremble. He let her cry; it might do good, and in any case he was lost for words. She had grown fond of him, while for his part he was unsure of his feelings still. Perhaps, until he was sure, he should not have gone out of his way to seek her company. He was to blame; and over all loomed the arrogant and disapproving figure of Major Lord Brora, from whose guardianship Fiona might well see him as a release. And as to Brora . . . she was probably right that he would not succeed Lord Dornoch. The War Office was not stupid, nor was the Commander-in-Chief blind in his office at the Horse Guards . . . majors who fell out with men of Cunningham's stamp were unlikely to have a battalion delivered into their hands. Lieutenant-Colonels were far from being two a penny, but very many were the majors who competed for their shoes . . . Fiona's sobs subsided and she lay quiet in his arms and he smelled the scent of her hair as it lay against his cheek. He believed she was sleeping after a while, but knew he must disturb her in the interest of his duty. He disengaged an arm and was starting to withdraw himself as gently as possible when through the tunnels in the distance he heard his name being shouted.

"Captain Ogilvie . . . where is Captain Ogilvie?" It was MacTrease's voice. Ogilvie scrambled to his feet, dalliance forgotten, and moved at the double towards the shouts. He saw light ahead, the light of a flare that showed MacTrease, and he called out.

"Here I am, Colour. What is it?"

"Captain Ogilvie, sir! I've found an exit, sir."

"Where?"

MacTrease came closer. "A long way, sir Half a mile from where we are now – and back the way we came along the pass, sir. There's daylight . . . I put my head out, sir, and saw no Pathans, and I made a small reconnaissance of my own. The exit's well hidden and it appears to me the Pathans knew nothing of it."

"Why's that, Colour?"

"Well, sir, if they'd known of it, they'd have entered – you see, sir, the exit lies just to the north of the pass we came along, where the attack came. In the pass close by is Mr

187

Faulkner and Sar'nt Davison's section. All dead, sir. Dead at their posts."

Seventeen

The sun stood at high noon and the long column out of Murree sweltered and suffered. Reports coming back from the extended scouts had indicated no enemy in sight ahead: the land lay peaceful, burned merely by the sun. Sir Iain Ogilvie stared through his field glasses, sweeping the surrounding country as though intent upon finding some sign missed by the scouts. Then he brought his glasses down, snapped them into their leather case, and informed his Chief of Staff that he intended riding down the column for a personal word with the various units. He turned away through the vast dust-cloud that enveloped the marching men and the guns and limbers, and rode down at a walk to pull his horse alongside that of Sir Clarence Farrar-Drumm, whom he courteously saluted, putting age above rank. Poor old Farrar-Drumm, he noted, appeared glued to his saddle, quite unable to dismount without assistance, and looked uncomfortable.

"All quiet," Sir Iain remarked.

"Yes. Wild goose chase probably."

"I trust not!"

"You younger generals always act impetuously, rushing after shadows and will-o'-the-wisps. In my day, we used to think well about it before we committed large bodies of men, doncher know." Farrar-Drumm coughed for a spell. "Take Wellington. One of his maxims: action needs well thinking about."

"Really? I'm surprised."

"Well, it may not have been him, one forgets, doncher know. Time . . . funny thing, time. When I was younger. . ."

188

Farrar-Drumm's thoughts trailed away. "Blasted bony horse. I should have been provided with something less damn lean, in my opinion. Could be the blasted rheumatism, of course."

Sir Iain reflected that Farrar-Drumm could well have entrained his own charger from Ootacamund, but forbore to say so. Instead he made a polite enquiry. "You find the rheumatics troublesome, Sir Clarence?"

"Very! Damn leeches . . . have you any reliable leeches, Ogilvie?"

"I have."

"H'm. I may submit my bones to them, perhaps, though I doubt if they're any better than my people." Farrar-Drumm gave a sudden cackle. "Never trust a leech, my dear fellow, never, they take advantage of one's lack of medical knowledge to recommend all manner of stupid potions. Sometimes one is cured and then they take the credit for sheer coincidence. Dreadful lot!"

"Indeed," Sir Iain said drily. "If you're in trouble, General, I can place a commissariat cart at your disposal—"

"Cart? Rubbish! I'm as fit as a fiddle really and I'm damned if I shall advance upon the enemy in a cart."

Sir Iain turned his horse and continued down the line, passing His Highness of Kohat, who grinned and nodded from his *howdah*. Sir Iain intended to have an unofficial word in the ear of Brigadier-General Shaw even if it did cut across that old fool Fettleworth's prerogative: James's report, the one that should not have been made to him, had worried him considerably, as had a talk afterwards with Lord Dornoch. He had an enormous regard for Cunningham and would believe no ill of him at all. However, the 114th's second-in-command had made certain representations and military necessity obliged him to take note, or would do so once the Brigadier-General had passed those representations on, as he in turn was also obliged to do. In the meantime, a word might help. In the event, it didn't: Brigadier-General Shaw was being correct and adhering strictly to Queen's Regulations, to the letter of the military law. His formal report would reach Northern Army via

General Fettleworth's HQ as soon as he had been able to conduct his own full investigation, and in the meantime he preferred to say nothing further. And with that Sir Iain Ogilvie, General Officer Commanding or not, had to be content.

*   *   *

General Fettleworth had somewhat surprisingly made a fast recovery. He had both slept and sweated mightily and this seemed to have done the trick. He was weak still but his illness was evidently not, he said, of a fatal character. Either that, or his constitution was strong. He could do with a bath, a *chota peg,* and a meal. The first two needs could not be provided, and food was a hunk of bread and some wild berries. Fettleworth was disconsolate but reasonable: Lady Dornoch had done her best and he was grateful. He thanked her.

"It was nothing, General Fettleworth." She turned and glanced upwards at Ogilvie, who was waiting upon the Divisional Commander with his report. "Captain Ogilvie would like a word with you, but after that I think you should rest and not get up straight away."

"Yes, you may be right, Lady Dornoch. Well, Captain Ogilvie, what is it?"

"An exit's been found, sir." Ogilvie explained in full. Fettleworth's face showed sadness at the loss of Faulkner and Sergeant Davison and his section. They had proved stout fellows, he said, holding the natives back so that Ogilvie's company could reach the cave. They would be mentioned in his despatches, and in the meantime would be decently buried: Captain Ogilvie was to detail burial parties.

"I shall, sir. After that I propose—"

"*You* propose?" Bloody Francis sat up a little straighter and found it not as much of an effort as he had feared it might be. His voice, too, grew stronger. "*You* propose, Captain Ogilvie? *I* am the Divisional Commander."

"I'm sorry, sir. I believed you to be sick, and as the next senior officer—"

"Yes, yes, yes, I understand, naturally. You have acted properly I don't deny. However, I am not now sick and never mind what Lady Dornoch has to say about that."

190

Fettleworth pondered for a moment and began to do up the buttons of his scarlet tunic. "You may as well tell me what your proposals would have been, Captain Ogilvie."

"Yes, sir. I intended – that is, my proposal was that scouting parties should be sent out to reconnoitre for the enemy, and other parties to scavenge for food and water, the rest of my company continuing to form the cave guard with the Kohat soldiers. As to the women and children, sir . . . I suggest they're allowed out in small parties, kept close to the entry, of course—"

"May one ask for what purpose, Captain Ogilvie?"

"In order to get some fresh air, sir, and sun."

"Oh, rubbish, my dear fellow, they'll be getting plenty of that when we move out."

Ogilvie stared. "I beg your pardon, sir?"

"If you are not deaf," Fettleworth said irritably, "you must have heard what I said." He looked down at his tunic: a button was missing . . . damn natives! No respect at all. "Are you suggesting we hold the women and children here in the cave?"

"Yes, sir. That was the order of the GOC in Murree . . . or rather, his suggestion. I should hold the cave and await relief."

"From Murree?"

"Yes, sir."

Fettleworth shook his head. "That's no good. Murree'll be in no position to send reliefs to anyone – they're very badly depleted, and no one else knows where we are. Meanwhile, the GOC may be the GOC, but I'm the Commander of the First Division and I'm here, he's not."

"But if we leave, sir, where shall we go?"

Fettleworth pondered again, fingering his stubble with distaste. "Not Peshawar certainly. Nowshera may be under attack by now, too. Rawalpindi . . . but we'd reach Murree first." He came to a decision. "We shall march out, Captain Ogilvie, as soon as those gallant fellows are buried, for Murree."

"Murree, sir?"

"Murree." Fettleworth glared. "Am I to take it you have some objection?"

191

"Yes, sir! The Star of Islam's marching his army on Murree—"

"You are afraid of action, Captain Ogilvie?"

"Certainly not, sir, but the women and children—"

"They will be in no danger unless we meet the Pathans, which we shall not."

"But the Pathans *are* heading for Murree, sir!"

With dignity Fettleworth said, "I have formed the view that they are not, and there is no more to be said. I believe you're already aware that my person has been more recently than yours in the hands of this Star of Islam himself?" he asked sarcastically.

"Yes, sir—"

"Then kindly accord me some knowledge superior to your own. *You* make assumptions, *I* speak from observation. I believe the Pathans to have made a mere deviation for the particular purpose of retaking their hostages, and that the force concerned has now been withdrawn to the Nowshera perimeter to attack and consolidate before any further advance is made towards the Indus. They'll be thinking the hostages are securely sealed within the cave, my dear Ogilvie. We shall have a clear march to Murree, you may be sure."

"But—"

Fettleworth waved an arm in the air. "There are no buts. You'll do as you're told. Damn it, do you expect your Divisional Commander to skulk in a blasted cave, safe underground while gallant hearts fight for Her Majesty and the Raj?"

Ogilvie saluted and turned away: the orders were clear and must be obeyed. Fettleworth glared after him angrily: young puppy! Still wet behind the ears. Divisional Commanders did not skulk, they marched. Skulking brought no honour but resolute marching did. And there was honour yet to be retrieved: it was unusual for Divisional Commanders to be handed over like a bag of beans to the enemy and addressed thereafter as a fat pig. All that would shortly be forgotten, submerged by his glorious advance upon Murree with the women and children intact, seized by sword and valour from the savage, bloody hands of the Pathan. Fettleworth felt a good deal better. He surged to his feet and after an alarming moment of swaying, stood firm.

* * *

"What is it? You there, that blasted man!" Farrar-Drumm tried to stand in his stirrups as a staff officer came down hell for leather from the van of the column. "Come here, I say!"

The rider, who was in any case heading for Sir Clarence's brigade, pulled up his horse in a lather of sweat and sliding hooves. "The enemy has been sighted, sir."

"What?"

"The enemy, sir. A cloud of dust on the horizon to the west ahead of us."

"Good God!"

"There are orders from the GOC, sir. After saturation by the gun batteries, the cavalry will ride ahead and charge the line, with the infantry in support—"

"Squares?"

"Not squares, sir. They will deploy and advance in line behind the cavalry." The staff officer paused. "The General orders that the enemy will be held and then destroyed, and the column will fight to the last man."

"Well, of course," Sir Clarence said irritably. "What a stupid thing to say." The staff officer saluted and turned towards the rear. Within minutes the trumpets and bugles were sounding as the column deployed and the mounted squadrons took position to await the order to advance at the charge. In front of the extending ranks of the infantry, the horse artillery batteries swung to right and left, trundling with a rattle of equipment and a creak and jingle of harness into their stations for bombarding the advancing enemy. The dust-cloud ahead grew larger and came menacingly into the view of Sir Clarence Farrar-Drumm, who lifted a hand from his reins and brandished a fist at it. Then he drew his cavalry sabre from its scabbard and waved that. As a regimental officer he had served with Her Majesty's Fourth Dragoons, and still retained his sabre and to hell with regulations. The savage waving of the sabre, which was immensely heavy, did something untoward to his rheumatic backbone, and he replaced the weapon in its scabbard, grimacing with sudden pain. Growing old was damnable, really damnable ... then the artillery opened and the gun-flashes dappled the hard earth and the uniforms of the soldiers as the sound of their thunder echoed and re-echoed. The shells took the enemy mass in great upsurges of flame, red and orange that seemed to expand like swiftly-growing flowers, one after another as though driven from some enormous pump as every battery fired its guns and reloaded and fired again. Back from the Pathans came return fire: the casualties had begun now. Farrar-Drumm sat his horse like some ancient demon, looking quite unworried as the flashes and explosions flickered over his white whiskers. After a fearsome pounding of the enemy the guns fell silent on the order from the GOC and then the bugles sent the infantry forward as the cavalry, beneath its guidons and with the lance-points thrusting and the trumpets sounding, moved on at a canter that become a gallop and then a charge. Farrar-Drumm shouted encouragement at his brigade, loudly and hoarsely between spasms of coughing reminding them of Wellington and Waterloo, of the Light Brigade and Lord Cardigan, of Lord Roberts and his brave march from Kabul to Kandahar against the worst the stinking Afghans could hurl at him. Within minutes, mounted or not, he found himself shouting from behind the line of advance. His blasted horse had cast a shoe.

*　　*　　*

Under the command of Lieutenant-General Fettleworth mounted upon a transport mule, B Company of the Royal Strathspeys had formed a guard for the women and children and had begun their march to Murree. They moved past the sad cairns of stones that marked the graves of the dead who by their dying had made possible the relief of the hostages. When the mail reached home there would be much sadness in Invermore and in the mountains and glens around the depot. Letters would have to be written as soon as possible to parents and widows; always an unwelcome task. Fettleworth's mule was not fast; Ogilvie marched alongside it, bidden to converse with his General. Somewhat embarrassingly, Bloody Francis wished to discuss the 114th's Sergeant-Major, a subject Ogilvie had so far steered clear of in case Lord Dornoch had found a way of blocking a report to Division. However, Fettleworth seemed merely to be suffering from a fading memory and his interest was confined to the one point only: he had recollected, he said, a report to the effect that Mr Cunningham had been left behind in Peshawar when Lord Brora had withdrawn his unauthorised attack. Now he had turned up again and had saved his General's life, a a noble act. What had happened in Peshawar?

Patiently Ogilvie repeated the facts, reflecting that possibly Bloody Francis was less well than had appeared to be the case. Fettleworth was much astonished. "Indeed, indeed?" he said. "Dammit, so far as I recall, the subsequent despatches failed to make mention of Cunningham, though possibly I was too busy to take note . . . why have you not told me this before, Ogilvie?"

Ogilvie coughed. "I did, sir, shortly after we entered the cave. I—"

"Well, I don't remember," Fettleworth broke in crossly. "I can't damn well be expected to remember everything! I've had much on my mind as you know. Cunningham now . . . no doubt he conducted himself bravely and in manly fashion whilst in that bugger's hands?"

"He did, sir."

"The man who killed his wife as I remember – poor fellow, a most dreadful situation! It's a hard thing, Ogilvie, to serve Her Majesty."

"Yes, sir."

"But nevertheless splendid." Fettleworth jogged on, looking cleaner than the night before. His uniform had been tidied, and a razor had been found to deal with his stubble. Mr Cunningham, he said, would be mentioned in his despatches together with the men who had died fighting in the pass; and Cunningham would be recommended for the award of the Medal for Distinguished Conduct in the Field. Ogilvie reflected that if and when Fettleworth received Lord Brora's submissions about the RSM the picture could change. Brora could certainly be relied upon to make the most of his charges, and generals could be difficult and sticky when it came to matters affecting discipline; it was customary with many of them to support a holder of the Queen's Commission against all comers as it were, so that iron discipline should remain unbreached. Yet Bloody Francis Fettleworth could be warm-hearted at times and undoubtedly regarded his life as important to the Raj. For Cunningham, time would tell.

Meanwhile Cunningham's voice could be heard encouraging the women and children along as the straggle towards Murree proceeded. Turning, Ogilvie saw that the RSM was carrying one of the children upon his shoulders – a small girl, very conscious of her importance as she clung to the head of no less a personage than the Regimental Sergeant-Major and dangled her legs down his tunic and Sam Browne belt. Cunningham was looking happier than for many days past.

After a couple of hours Fettleworth called a halt for rest, and slithered off his mule. The men fell out and pipes were lit as they sprawled on the hard, sun-baked ground. Blue smoke curled up and the children played, shouting and laughing. For them the ordeal was over, and the march with the Scottish soldiers was fun, something to be remembered afterwards. The women's faces were less happy: they were desperately tired and hungry, and the haunting anxiety for their menfolk was ever present. Ogilvie circulated, having a word here and there, smiling and cheerful, doing his best to keep their spirits up. Fettleworth took a few turns up and down, easing away the stiffness brought by the wretched mule, then sat upon a boulder and sweated into his scarlet-and-blue, his mouth watering for *chota pegs* by the dozen, and ice . . . he stared down the line towards Ogilvie: an efficient young man, but inattentive to his General. The women could get on perfectly well without him. Fettleworth frowned and looked the other way; then swivelled back again upon his boulder: someone was shouting, and where the devil was Ogilvie now, he'd suddenly vanished. Then he reappeared, running forward and calling to Cunningham, and the men began scrambling up.

"What is it, Captain Ogilvie?" Fettleworth demanded loudly.

"A report by heliograph from the scouts, sir: a dust-cloud ahead."

"The relief column after all!" Fettleworth mopped at his face, showing much surprise.

"Perhaps, sir—"

"Why perhaps, for God's sake? I confess I didn't expect them, but who else could it be?"

"The enemy, sir."

"Oh, rubbish!" Fettleworth said irritably. "I'm positive the buggers aren't to be found in this sector, quite positive. If you'll kindly fall the men in, I shall advance to meet the relieving column. I shall require smartness, Captain Ogilvie, and I think your pipes and drums would be appropriate." He got to his feet with dignity and fastened the collar of his tunic. As he did so, the unmistakable sound of heavy artillery in action swept down from ahead and Fettleworth's face grew purple, flesh bulging over the tight neckband's gold lace. "Damned if I can make head nor tail of this!" he said. "D'you really think it's the damn Pathans, Ogilvie?"

"Yes, sir."

Fettleworth blew up the ends of his moustache. He was much agitated now. "They're plainly not firing upon us. Possibly they've engaged the relief column. Indeed, that must be so and I shall assume that it is. Captain Ogilvie, you will conceal the women and children as best you can behind the boulders and detach one section to guard them. The remainder of your company is to advance and attack the enemy and pincer them between ourselves and the column out of Murree."

Ogilvie objected. He said, "We'll be a pretty poor pincer, sir. I suggest the whole company forms the line to stand between the Pathan and the families—"

"You have your orders, Captain Ogilvie. Kindly carry them out."

*　　*　　*

Sir Iain Ogilvie seemed to be everywhere at once, shouting

the infantry on as they doubled with fixed bayonets behind
the cavalry charge. That charge cut swathes through the
native ranks already carved by the exploding shells from the
guns: the riders swept through with lances spitting native
bodies, sabres slicing necks, and carbines shattering faces
and arms and stomachs. Riding out to the enemy's rear, the
cavalry turned and came back in, cutting again through the
howling mob and then extending to the flanks as once more
the guns thundered into action. Then, as the infantry
brigades pounded up, the guns withdrew again and the
bullets and the steel of the shining bayonets took over.
Shouting and yelling, with the Scots pipes playing them on,
the soldiers took the enemy line and surged into it and the
hand-to-hand fighting began with all its blood and savagery.
The Pathans had been severely hit by the artillery, much
more so than had the British by the natives' return gunfire:
the native aim was wild and many of their ancient pieces had
exploded in their own faces, killing the gunners and blowing
up stocks of ready-use ammunition to add to the slaughter.
The infantry swept into a very softened-up position. As the
army from Kohat was deployed by order of Sir Iain Ogilvie
to the left flank, and Farrar-Drumm's brigade to the right
to squeeze the enemy inwards, Brigadier-General Shaw, with
Lord Brora in his capacity of Brigade Major, led the attack
upon the centre. Brora was in his element, his eyes shining
madly, his broadsword whirling as it had whirled in
Peshawar and with as good an effect. It was as though he had
appointed himself a one-man execution band. He seemed
impervious to bullets and the thrust of knives and bayonets
as he hurled his horse into the mob. Behind Lord Dornoch
the Royal Strathspey and their brigaded battalions fought
like maniacs also: they had their women and children in
mind and word had spread that the Star of Islam had
advanced by way of the cave where they were held. What
might have happened they didn't know; but, just in case of
the worst, the Pathans were going to feel the full weight of
British displeasure. On the right flank, Sir Clarence Farrar-
Drumm did noble work, not flinching from the fight.
Though his sabre was not so nimble as Brora's broadsword

he used it well enough and made his first kill since the Zulu War. This much heartened him, and he rode his limping horse on into the fray with a grim determination visible upon the white-framed leathery face, his voice raised loudly to shout his men on until something jolted his back and his rheumatism propelled him from his horse. He took the ground winded but intact, though in pain, and could find no one with the time to help him remount. Cursing his luck, he dragged himself into the lee of a dead bullock and was forced to allow the battle to continue over his head.

To the left, the British officer detailed by Sir Iain to keep a watch over the Rajah's loyalty had performed something like a circus act insofar as he had balanced himself in a standing position on the back of his horse and from there had leapt upon the Rajah's elephant, got a grip on the framework of the *howdah,* and pulled himself in. Seated, he had brought out his revolver and aimed it at His Highness's stomach. It had not been necessary to explain its purpose.

*　*　*

With the women and children left behind under their totally inadequate guard, the depleted company of Scots advanced at a fast pace towards the sound of the guns. The dust-cloud reported by the scouts was in view of the main body of the company shortly after they moved out; and through it could be seen the gun-flashes and the explosions of the shells. As they came nearer, apparently unseen as yet, Fettleworth passed the order to advance at the double with bayonets fixed. B Company pounded on, every man considering the General's order to be suicidal but none hanging back: the Regimental Sergeant-Major in rear saw to that, though he, too, thought Fettleworth must have taken leave of his senses to abandon the women and children, who should be his first concern, to the care of a mere section. It failed to make sense, and Captain Ogilvie's suggestion, overheard by Cunningham, should have been accepted ... all the same, the Regimental Sergeant-Major found excitement in his very guts: ahead of him now, ahead of the revolver in his hand, lay the man known as the Star of

199

Islam; and Cunningham was out to get him personally if it was his last act on God's earth.

The Scots took the enemy rear unseen: all the attention was on the front and flanks, and the men of B Company, forming line to Ogilvie's shouted orders, went in to kill. Fettleworth, still upon his detested mule, rode bravely on, firing at everything that appeared before him. The effect of the sudden and unexpected attack from the rear was beyond all proportion to its size, though it was likely enough that the natives imagined them to be the advanced guard of a larger force; havoc was created in the rear, the Pathans pressing away to be taken by the men of the front attack or the inward-thrusting flank brigades. Ogilvie, fighting through closely with his company, saw through the rising dust and the gunsmoke the tartan of his regiment as Lord Brora, fighting still though streaming blood from a scalp wound, laid about him with his broadsword. Briefly he saw his father also, then Sir Iain turned his horse away and rode out of sight through the swirling clouds of dust. A moment later Ogilvie heard the bugles blowing retire, and heard his father's carrying voice ordering the guns to open again as soon as the infantry and cavalry had withdrawn, and to finish off the Pathan army.

Ogilvie found himself beside Bloody Francis, who grasped his arm and shouted in his ear, "We appear to have achieved notable success, Ogilvie, my dear fellow! Kindly withdraw your company to the rear, and we shall watch the effect of the artillery . . . I have no doubt we shall be needed again."

Ogilvie acknowledged the order breathlessly and looked round for the Regimental Sergeant-Major. He failed to see him. He put a hand on his bugler's shoulder. "Sound the retire for our men, young MacKay. They may not consider the GOC's order was for them." The fight seemed to be dying around the Scots as the troops from Murree withdrew as fast as possible and the notes of the bugle blared out. Then Ogilvie saw the Regimental Sergeant-Major running like a madman back into the heart of the native army. At the same time he saw Lord Brora, still whirling his broadsword about his head, and saw that both he and Cunningham appeared to be converging on the same man: a tall Pathan, mounted, in the centre of a group of henchmen ... a big bastard, in Cunningham's original words, more than six feet of him, with a great hooked nose, dressed in a white gown ... Ogilvie failed to see the branded star but knew well enough who he was and knew that both Cunningham and Brora had also recognised him. Then the clouds of dust rolled again and the scene was lost, and as Ogilvie shouted into the confusion for Cunningham to obey the order to retire before the barrage started, the ominous and earth-shaking sound of the artillery was heard as the gunners began their final blasting of the Star of Islam's army. Whistles were heard overhead shortly after, and the dust was lit again by the explosions as the shells landed and the shrapnel sliced into flesh.

Eighteen

Cunningham went flat as the shells exploded around him. Debris flew, as did limbs and the shattered trunks of bodies. The whole air seemed filled to the point of torment with the screams of the wounded and the dying. Cunningham scrambled to his feet again and ran on, stepping on bodies both British and Pathan, keeping the Star of Islam in view all the while. Away to his right he saw Lord Brora, on foot now and staggering a little as though wounded. Evidently his horse had been cut from under him; but he, too, was keeping his eyes firmly on the Star of Islam, who sat his horse in the middle of his protective group like a defeated Napoleon surveying the battlefield of Waterloo.

One quarry!

Cunningham set his teeth: again he was disobeying orders but to hell with it. There would be no retreat now: all too clearly he saw Bessie, saw her in their shared life and saw her in death as well. There would be no peace for her or him until he had cut down her murderer. He went forward at a crouching run, his kilt bloody with the blood of many men, blood that could never dim the glory of the tartan. In his ears now he heard, and knew not whether it was mere fancy, the sound of the pipes and drums from the fringe of the battle. It was good to hear that, but he had no need of stiffening. Now he was not so far off the Pathan leader, who remained quite motionless on his horse as though in his hour of defeat he wished for nothing more than death from the pounding British guns. Honour would not permit him to return in humiliation to Afghanistan, nor to fall into the hands of the hated Raj. Maybe the bastard would commit suicide, but not if Cunningham had anything to do with it.

Then back into the picture came Lord Brora, who had temporarily vanished. The Major was mounted again, now upon a horse whose rider had been killed. Brora was making straight for the Star of Islam, was flinging his broadsword about in all directions as it seemed . . . he reached the perimeter of the leader's personal guard at the same moment as did Cunningham; and seeing Cunningham he gave a harsh laugh, an insulting laugh, and cut savagely through the guard. Cunningham was almost within range when Lord Brora's sword took the neck; the head seemed to rise into the air and spin from the slicing impact, then it fell and took the ground close by Cunningham's feet.

"Beaten to the draw, I think, *Mr* Cunningham," Lord Brora said icily. "And there's still the matter of your attempt to do away with *me,* is there not?"

*   *   *

It was, of course, all over: with the death of their leader the remaining Pathans streamed away, pursued by the British cavalry until the General Officer Commanding decided that a disorganised rabble running and riding to all points of the compass was too fragmented for worthwhile action, and ordered his force to disengage. As the fighting ceased the field ambulance sections picked up the wounded, and burial parties were at once detailed to scrape out the many shallow graves for the dead. While this was going on the column from Murree was joined by B Company of the Royal Strathspeys together with General Fettleworth and the retrieved families. There was a burst of cheering as the women and children were seen approaching through the lingering dust-clouds, and men ran to greet and embrace them. Fettleworth meanwhile lost no time in reporting personally to the Northern Army Commander, surging importantly up on his mule. He would be obliged, he said, if he could be returned forthwith to his headquarters in Nowshera so that he might take command of whatever might be the situation there.

"You shall be," Sir Iain promised. "It's my intention to follow up and take my column westward to Nowshera."

"You'll not return to Murree, then?"

"No." Sir Iain lifted himself in his stirrups and gazed around the bloody battle scene: the brown earth itself seemed reddened. "I shall send the women and children back to Murree under escort of battalion strength."

"Ah! Then I shall accompany your column to Nowshera. And a horse, if you would be so kind, General." Fettleworth blew out his cheeks. "Mules have their purposes, but they are not for me."

A horse was provided and Fettleworth, next in seniority to the Army Commander, sat close to him in proper state and style. When the men had had their opportunity to talk to their womenfolk, the Royal Strathspeys were detailed as the escorting battalion for Murree. Lord Dornoch, with Brora, who was riding with a foot in bandages, led the escort out to the sound of the pipes and drums. Sir Iain's column moved out westwards, still accompanied by the Rajah of Kohat whose assistance might well be required outside Nowshera. Sir Clarence Farrar-Drumm, wounded in an arm during the action in spite of the dead bullock into the lee of which he had crept, was drawn in a *doolie* protesting loudly that he was perfectly fit to ride. As they went, Fettleworth had many words with Sir Iain. B Company of the 114th under Captain Ogilvie had done splendid work; and the Regimental Sergeant-Major had saved his, Fettleworth's, life.

"Indeed?" Sir Iain enquired sharply. "That's interesting!

I'd be obliged if you'd tell me the circumstances."

Somewhat stiff-faced, Fettleworth did so; his arrival outside the cave mouth had been undignified and he found he disliked having to refer to it in detail. Sir Iain listened and nodded at intervals; then told Fettleworth that a certain report would reach him shortly from Brigadier-General Shaw. He indicated the nature of this report, and Fettleworth's cheeks seemed to swell with indignation.

"Stuff-and-nonsense, my dear sir!"

Sir Iain grinned. "Don't blame me."

"The man's splendid, first-class! Not a murderer at all!"

"I agree."

"As for Brora, words fail me. Such a boor – damn rude at times."

"A good fighting officer, Fettleworth. We must be fair. Fair to both sides in an unsavoury dispute." Sir Iain lifted his field glasses and stared ahead. The terrain stood empty now, and again at peace, but fighting could still lie ahead around Nowshera, and Mardan was yet to be relieved. But the momentum would have gone out of the Pathans, he felt sure of that, and the Raj was secure . . . it was most unwelcome that victory should be spoiled by an arrogant officer's attempt to damn the career and reputation of one of the best warrant officers Sir Iain had known in all his years of service.

*　　*　　*

Murree was reached without incident; during the march back Ogilvie made his report to Lord Dornoch, informing him of Cunningham's action in saving the life, under fire, of the Divisional Commander. Upon arrival the women and children were taken to the married quarters, where they were warmly welcomed and absorbed by the garrison pending their return to the Peshawar cantonment. The 114th were allocated the quarters vacated by the troops absent on the march to Nowshera; and when they had settled in Ogilvie was sent for by Lord Dornoch who wished a word in private.

Filling his pipe, the Colonel said, "Your report about Cunningham, James. When you made it to me on the march, I had the feeling you thought it might help to turn away the Major's charge against him. Am I right?"

"Yes, Colonel."

Dornoch shook his head sadly. "I fear not. Things don't quite cancel out in the army, you know. A charge is a charge, and this is a serious one on the face of it."

"And the Major's going ahead?"

"I'm afraid he is," Dornoch answered. "I've just had words with him and he's adamant. My hands are tied, as you'll appreciate. I can't block Lord Brora's path to Division – the matter's already at Brigade, of course, and that cuts me out in any case. When we're back in cantonments, the Brigadier-General will pass his recommendation for a medical board to Division . . . that's bad enough, but General Fettleworth may decide upon Court Martial."

"Of the man who saved his life, Colonel?"

Dornoch signed. "I've already made the point that things don't cancel out. Even the Divisional Commander must follow Queen's Regulations."

"It'll break Cunningham's heart."

"It's broken already," Dornoch said. "This will be the last straw, that's all. I'm desperately sorry . . . the army's all he has left – the army and the regiment."

"Is there no way, Colonel?"

"None that I can see. None!"

Ogilvie said, "Suppose the Major did withdraw the charge, Colonel. That'd finish the matter?"

Dornoch gave a hard laugh. "He's in no mood to withdraw. You can dismiss that from your thoughts, James."

Ogilvie's face was bleak as he left the Colonel's quarters. There was one thing left to try, and, unpleasant as it was, he was determined to go ahead with it. It must be settled between Brora and himself alone, and the Colonel must not be involved. An opportunity would come; and in fact it came next day when news reached Murree on the field telegraph line now repaired by the sappers of Northern Army: the Dargai Heights had been retaken by a brigade from Nowshera, and the district around Nowshera itself had been cleared after a vigorous assault upon the Pathans by Sir Iain Ogilvie's column. The armies of the Raj were now advancing upon Mardan, and the indications were that the siege was already breaking up as the Pathans began leaving the lines and retreating back into the Afghan hills taking with them the tidings that the Star of Islam had fallen to the Raj. The news was excellent and it was duly celebrated in the officers' and sergeants' messes and in the barrack-rooms. It was much celebrated by Lord Brora in the privacy of his quarters; and late in the evening a message reached Ogilvie in the ante-room that the Major wished words with him.

He found Brora alone and very drunk. The Major was sprawled in a basketwork chair, a glass in his hand, his tunic rumpled and undone, hair awry, face a fiery red. An almost empty bottle of whisky was on a table beside him; another lay smashed in a corner of the room. There was a smell as of a distillery. Saliva drooled from a corner of Brora's mouth as he stared at Ogilvie from bloodshot eyes.

"So you can obey an order when you've a mind to." Brora glared. "Well, answer me, damn you!"

"I don't see what there is to answer," Ogilvie said.

"Oh, you don't? Well now, look here." Brora swept an arm towards Ogilvie, and whisky spilled on his uniform. "I just want to say this. We have orders to march back into cant-onments tomorrow . . . when we get back, Captain Ogilvie, there's to be no more damn poodle-faking. You'll keep your distance from my – from my niece, d'you hear me?"

"I—"

"Young puppy! That's what you are . . . sniffing round the women instead of getting on with a soldier's job." Brora's voice was slurring badly, "Well, I'll not damn well have it. I'm your Major. You'll keep your hands to yourself." Once again he swung the whisky glass. "The girl's marrying no one."

"No one's asked her to!" Ogilvie snapped.

Brora took another mouthful of whisky. Ogilvie went on, furious now, "Give me credit for behaving as a gentleman, Major. If I'd thought of marriage, I'd have gone first to Miss Elliott's mother."

"Mother!" Brora sneered. "That stupid bitch. What about her father, may I ask? No, don't answer that. Just hold your tongue, Captain Ogilvie, and listen to what I have to say." Brora lurched to his feet, staggered a little and steadied himself on the table beside his chair. The table went over and the whisky bottle fell to the floor. Brora managed to recover his balance and stood swaying. He opened his mouth, then closed it again; it was as though he had thought better of some intended utterance. He stared at Ogilvie from bloodshot eyes for some moments then asked in a thick, slurred voice, "Well, what the devil do you want now, hey?"

"You sent for me, Major." Ogilvie took a deep breath: he believed that the moment had come. Disliking even now what he had to do, he said steadily, "Since I'm here, Major . . . I think I should tell you that I may see it as my duty to make a certain report to the Colonel."

"What report, pray?" Brora reached out a hand to a chair back.

Ogilvie said, "On the night of the attack on Peshawar by our brigade, mounted runners from the Guides were sent by General Fettleworth to call off the attack—"

"Really."

"I have an eye-witness who says you were personally contacted by a *sowar* of the Guides on the perimeter, and that a conversation took place, the *sowar* appearing to be making a report to you."

"I deny it!" Brora shouted.

"On that night many of the battalion were killed – men who would not have been killed had General Fettleworth's message been delivered to Brigade. Since no one of the Guides other than the man you spoke to was present at the assault, it's clear the *sowar* came from General Fettleworth."

"Damn you to hell, he was too late, there was no time. . ." Brora's voice died away and his face grew mottled, patched red and white. His body shook. "Yes, now I see. Do I take it you're uttering threats and blackmail?"

"You may take it as you wish," Ogilvie answered coolly. He paused. "I shall make my report, and produce my witness, to the Colonel in the morning, unless you yourself go to him and withdraw all charges and insinuations against Mr Cunningham."

*   *   *

It had been a close thing: it was perfectly possible that Fettleworth's runner had indeed arrived too late for the brigade to disengage, but if not, and had they then

207

withdrawn in accordance with the orders rather than proceed without the expected support, then many lives would have been saved. In any case, to fail to pass on orders was a serious matter in itself; and evidently Lord Brora, when the whisky had drained away in the morning, had been unwilling to take the risk of his name stinking throughout the sub-continent as an officer whose dereliction of duty had caused many unnecessary casualties. Next morning Brora was seen to go to the Colonel's office; and after he had left with a face like thunder, the RSM was sent for. Later that morning the regiments formed up for the march back to Peshawar, where the Hindus had long since withdrawn their siege line and the city was peaceful if scarred. As the pipes and drums played them away from Murree, Cunningham had words with Ogilvie.

"I shall never understand it, sir. The Major must have his good side, if you'll excuse a seeming impertinence."

Ogilvie grinned. "It's possible, Bosom. Anyway – all's well that ends well."

"Aye, sir, it is." Cunningham still looked puzzled. He marched away busily to overlook the colour-sergeants, the set of his shoulders once again as straight as ever. The return to cantonments would be a sad one, but he remained the Regimental Sergeant-Major. Ogilvie felt a lump in his throat as he watched the swing of Cunningham's kilt, the swing that seemed to keep time with the pipes and drums as they sent their message of a continuing Raj out over the sun-browned Indian countryside. Turning out of the line, Ogilvie rode back to come alongside one of the wagons that was carrying the women and children, and lifted a hand to Fiona Elliott, who smiled at him. At some moments – though not usually when smiling – she was very like her uncle ... a shadow passed across Ogilvie's face. Last night, Brora had seemed to be on the point of saying something in his semi-stupefied condition but had not come out with it, and it had clearly been intended to concern Fiona. Ogilvie shrugged his thoughts and wonderings away; it had probably not been all that important. He rode his horse towards Fiona's wagon, and the devil take Lord Brora.